Lisa B. Kamps

THE DEFENDER: RYDER

Cover Six Security, Book 3

LISA B. KAMPS

Lisa B. Kamps

Dedication

For Jackie Howerth Forquer, who's always ready with a keen eye and a shoulder to lean on.
Thank you.

Lisa B. Kamps

THE DEFENDER: RYDER
Copyright © 2019 by Elizabeth Belbot Kamps

All rights reserved. Except for use in any review, the reproduction or utilization of this work in whole or in part in any form by any electronic, mechanical or other means, now known or hereafter invented, including xerography, photocopying and recording, or in any information storage or retrieval system, is forbidden without the express written permission of the author.

Cover Six Security™ is a fictional security company, its name and logo created for the sole use of the author and covered under protection of trademark.

All characters in this book have no existence outside the imagination of the author and have no relation to anyone bearing the same name or names, living or dead. This book is a work of fiction and any resemblance to any individual, place, business, or event is purely coincidental.

Cover Design by Jay Aheer of Simply Defined Art
https://www.simplydefinedart.com/

Photographer: Christopher John of CJC Photography
http://www.cjc-photography.com/

Cover Model: Brian L.

Cover Six Security Logo Designed by Benjamin Mangnus of Benjamagnus Design Ltd.
http://www.benjamagnus.com/

All rights reserved.
ISBN-13: 978-1096856757

CONTENTS

Title Page iii
Dedication v
Copyright vi
Other titles by this author ix
Special Acknowledgement xi
Prologue 13
Chapter One 18
Chapter Two 30
Chapter Three 40
Chapter Four 52
Chapter Five 65
Chapter Six 77
Chapter Seven 87
Chapter Eight 100
Chapter Nine 111
Chapter Ten 114
Chapter Eleven 126
Chapter Twelve 134
Chapter Thirteen 143
Chapter Fourteen 153
Chapter Fifteen 164
Chapter Sixteen 174
Chapter Seventeen 184
Chapter Eighteen 194
Chapter Nineteen 207

Chapter Twenty	218
Chapter Twenty-One	226
Chapter Twenty-Two	237
Chapter Twenty-Three	249
Chapter Twenty-Four	262
Chapter Twenty-Five	268
Chapter Twenty-Six	277
Epilogue	287
About the Author	289
The Protector: MAC	291
The Guardian: DARYL	292
The Warrior: DERRICK	293

Other titles by this author

COVER SIX SECURITY

Covered By A Kiss, A CSS Novella, Book 0
The Protector: MAC, Book 1
The Guardian: DARYL, Book 2
The Defender: RYDER, Book 3
The Warrior: DERRICK, Book 4
The Rescuer: SEBASTIAN, Book 5

THE BALTIMORE BANNERS

Crossing The Line, Book 1
Game Over, Book 2
Blue Ribbon Summer, Book 3
Body Check, Book 4
Break Away, Book 5
Playmaker (A Baltimore Banners Intermission novella)
Delay of Game, Book 6
Shoot Out, Book 7
The Baltimore Banners 1st Period Trilogy (Books 1-3)
The Baltimore Banners 2nd Period Trilogy (Books 4-6)
On Thin Ice, Book 8
Coach's Challenge (A Baltimore Banners Intermission Novella)
One-Timer, Book 9
Face Off, Book 10
First Shot At Love (A Baltimore Banners Warm-up Story)
Game Misconduct, Book 11
Fighting To Score, Book 12
Matching Penalties, Book 13

Lisa B. Kamps

THE YORK BOMBERS

Playing The Game, Book 1
Playing To Win, Book 2
Playing For Keeps, Book 3
Playing It Up, Book 4
Playing It Safe, Book 5
Playing For Love, Book 6
Playing His Part, Book 7

THE CHESAPEAKE BLADES

Winning Hard, Book 1
Loving Hard, Book 2
Playing Hard, Book 3

FIREHOUSE FOURTEEN

Once Burned, Book 1
Playing With Fire, Book 2
Breaking Protocol, Book 3
Into The Flames, Book 4
Second Alarm, Book 5

STAND-ALONE TITLES

Emeralds and Gold: A Treasury of Irish Short Stories
(anthology)
Finding Dr. Right, Silhouette Special Edition
Time To Heal
Dangerous Passion

Special Acknowledgement

The idea for the Cover Six Security series came about when I started the Chesapeake Blades series—particularly book 2, *Loving Hard*. And the more I played around with it, the more it drew me in.

I had the story ideas. Names for the guys on the team. Their backgrounds. I was ready to go, my fingers itching to get the words on paper.

What I didn't have was a name for the security company. Ideas came to me, only to be deleted because...well, frankly, because they stunk. Then I got stuck.

Like many authors, I have a fabulous reader's group on Facebook: Kamps Korner. And that's where I turned to for help. I threw the question (okay, I begged) to the greatest bunch of readers I know—and they totally came through for me!

There were dozens of suggestions, all of them fantastic—which led to another dilemma: how do I pick one? There were a few that really stood out so I did what any smart author would do: I created a poll and let the readers pick...

And Cover Six Security was born.

Thank you to everyone who offered suggestions—there were so many great ones! And special thanks—and my undying gratitude—to Elizabeth Roney and her Marine husband for the wonderful suggestion! It totally fits. And in Elizabeth's words: "He [her Marine husband] said it would be a good pick up line explaining to the ladies what cover your six means!"

And it totally is—as you'll see in several of the upcoming books!

Elizabeth and your Marine husband—this one is for you! Thank you <3!

Lisa B. Kamps

PROLOGUE

Anger ripped through him, coupled with an extreme distaste that curdled his stomach and filled his mouth with acid. Did the insolent *nobody* in front of him actually think he could get away with making ultimatums? With *blackmailing* him?

It was bad enough that he'd tried to have this conversation on the beach. Out in the open, where anyone could see them. Not that they'd be overheard, even with the way the bastard had been yelling. But it was still a careless risk. A worthless one.

And then he'd dared to try to shove him!

Which only proved how stupid the sniveling little twit really was.

Blue eyes stared back at him, the first hint of fright wavering in their depths. So, he wasn't *that* stupid, was already beginning to regret the words that had tumbled from his worthless mouth.

Good. Let him regret them. Not that it would do any good. The blackmail attempt had been a slight.

And he never allowed a slight to pass without retribution. Doing so would only undermine his authority.

Even so, part of him had to give the sniveling little bastard credit. He wondered how long it had taken the man to work up the courage to say what he had. Days? No, longer than that. The man was as spineless as a jellyfish and nearly as worthless. He'd probably been working up the courage for the past two weeks.

Too bad it would do him no good.

He didn't know that. Not yet.

But he would, soon enough.

He leaned against the wall of the cave, careful not to get dirt on his shirt. He had no problem getting dirty in general—it was part of his cover, after all—but the muck that lined these cave walls was different. Someone might notice.

Not that any of the do-gooders he was surrounded by was smart enough to tell the difference. They were all too preoccupied with their precious volunteer work. Too wrapped up in helping others and paying for the privilege, thinking that it made them better than everyone else. They were clueless. Pathetic. Naive and stupid.

The sniveling bastard in front of him was proof of that. Why, none of those do-gooders had a clue what the twit was doing! How he was lying to them all, charming them with smooth words and an even smoother smile. Weaving a web of deception right in front of their stupid, naive noses.

Pathetic.

But still, he couldn't take a chance that someone might notice an odd smear of dirt on his shirt that didn't quite match the other smudges. That wouldn't do. Not at all.

At the same time, he couldn't do what he wanted to the sniveling little bastard who had dared try to blackmail him. Someone might notice him missing. Not *might*—they'd definitely notice him missing. And if he went missing, the entire operation might be put at risk. People might start poking their noses where they didn't belong and asking questions.

That wouldn't do, either.

He glanced at the second man, the one who was

surprisingly smart enough to realize the bastard had crossed an uncrossable line. Surprising because there were definitely more brawns than brains with that one.

Which was a shame. That brawn had come in handy. Would come in handy again over the next two weeks. The man was strong, carried more than his share of weight despite the fellow missing a leg

The man sighed. Well, there was nothing to be done about it. A slight *was* a slight, after all. He couldn't let it slide, not without undermining his own authority.

He offered the sniveling bastard a pleasant smile, watched with satisfaction when some of the tension left the man's shoulders. "You think you're entitled to a bigger cut, is that right?"

"Yeah. Yes."

"And why is that?"

"Because—" The bastard paused. Sucked in a deep breath and squared his shoulders. "The risk I'm taking. If someone finds out—"

"The risk *you're* taking? And what risk is that?"

"Well, you know. By letting you hide this stuff here. If someone found it—"

"And who would find it? You *are* doing your job and keeping everyone away, aren't you?"

"Yes, but—"

"Then there's no risk, now is there?"

Anger pushed away some of the fright in the man's eyes. "Now listen here. I've busted my ass to get this thing running. I've worked for months—*months*—to make this work. Living in squalor. Playing nice with everyone. So yeah, I think I deserve a little more for the risk I'm taking."

He tilted his head to the side, pretending to contemplate the issue. He finally nodded, offered the man another smile. "Possibly—"

"Good. I knew you'd agree—"

"I'll let you *keep* the money you've stolen and not report you. How does that sound?"

"But—you *can't* report me. If you do, I'll tell them about—"

"No, I don't think you will." He pushed away from the wall and moved toward the second man, the one who wasn't quite smart enough to realize what was about to happen.

Then again, neither was the sniveling bastard because he was still stammering, indignation turning his face red.

"I will. You can't stop me."

"Oh, but I think I can." He swung his arm out and hit the second man in the back of the head with the rock he'd been holding. The man's eyes widened, knowledge of what was happening slowly flaring in their depths. The man started to move but it was too late. He hit him again, then a third time before the fellow finally crumpled to the ground.

The bastard just stood there, his mouth gaping open, urine soaking the front of his pants as he pissed himself.

Such disgusting behavior.

He stepped out of the cave and made his way to the water. Tossed the rock into the waves and watched it sink below the surface. He brushed his hands off, checked to make sure there was no blood on his clothes, then moved back to the cave.

The sniveling bastard was still standing there, his mouth still hanging open in the most unbecoming way.

"There will be no more talk of bigger cuts or sharing profits, is that clear?"

The sniveling bastard snapped his mouth closed, quickly nodded.

"Good. Now get rid of him. Not here. Take him to the other side of the island and dump him."

There was no hesitation at all this time.

"Y-yes, sir."

"Good." He turned and walked out of the cave, his steps light, his conscience clear.

It was time to get back. Dessert was waiting for him.

CHAPTER ONE

"*Treasure?*"

Ryder "Boomer" Hess forced the word between clenched teeth. For all that he was seething inside, he was damn impressed with how calm he sounded. So what if the volume of his voice was a decibel or two louder than it should have been? He blamed that on needing to compete with the sound of the surf lapping against silky white sand fifty yards to his right.

He turned his head to the right and stared at the surf in question. Squinted against the bright sun reflecting off crystal blue water. Clenched his jaw a bit tighter. Jammed his fists into the pockets of his tan tactical pants.

He would not blow up.

He would *not*. Blow. Up.

He sucked in a deep breath, released it entirely too fast to derive any calming effects from it, then turned back to the woman standing five feet away from him.

"You fucking called me down here for fucking *treasure?*"

The woman didn't even flinch. Of course not—she was too damn stubborn. Too damn mule-headed. Too damn sure of herself to be intimidated by his outburst.

And too damn use to those outbursts to be even remotely fazed.

She crossed her tanned arms in front of her,

clenched her own jaw and tilted her head back to glare at him. Silence hung in the still air, thick with tension.

Heavy with her own imminent explosion.

Ryder braced himself for it. Narrowed his own gaze behind the dark sunglasses and rolled his shoulders back. Shifted his weight to the balls of his feet. Waited...and waited some more.

Instead of the expected explosion, the woman closed the distance between them and abruptly jammed one long finger in the middle of his chest. Hard. And damn, that fucking hurt, especially when she kept doing it, punctuating each word with another jab.

"Treasure *hunters*." *Jab*. "And *you* have a foul mouth." *Jab*. "Do you know that? Mom would wash your mouth out—" *Jab*. "—with soap if she heard you—" *Jab*. "—talk that way!"

His patience with his sister finally snapped and he grabbed her hand before she could add even more bruises to his sternum. She struggled against his gentle hold and tugged her hand from his, muttered something under her breath, then pulled one leg back and kicked him in the shin—

With her bare foot.

She gasped in surprise then bent over, cradling the injured foot with one hand while she hopped around. Ryder rolled his eyes and stepped back, just in case the whole hopping-around thing was an act to get him to drop his guard.

"Holy hell, Allison. What the hell did you think would happen? You don't kick someone with your bare feet."

She stopped hopping around long enough to glare at him. "I'm wearing flip-flops. And you're an ass."

"Those aren't real shoes. And I'm not the one with a broken toe."

"It's not broken. I should have kicked you in the head!"

"Why? So you could break your foot instead?"

"No! So I could knock some sense into that damn thick skull of yours!"

Smothered laughter came from behind him, the sound quickly choked back when Ryder turned. Colter Graham—otherwise known as *Ninja*—stood perfectly still, his head turned to the side, seemingly preoccupied with the sight of the waves crashing against the beach.

Yeah. Right. Sure he was.

The ass.

Ryder turned back to his sister. "You said it was an emergency."

"It is—

"You said you needed help—"

"We do."

Ryder ignored the *we* part because no way in hell could he even go there right now. He hadn't even bothered to look at the other woman standing a few yards away. If he did, he would totally lose his fucking shit—and not just because his sister had called him down here to this quasi-remote island in the middle of fucking nowhere on false pretenses.

He advanced on Allison, not bothering to hide his anger. "Ninja and I just spent the last twenty-fucking-four hours breaking our necks getting down here because *you* said it was a matter of life-or-death!"

Allison's gaze dropped to the ground. "I didn't exactly say that—"

"The hell you didn't. 'Ryder, this is life-or-death. I need your help.'" He mimicked her voice then clenched his jaw again and sucked in another deep breath. "Or don't you remember saying that? Right before the damn phone went dead!"

"Phone service down here isn't always reliable—"

"Dammit, Allison, this isn't a joke. Do you have any idea what the hell was going through my mind after you called?" No, she probably didn't. And knowing his little sister, she probably hadn't even given it much thought. *He'd* been going through pure hell the last twenty-four hours, not knowing what the hell was going on or what the hell he was going to find when he got down here. Twenty-four hours' worth of commercial flights, layovers, delays, and fucking *waiting*.

Only to learn that she was worried about *treasure hunters*?

What. The. Fuck.

Ryder spun on his heel, grabbed his pack from the gravel lot where he had dropped it fifteen minutes earlier and tossed it over his shoulder. "Ninja, we're done. Let's go—"

"*Go*? You can't leave! You just got here."

"Don't care—"

"Ryder, wait!"

A hand closed over his arm, the touch light yet desperate. He clenched his jaw, counted to three, then turned back to his sister. "Allison, I'm really not in the mood—"

"But this is important." She blinked and damn if he didn't see tears filling her eyes. Big and wide, their brown color just a shade lighter than his own. And dammit, why did she have to pull the tears card? He fucking hated that—

And she knew it.

"Allison—"

"I wouldn't have called you if it wasn't important."

"Treasure hunters *aren't* important, Allison. And they sure as hell aren't 'life-or-death'. Not to me. Not to anyone else, either. Hell, they're probably a dime a dozen down here." Maybe that was the truth, maybe it wasn't. Either way, he didn't care. And why should Allison? If some lame ass group of tourists wanted to break their backs digging in the sand searching for buried pirate treasure, more power to them.

"But they're not. And where we saw them—" She hesitated, glanced over her shoulder at the other woman, then looked back at Ryder. "It's too close to where the kids play."

Ryder blinked, wondered if maybe he was more fucking tired than he realized because no way in hell did he hear what he just thought he heard. "Kids?"

"Yes, the kids."

He wasn't going to ask. No way in hell would he ask. Asking would only encourage Allison. Give her a false sense of hope. Make her think he cared when he didn't.

"What kids?"

Ryder tossed a narrow-eyed glance over his shoulder at Ninja. Why the fuck had the man even opened his mouth? Why couldn't he just stand there and say *nothing*, like he usually did? Hell, that's why he had the nickname—because he was usually silent as a monk. Unseen. Unheard. Unnoticed.

Until he opened his fucking mouth.

Allison picked right up on it, too. Her gaze shot to Ninja and she offered him a small smile, like she was silently thanking him. And that sparkle in her eyes—oh, hell no. No way was she going to flirt with Ninja.

Uh-uh. Not happening.

"The kids at—"

Ryder advanced on his sister, cutting her off with a dangerously low voice. "No. Don't even answer that. Don't care."

Allison narrowed her eyes at him then turned back to Ninja with that soft smile. "The children at the school we're helping to rebuild."

Dammit!

Ryder fought the urge to slam his pack to the ground then drop-kick it into oblivion. Dammit. And damn her. He was losing the battle, he knew it.

Kids.

And a rebuilt school.

Fuck.

Next, she'd probably tell him they were orphans or some shit like that—

"Most of them are orphans."

"Oh, come on!" Ryder threw his hands up in the air, dropped them to the back of his neck and tilted his face up to the clear sky overhead. "Really? *Really?*"

Allison jabbed him in the chest again. "What is your problem?"

"Nothing." Ryder stepped back and shook his head. "Not a damn thing."

"Then stop acting like some damn Neanderthal."

Ryder opened his mouth, stammered, slammed it shut before he said something he'd regret. And before Allison could jam that damn finger in his chest again.

He tossed another glance at Ninja then swore under his breath. Shit. The other man was just standing there, watching him with that quiet gaze. And fuck, he could *feel* the other man trying to sway him. To get him to change his mind.

Shit.

Ryder blew out a deep breath between pursed lips then turned back to his sister. "What are you even doing down here?"

"We're volunteering."

"Volunteering?"

"Yes, volunteering. You know—where you give up some of your time to help others without expectation of being given anything in return? Volunteering." She tilted her head to the side and smirked. "You should try it sometime. It might do your black heart some good."

His black heart? Really? Is that what his sister really thought of him? Or was she simply repeating what she'd been told?

He started to glance at the other woman then quickly stopped himself, focusing instead on the gravel under his feet. Fuck. He didn't understand the need to look at her—he shouldn't want to. Shouldn't even be wondering what the two women had discussed—if they had discussed anything. It had been a long time ago.

A lifetime ago. She should be over it by now. Hell, *he* should be over it by now.

Yeah, sure. That's why he couldn't even look at her. That's why heat that had nothing to do with the warm climate filled his face.

"Ryder, please. You're here. Can't you just look into it for us?"

He didn't miss the pleading in his sister's voice—or the way she kept saying *us*. He should say *no*. He *needed* to say no. Needed to head back to the aging dock and catch the next ferry to the other island and hop on the next plane back to the states.

Yes. That's exactly what he *needed* to do.

So why wasn't he moving?

He shifted his weight from one foot to the other. Ran a hand through his hair. Blew out a deep breath.

And made the mistake of finally looking at the other woman.

Thick hair the color of honey was pulled back in a ponytail. A few long strands had come undone and curled around her oval face, framing high cheekbones and a full mouth. Loose khaki shorts hung from curved hips, the hem stopping mid-thigh. Like his sister, she was wearing a dark green tank shirt embroidered with a small logo he couldn't quite make out. Unlike his sister, she was wearing sandals, the heavy-duty kind that you could hike in.

Ryder allowed himself a brief second of male appreciation as his gaze roamed from the top of her head to the painted tips of her toes and back up again. Why shouldn't he? It wasn't like anyone could see his eyes behind the dark sunglasses.

And she was beautiful. Not in the modern supermodel sense but in the classical sense, with curves in all the right places and skin kissed by the sun. An outdoors girl who wasn't afraid to let the wind mess up her hair. A girl who wouldn't think twice about baiting a hook or climbing a tree.

Hannah Montgomery. His kid sister's best friend. The girl whose virginity he had stolen eleven years ago under the stars of a Springtime night. The girl whose heart he had broken three months later when he left, acting like what they'd had was no big deal.

Yes, she was beautiful. Had always been beautiful—but she wasn't a girl. Not anymore. Hadn't been for a long time. She was a woman.

And she was watching him with those beautiful eyes that still haunted him in his dreams, even after all these years. Eyes the color of warm tea focused on him, filling him with heat of another kind and making him wonder what she saw when she looked at him. Making him wonder if she—

A hand darted into his line of vision, the fingers snapping dangerously close to his nose. Ryder jerked back, turned his gaze to his sister and frowned when she rolled her eyes at him.

"Did you hear anything I just said?"

"Of course I did." At least, he thought he did. She had asked if he could stay and check things out. "And the answer is *no*."

A slow smile wreathed Allison's face. The sight was enough to make his stomach clench in dread and Ninja's choked laughter only made the sensation worse. What the hell? Had he screwed up somehow? Said something he shouldn't have?

"Perfect. I knew you'd agree."

"Wait. What? Agree to what? I didn't *agree* to anything."

"Yes, you did. Just now."

"No, Allison. I didn't."

"But you said *no*."

"Exactly. *No*. Absolutely not."

"Then you *do* agree."

"I—" Ryder stopped before he dug himself in deeper. This was a trap, he knew it. He had missed something—something important. He just couldn't figure out what. He turned to Ninja, frowned when he saw the other man's grin. "What?"

"She asked if we were going to leave."

"Yeah? And?"

Ninja shrugged. "That's what you just said *no* to."

Shit. He turned back to Allison, shuddered at the broad smile she was giving him. Wide. Sweet. Innocent.

Bullshit. He knew better.

"Not happening. I know all about your games, little sister, and I'm not playing. We're not staying." He readjusted the strap of his pack and spun on his heel. "Ninja, let's go—"

"You can't."

He didn't bother to look back at his sister when he answered, just kept walking. "We can. And we are."

"But you can't. I mean, you really can't. At least, not until tomorrow."

Ryder halted, closed his eyes and counted to three. Took a deep breath and extended the count to ten then slowly turned around. "And why can't we?"

He didn't miss the satisfied smile curling the corners of Allison's mouth when she pointed toward the dock behind him. "Because the ferry only comes twice a day and you were on the last one. You're kind of stuck here."

Twice a day? She had to be fucking kidding.

Ryder swallowed back an oath as he stared at the empty dock. Empty? Hell, it was beyond empty. The few people who had been on it with them were nowhere to be seen. In fact, they were the only four people in the immediate area.

That struck him as odd. This was an island in the middle of fucking paradise. Isolated and remote, maybe, but still—there should be other people around. Where the hell were all the tourists? The vendors? Hell, even the locals.

He started to ask Allison where everyone was

when she moved past him, a teasing grin on her face. "Suck it up, big boy. You can handle one night of roughing it."

"*Roughing it?* What the hell do you mean, *roughing it?*"

"Just what I said. This isn't a tourist spot like the other islands. Things are a little more primitive around here." She elbowed him in the side and kept going. "But at least I already made arrangements for your accommodations."

He stared after her, wanting to ask what kind of accommodations but stopping himself. Not because he was afraid of the answer but because Hannah had moved past him, her steps hurried as she raced to catch up with Allison.

Ryder stared after her, his gut clenching with need—and remorse—as his gaze locked on the round curves of her ass. Something hit him from behind and he stumbled forward, caught himself then whirled around to face Ninja. "What the hell was that for?"

The other man hoisted his pack higher on his shoulder with a shrug. "You might want to wipe the drool off your chin."

Ryder started to raise his hand, dropped it and glared at Ninja. "Real fucking funny. I'm not drooling."

"Yeah, uh-huh." Ninja took two steps, stopped and turned back. "And for future reference, if you're going to ogle someone, you need to learn to be a little more discreet. Hell, that look you were giving her was giving *me* a fucking hard-on."

What the fuck was he talking about? "What the fuck are you talking about?"

Ninja chuckled, tapped the top of his head with one finger, then pointed that same finger at Ryder. No, not at him—at his *head*. He frowned, reached up—and touched the frames of the sunglasses perched on the top of his head.

"Fuck."

"Yeah, apparently. And I expect to hear the full story."

Ryder dropped the sunglasses back in place and stormed past Ninja. "There is no story."

"Uh-huh. Sure there isn't. I still expect to hear it."

"Not happening." Because there was no story, no matter what the other man thought. There was just regret—

And no way in hell was Ryder going to share that. Not with anyone.

CHAPTER TWO

The decrepit van bounced over another rut, sending the rear passengers scurrying for any kind of handhold. Hannah bit back a smile when Allison glanced at her, a silent question in her gaze.

Maybe Hannah *was* driving a little more recklessly than usual. No, it wasn't exactly safe, not on these dirt and gravel paths that crisscrossed the island and passed for roads—but she was in a reckless mood and didn't care.

Ryder was here.

She hadn't expected him to show up at all. Had figured he'd make some excuse and completely blow Allison's request off—even if she *had* made the situation seem a little more dramatic than it really was. Life-or-death? Hannah still couldn't believe she'd gone that far.

But it worked. Ryder was here.

And now she had no idea what to do. How to act. What to say.

Did he remember her? That was a stupid question. Yes, of course he remembered her. They'd known each other for—she frowned, doing the math in her head. Fifteen years? Had it really been that long? No, that wasn't possible—

The van bounced over another rut and Hannah softly swore. She tightened her grip on the steering wheel and eased up on the gas until the ride smoothed out then returned back to her thoughts.

Fifteen years—only that was wrong, it was probably closer to sixteen. Maybe even seventeen. She had been ten—maybe—when Allison and Ryder had moved in several doors down all those years ago. That would make it—

Yikes. Seventeen years ago. When had she gotten so freaking old?

She mentally rolled her eyes and called herself a fool for skirting around her main worry. Ryder was *here*, sitting a few feet behind her. Close enough that she could smell the faintest hint of his soap, mixed with the tangy salt in the humid air and his own unique scent, something masculine and strong and entirely too distracting. Close enough that if she looked in the rearview mirror, their gazes would meet and her heart would slam into her chest again—not that it mattered since he had lowered those dark sunglasses over his eyes. But earlier, when those intense brown eyes had raked her from top to bottom and everywhere in between?

Yikes. Her skin had prickled with awareness and it had taken more control than she expected not to throw herself into his arms.

It was either that or deliver a roundhouse kick upside his head. She still wasn't sure which one held more appeal.

Ryder was *here*, after all these years.

And she had no idea how to act. What did one say to the guy who took your virginity when you were not-quite-seventeen-years-old? *Nice to see you? How have you been?*

Want to find a secluded spot and reenact that long-ago night?

Hannah swallowed back a groan and readjusted

her grip on the steering wheel. No. No, no, no. That was precisely what she *couldn't* say. But wow, it was hard not to—because *Ryder* was hard. Every inch of him, from the defined muscles of the biceps stretching the sleeves of his snug polo to the steely strength of his thighs encased in the light fabric of those cargo pants he had on. There wasn't an inch of fat on him anywhere that she could see. Yes, he was hard. Even his eyes had a hardness to them that hadn't been there all those years ago. Definitely hard.

Probably hard everywhere in between, too.

And *no*! No, she absolutely could *not* be thinking like that.

She chanced a glance in the rearview mirror. Her pulse quickened as she studied the strong line of his stubbled jaw, the chiseled cheekbones and sinfully full mouth. How could he be even more ruggedly handsome than he had been all those years ago? Back then, he'd just been starting to fill out, his body only hinting at what was to come. She'd thought him just a little bit dangerous back then. But now?

Oh, he was more than just a little dangerous. And more than just a little sinful. He was trouble with a capital T and a whole lot of heartbreak and if she were smart, she'd pull the van over and kick him out right now and run like hell in the opposite direction and—

They hit another rut, this one even deeper. The van bounced and swayed, tires spinning on loose dirt and sand. Hannah hit the gas and jerked the steering wheel and the van shot forward with another final bounce.

The passengers in the back—Ryder and the other man whose name she didn't know because nobody had bothered to make introductions—both swore. Even

Allison muttered under her breath and shot Hannah a meaningful look.

"Eyes on the prize, Hannah."

Yes, she knew that. And *that* was the problem. Her eyes *had* been on the prize—it was just the wrong one.

But that led to an entirely different problem. How were they going to explain the men's presence when they got back to what passed for their base of operations? It wasn't like they could just say they ran into them and brought them back for a visit. Allison had been right when she told Ryder this wasn't a tourist kind of place. This remote island, more than an hour east of all the others, had sustained significant damage from the hurricane several years ago. It was still recovering, would probably be recovering for the next five years, maybe even longer. The island wasn't home to any hotels or restaurants. It didn't have any fancy nightclubs or popular cultural attractions.

What it had was a small village nestled on the southeast side of the island and some private homes scattered here and there. Everything else was preserved as a nature sanctuary. People didn't come here to visit, not really. If they came here at all, it was to get away. And that didn't happen very often, either.

Hannah had no idea how her best friend was going to explain their presence—she could only hope Allison had some kind of plan because they were pulling up to their home-away-from-home now. Hannah had just placed the aging van in *Park* when the door to the main office—and the project coordinator's private quarters—opened. Kevin Wright stood just outside, his hands fisted on lean hips, brows pulled low over blue eyes. He stared at the van, no doubt wondering where they had gone and why.

Wasn't he about to be surprised?

Allison turned in the worn seat, a bright smile on her face. "Welcome home!"

Silence stretched from the back seat. A long, drawn-out silence that did not bode well for their survival. Hannah shifted, drummed her fingers on the steering wheel. Studied the few worn and aging buildings as if seeing them for the first time.

Nope. That brooding silence definitely didn't bode well for them.

"Home." Ryder's deep voice came from behind her, close enough that Hannah whirled in her seat. He braced his forearm against the headrest and leaned forward. But he wasn't looking at her, he was staring out the windshield, his dark eyes shielded by the even darker sunglasses.

What did he see when he studied the buildings? To him, they were probably nothing more than rundown bungalows constructed of concrete and in desperate need of paint.

Which was exactly what they were.

The colors—blues and greens and yellows—were faded from the sun that continuously beat down on them. In some places, paint was missing altogether, the surface chipped down to bare concrete. Lush vegetation surrounded the area, large palms providing shade that offered at least a little relief from the heat. A pavilion—nothing more than a corrugated tin roof braced on sturdy support posts—sat at the far edge of the tiny site. The community kitchen was inside the twenty square foot pavilion, tucked into the back against a make-shift wall. Mismatched tables and metal folding chairs provided a place to eat. Camp chairs—the heavy-duty nylon kind that folded up—provided a place to lounge in the shade.

Hannah had no idea what Ryder had been expecting. Five-star accommodations? Probably not. But from the stony expression on his face, it was a safe bet he hadn't been expecting the small scattering of buildings spread out in front of them.

He tucked one long finger behind the top frame of his sunglasses and slowly nudged them down his nose, just enough that his eyes were visible. And thank God that hard glare was focused on Allison instead of her.

"Home." Ryder repeated the word—a statement, not a question—in an ominously quiet voice. Hannah shifted in the seat, her gaze briefly meeting Allison's before sliding past and landing on Kevin. He was still standing outside his quarters, a frown creasing his tanned face as he stared at the van.

"Yes. *Home*. I told you this wasn't a tourist hot spot."

"This isn't any kind of spot, hot or otherwise." Ryder's arm brushed against her shoulder as he lowered it. Hannah stiffened, cursed the prickle of awareness shooting through her just from that brief touch. She shifted then swallowed back another curse when Kevin started working toward them.

"Allison." Hannah whispered her friend's name and motioned out the window. Allison glanced over her shoulder, muttered something when she saw Kevin, then quickly turned back to her brother.

"Just do me a favor and don't say anything, okay?"

"What the hell are you talking about? Say anything to who?"

"Ryder, please." Allison reached for the handle and pushed the door open, swung her legs to the side and hopped down with a bright smile.

Ryder swore to himself then turned to Hannah, pinning her in place with his dark gaze before she could make her own escape. "Who's that guy?"

"His name is Kevin. He's the project coordinator."

"What project? What the hell is going on?"

Hannah ignored him and opened her own door, climbed down then reached for the handle to slide open the passenger door. She didn't wait for Ryder or his friend to get out. Why would she, when she was certain he'd pin her in place with another glare and ask more questions? It was safer to let Allison deal with him—right after she dealt with Kevin. From the low sounds of conversation coming from the other side of the van, that might be a while.

Hannah pocketed the keys, forced a smile she didn't feel to her face, then stepped around the van to join Allison. Kevin paused in whatever he was saying to look at her, some of the tension leaving him.

"Hannah. I was wondering where you had disappeared to." He stepped a little closer, his smile deepening. "Maybe you can explain what's going on because Allison isn't making any sense."

"Um—" Hannah tossed a helpless glance at her friend. What had Allison told him? What excuse had she given him? Hannah wasn't sure and had no idea what to say, worried that she might say the wrong thing. This wasn't part of the plan. As far as Hannah knew, there *was* no plan because up until an hour ago, neither one of them had been sure that Ryder would even show up.

"Just what I told you, Kev. My brother and his friend are on vacation and wanted to stop by and say hello."

And yikes. *That* was the story she had come up with? Even Hannah would have a hard time believing that one. From the looks of it, Kevin wasn't buying it either. His clear gaze moved past both women, his eyes narrowing at something behind him. Hannah didn't need to turn around to know that Ryder had finally stepped out of the van. Didn't need to look to know that he was now only a few feet behind her. She could *feel* him there, a looming presence. Tall. Broad. A study of male perfection.

And about as inconspicuous as a brick wall.

Tension swirled around them, growing thicker with each passing second as the men studied each other. Hannah exchanged a quick glance with Allison, smothered a smile when the other woman rolled her eyes at the obvious display of male competition. The only thing missing was a few low growls and the baring of teeth.

No, scratch that. Kevin must have realized he was badly outnumbered—and out-manned—because his fake smile grew wide enough to show teeth. He studied the other two men in silence then turned that smile on Allison.

"This isn't a place for vacationers, Allison, and you know that. We *work* here. I can't afford to—"

"They know that and they've already agreed to help out. And pitch in with money." Ryder started to say something but Allison kept talking, raising her voice just enough to drown out his objections. "It's only for a few days, Kev. And you know we could use the extra hands, especially this late in the season."

"I need to get approval—"

"No, you don't." Allison stepped closer and playfully nudged him. "Like I said, it's only for a few days. Besides, this is no different than when your buddy comes around to hang out and I *know* you don't get approval for that."

Did Kevin hear the underlying threat in Allison's voice? Maybe. Or maybe he could just feel the simmering threat from Ryder himself—although Hannah was fairly certain *that* was aimed at Allison and not Kevin.

In the end, it made no difference because Kevin finally stepped back with a curt nod. "Fine. Just a few days. But I expect them both to work, and to pay their share of the fees. No excuses."

"Of course. I said they would, didn't I?"

Kevin frowned then slowly shook his head. He turned to Hannah, a smile replacing the frown as he reached for her. A hand closed over her arm in a gesture of familiarity that made her inwardly wince. "Now that you're back, I need your help with the weekly report. It shouldn't take long." He tugged her along, easing her away from the small group—and the curious gazes of the two men.

No, not the *two* men—just one in particular. And the look in Ryder's dark gaze was anything but curious.

For a brief second, Hannah considered telling Kevin *no*. He didn't need her help and they both knew it. This was just another ploy to get her alone so he could ask her out. Again. Any other time, she'd make up an excuse to avoid him, or offer to take the reports back to the bungalow she shared with Allison and do them herself.

The words were on the tip of her tongue, ready to fall from her mouth—and then she caught Ryder's gaze. Dark. Intense.

Irritated.

She knew that look, remembered it from the years they'd spent together growing up. Ryder was ready to explode. To start shouting and demanding answers. Allison was the one who had conned him into coming down here—let *her* deal with him and the hundred different questions he no doubt had.

The excuse she'd been ready to utter died on her lips and she quietly followed Kevin without a word, the heat of Ryder's dark gaze following her every step of the way.

CHAPTER THREE

Allison hurried away from him before he could say anything—probably a smart move on her part, one born from survival instinct. Not that Ryder couldn't have caught up with her because he could. And he would—as soon as he figured out where Hannah was going with that slimy little weasel.

His frown deepened when he saw the two of them disappear into one of the buildings. It was bigger than the others, though not by much, which wasn't saying a whole lot. All of the buildings—Ryder counted eight from what he could see—looked identical, except for the faded colors of the paint covering their concrete exteriors. The one Hannah just went into was a pale green, the paint fresher than the others.

And damn. The weasel closed the fucking door, but not before tossing a fucking smirk at Ryder over his shoulder.

He took a step toward the building—no idea why, unless it was to ram his fist into the weasel's face before grabbing Hannah—but a hand on his arm stopped him. Ryder stared down at the hand then looked at Ninja, a silent threat in his eyes. The other man totally ignored the warning and pulled him in the direction Allison had headed.

"Down, boy."

"Fuck you." Ryder shook his arm free then shifted the pack on his shoulder. "I don't like that guy."

"Yeah. No shit. But before you start breaking

limbs, don't you think you should figure out what the fuck is going on first?"

Ryder grunted in agreement and lengthened his stride, reaching the small building where Allison was standing in a matter of minutes. She frowned and quickly shook her head, then pushed open the door and motioned them both inside.

"Allison—"

"Keep your voice down."

"I'm not yelling—"

"Maybe not yet but you're close." She followed them inside then quickly closed the door behind her by ramming her hip against it. Ryder started to say something, made the mistake of looking around the small room, and swallowed back the roar that threatened to erupt.

What. The. Fuck.

The building was set up like a hotel room. Maybe. Two double beds were shoved against the far wall, separated by a single nightstand that had definitely seen better days. A large window, currently closed and shuttered, was directly above the beds. There was even a curtain hanging from the window, some kind of gauzy material in a pale yellow that was probably meant to add a homey touch to the depressing decorating scheme.

Two doors were set into the wall at the right. Ryder frowned at his sister then moved toward them, opening the first to reveal a small closet. He slammed it shut and opened the second, clenched his jaw at the sight of the tiny bathroom.

Sink. Toilet. Shower stall that would take a lot of contorting to fit in without banging his elbows and shoulders.

"Shit."

He slammed that door and looked around but there was nothing else to see except painted concrete walls, faded tile floor, and a worn dresser pushed against the outside wall. That's where Allison stood—which just happened to be in front of the door. Did she really think blocking the door would stop him from leaving if he wanted to? Had she learned nothing when they were growing up?

Judging from the mutinous expression on her face, probably not.

Ryder folded his arms in front of him and stared. "Start talking."

"This is your bungalow—"

"Is that what you're calling this thing?"

She ignored him and kept talking, her gaze focused on a spot over his shoulder. "I probably should have told you to bring some sheets with you but that's not a big deal. I have some extras you can borrow—"

"Allison—"

"The kitchen is in the pavilion. Breakfast is usually fruit and coffee. Lunch is provided at the job site. Everyone is expected to pitch in—"

"Allison—"

"—for dinner." Her gaze slid to his, quickly skittered away as she shifted her weight from one foot to the other. Ryder clenched his jaw and sucked in a deep breath before he exploded. He shot a look at Ninja but the other man was just standing there, studying the nylon strap of his watch like nothing was amiss.

Ryder dropped his arms to his side and moved closer to Allison, close enough that she actually backed up a step and collided with the door. Her eyes widened a fraction of an inch then quickly narrowed. She placed her hands against his chest and pushed. Frowned when he didn't budge and pushed again. Then damn if she didn't poke him in the sternum with that damn finger of hers.

Jab. "Don't even think about trying that stupid intimidation tactic with me because it won't—" *Jab.* "—work."

He grabbed her hand and held it away from him before she could jab him again. "And don't even think of kicking me again because that isn't going to work."

"I wasn't."

"Liar. Now start talking."

She lifted her chin a bit but wouldn't quite meet his gaze. "About what?"

"About everything. Why you called. Why you dragged me down here." He released her hand and stepped back. "And God help me, if this was some kind of stunt to get some cheap labor—"

"It wasn't. It's *not*. Honest." Allison glanced over at Ninja and offered him a sweet smile, then turned back to Ryder. The sweet smile morphed into a scowl. "Not that we can't use the help—"

"Allison, I swear to Christ—"

"Okay, okay. Fine." She stepped around him and took a seat on the edge of one of the beds. Springs creaked, the sound echoing around the room as she adjusted her position and crossed one tanned leg over the other. She folded her hands together, stared at them for a few seconds then started playing with the edge of one nail.

Seconds stretched by and with them, his patience. "Allison, *now*."

"Okay, okay. You don't have to yell." She dropped her hands to the side with a loud sigh. "About three weeks ago, Hannah and I were down by the building site. We went back after dinner because I thought I left something there. Turns out I didn't, it was in the van the whole time but I didn't think to look there—"

"Allison, get to the point."

She nodded, ran one hand through her hair and nodded again. "The point. Right. Anyway, when we were down there, we noticed two men walking on the beach. They, um, they had shovels. And some kind of metal detector thing."

Ryder waited. Waited some more. A full minute went by but Allison didn't say anything else. He released a heavy sigh and curled his hands in frustration. "That's it?"

"Um, well—" She shifted on the bed, creating another round of creaking before stilling. "They, um, they kind of shouted at us and, um, started running toward us, so we left. Fast."

"Let me get this straight. You saw two guys on the beach with a metal detector and automatically thought they were treasure hunters up to no good?"

"Well, the metal detector thing is what made me think they were treasure hunters. It was the chasing part that made me think they were up to no good."

Ryder brought both hands to his face and rubbed. Up and down, up and down, the stubble on his jaw scratching his palms. Shit. He needed to shave. He needed a shower. He needed about ten hours' worth of sleep.

And he really, really needed not to throttle his sister. His parents would kill him if he did that.

He dragged his hands through his hair then let his

arms drop. "What time does the first ferry leave in the morning?"

"Around nine. Why?"

"Because we're going to be on it."

"What?" Allison shot to her feet, confusion and worry marring her face. "You're just going to leave? You're not even going to look into it?"

"Look into *what*, Allison? You saw two guys on the beach—"

"But they *chased* us!"

Ryder doubted that. Knowing his sister, she probably overreacted. The guys were probably doing nothing more than trying to meet two pretty women and hook up. And yeah, *there* was a thought he didn't need. The idea of any guy trying to hook up with his sister—with *Hannah*—was enough to make him turn hot under the collar.

He pushed the irrational jealousy away and moved toward the door. He had every intention of escorting his sister out so he could take that shower then figure out how they were going to make it back to the dock to catch the morning ferry. Hell, they'd walk if they had to.

But Allison must have guessed what he was going to do because she rushed to the door and stood in front of it. Her arms stretched out to the side and a mutinous scowl wreathed her face.

"You can't leave. Not without looking into it."

"Look into *what*, Allison? Something you *think* you saw three weeks ago?"

"But—" She stopped, ran her tongue over her lip then quickly shook her head. "That's not all we saw."

"Really? What else did you see? The Loch Ness Monster? Bigfoot? The Kraken?"

The desperation he had sensed thrumming through her a second ago quickly changed to impatience. "Do you always have to be such an ass?"

"Do you always have to be so damn melodramatic? This is just like that time you swore you saw a troll hanging outside your bedroom window."

"I was *eight*! I didn't know any better back then."

"And you don't know any better now, either—"

"Boomer."

The sound of his name spoken in a low tone silenced him. He turned, frowned when he saw Ninja standing right behind him. And fuck, he hadn't even heard the man move. Hadn't sensed him so close. If they were anywhere else—if it had been *anyone* else—Ryder could be dead right now.

Damn Allison for distracting him.

No—damn *himself* for allowing her to distract him. For letting his guard down.

He threw his hands up in the air in mock surrender and stepped away from his sister. "Fine. *You* talk to her. Tell her she's imagining things and that we're leaving in the morning."

Ninja shot him an unreadable look then reached down and closed his hand over Allison's. He gently tugged, leading her back to the bed she'd been sitting on a few minutes earlier. And damn if he didn't take a seat right next to her, close enough that their legs were touching.

Ryder ground his back teeth together and leaned against the wall, his arms crossed in front of him. His fingers dug into the flesh of his biceps hard enough to leave marks but he kept his mouth shut.

"You said you saw something else." Ninja's voice was low, mellow. Soothing. Allison shot a nervous glance at Ryder then looked back at Ninja, her shoulders relaxing just the tiniest bit as she nodded.

"Yes. We went back last week, around the same time, and saw them again. There was a third man with them, and they were arguing."

"What were they arguing about?"

"I—I don't know. They were too far away. Where we were—it's up high. You'll see tomorrow. When we go there."

"You couldn't hear what they were saying but you knew they were arguing." It was a statement, quietly phrased to put Allison at ease. Did she even realize that Ninja was working his magic and putting her into some kind of trance?

Not that the other man would ever admit to it. The only thing he'd say was that he was good at relaxing people. That it was all about the soothing tone of his voice and the way he held a person's gaze.

Yeah. Right.

"Yes, arguing. Their voices were raised, and one of the men tried to shove another one."

"Did you recognize them?"

Allison frowned, shook her head. "No. But...there was something about one of them—" She sighed, shook her head again. "No, I didn't recognize them. We were too far away."

"And they didn't see you this time?"

"No. We made sure to stay hidden. We waited until they went into the cave and then we left."

"What cave?"

"There's a cave down there. We didn't even know about it until we saw the men go inside it. We went back the next day and went down to the beach—"

"Shit—" Ryder bit off the rest of what he was

going to say at Ninja's quick look. Probably a good thing, because whatever he'd been ready to say wouldn't have come out very nicely.

Allison kept talking as if she hadn't been interrupted. "We went into the cave and looked around and that's when we saw it."

"Saw what?"

"The treasure chest. But it didn't look like a treasure chest, not like the kind in the movies."

Ryder swallowed back a curse, dug his fingers deeper into the flesh of his arms. Damn her. Damn them both. What the hell had they been thinking, to go wandering off by themselves, spying on men they both thought were up to no good? It was probably nothing more than some tourists but still—

Yeah, sure. That's why a sudden chill crawled along the back of his neck.

"What did the chest look like?"

"It was long. Metal. Dark green. And heavy." Allison shrugged and offered Ninja an apologetic smile. "We tried to lift it but we couldn't. And it was locked so we couldn't open it."

Treasure chest, his ass.

The chill creeping along the back of Ryder's neck spread and started dancing up and down his spine. He exchanged a quiet look with Ninja and clenched his jaw even tighter.

Ninja turned back to Allison and gently squeezed her hand. "What did you do then?"

"We left. But..." Her voice trailed off as a small frown creased her face.

"But what, Allison?"

"They found a body washed up on the other side of the island the other day. They said he hit his head and drowned. But..." She hesitated, pulled her lower lip between her teeth and chewed on it for a second. "I—I think it was one of the men we saw."

"Why do you think that?"

"Because he was missing his leg."

Ryder blinked. Swore to himself. Blinked again then opened his mouth. Closed it. Frowned. Opened his mouth one more time—

"You have got to be fucking kidding me."

Allison yanked her hand from Ninja's and pushed to her feet, anger staining her face pink as she pointed a finger at Ryder. "Why do you have to say it like that? Like I'm making this whole thing up?"

"Because that's exactly what it sounds like: a made-up story. Orphans. Buried treasure. And hey, let's throw in a fucking one-legged pirate while we're at it. Guess he screwed up and they made him walk the plank, huh?"

"Fine. Go ahead and laugh. Don't believe me. I don't care. I know what I saw—what we *both* saw. And I know the man who drowned was one of the men we saw on the beach—"

"How do you even know that?"

"Because the man who got pushed had on a prosthesis, that's why!" Allison stormed toward the door and twisted the handle. Hesitated then turned back to Ryder. "I called you because I thought you could help. That's what big brothers are supposed to do. But instead, you come down here and have to act all macho superior. Hannah was right—you really are an ass!"

She threw open the door, stepped out, and slammed it behind her before Ryder could react. He stared at the door long after the echo of its slamming died then released a loud sigh and turned toward Ninja. The other man was still sitting on the edge of the bed, an amused grin curling his mouth.

"I think I'm siding with your ex on this one."

"Fuck you."

"Sorry, buddy, but that was a dick comment and you know it."

Ryder swallowed back a growl and pushed away from the wall. "I know. It's just...shit, it's so fucking far-fetched nobody would believe it."

"Maybe." Ninja shifted on the bed and pulled one leg up to his chest. "But that description she gave? Not a whole lot of things that could be."

"Yeah. I know."

Long. Metal. Dark green.

It was possible they were both jumping to conclusions. Possible that treasure chest was something else entirely different than what they were both thinking.

That chill racing along Ryder's spine said otherwise.

Ninja's dark eyes bore into his. "Wouldn't hurt to stay a few days. Check it out."

Ryder grabbed his pack from the floor and tossed it on the bed next to the wall. "Yeah. I know."

"Our flight out isn't until Monday. That gives us four full days after today."

"Yeah. I know." Ryder opened his pack, rummaged through it until his hand closed over his small shower kit.

"So. What's the plan?"

"The plan is to take a shower and grab a nap."

"I take it that means we're staying?"

Ryder scowled at Ninja then stormed toward the

tiny bathroom. "Yeah, we're staying."
    He slammed the door closed on Ninja's laughter.

CHAPTER FOUR

Ryder stood just outside the pavilion and studied the small crowd. Ten people gathered around, talking and laughing, their low voices drifting on the gentle breeze that rustled the fronds overhead. Twilight teased the horizon, the soft light adding a mystical feel to the gathering.

Ninja, the damned traitor, stood next to Allison, his head cocked to the side as she talked to the weasel and an older woman wearing a loose sundress that drifted around her calves. To anyone else, it would look like he was simply listening, but Ryder knew better.

Ninja was studying every single face, committing features and voices to memory for use later. Ryder was doing the same thing, but he wasn't quite as subtle as the other man.

An older man, dressed in loose linen shorts and an even looser tropical shirt, stood just beside the older woman. His gray hair was slightly tousled, a little windblown. Ryder figured he was the woman's husband. Retirees, most likely.

His gaze drifted to the trio standing a few feet away from the first group. Two women, probably in their early twenties, and a man a few years older. Mid-twenties? Ryder tilted his head to the side and studied the man a little more closely.

No, late twenties, but with the attitude of someone who refuses to grow up and thinks the entire world is his playground. The guy was standing a little too close to the brunette, although his attention was bouncing between both women. Hedging his bets, just in case? Maybe. Or maybe he was playing both women. It didn't matter because the brunette's friend had definitely noticed and was doing her best not to scowl whenever she thought the first two weren't looking at her.

Ryder made a mental note to keep away from all three of them. That triangle had *disaster* written all over it.

His gaze drifted to the other side of the pavilion, back where the makeshift kitchen was set up. A large refrigerator was placed against the wall. Dim light from the bare bulbs overhead reflected off the surface, showing every scratch and dent and gouge. Three cabinets topped with a chipped countertop separated the refrigerator from the stove wedged into the corner. Not a regular stove—the behemoth was an industrial grill, the kind you might see in a burger joint somewhere, with two big burners on the side and a flat grill next to those. An old exhaust hood was positioned just above it. Ryder figured the hood was more for show than anything else since three of the four sides of the pavilion were already open to the great outdoors—and all the bloodthirsty bugs that went with it.

He slapped at one of the little fuckers feasting on his arm, flicked it away and went back to studying the kitchen area.

Or rather, the woman scurrying back and forth in the kitchen area.

Hannah stood in front of the grill, her back to him as she flipped whatever she was cooking. She leaned to the side and said something to the younger girl next to her, who nodded and walked away, disappearing around the side of the pavilion somewhere.

Hannah moved back to the grill and lifted the lid from a big pot. Steam drifted around her and she waved her hand in front of her face for a few seconds before leaning over the pot and looking inside. She frowned, closed the lid, then turned the heat up a little higher before turning back to whatever she was cooking on the grill.

Was this how they usually handled dinner? One person cooked while everyone else mingled around like it was cocktail hour? Or was Hannah the designated cook?

Somehow he couldn't see that. He remembered a trip home a few years ago, when he'd been forced to go with his parents and Allison over to the Montgomery's for dinner. He'd spent an uncomfortable two hours trying to make casual conversation while ignoring Hannah the entire time—something that had been harder to do than he thought it would be. It got even more uncomfortable when Hannah's mom had gently teased her about burning dinner the night before. She'd turned bright red and shot him a look of such misery and embarrassment that Ryder had taken pity on her and made up some lame ass excuse for why he had to leave.

Yeah, because he was honorable that way. So fucking honorable that he couldn't even stay in the same room with the girl who's virginity he'd taken eleven years ago.

Shit.

He clenched his jaw and started toward the makeshift kitchen. Ignored Allison's call and Ninja's smartass grin. Fuck it. He was thirty-fucking-years-old—more than old enough to move on from what had happened a lifetime ago. If they were going to be stuck on this fucking island for the next few days, he could at least pretend to act normal.

He leaned his shoulder against the refrigerator then cleared his throat. "Need help with anything?"

Hannah stiffened then whirled around, surprise flashing in her eyes. For a brief second, Ryder thought she might actually haul off and hit him with the oversized spatula in her hand. She lowered her arm and quickly turned away, but not before he saw the flush staining her cheeks.

"Um, no. Thank you. Everything's under control."

Ryder peered over her shoulder, frowning at the small slabs of pale meat on the grill. "What's that you're cooking?"

"Fish."

"Fish." Ryder leaned closer, sniffed. "It doesn't smell like fish. It smells like...nothing."

"Like nothing?"

"Yeah. Like nothing." He stepped closer and studied the filets spread out on the grill. "You guys have something against seasoning down here?"

"No. But with all the different tastes and dietary restrictions, we usually let everyone season their own stuff at the table."

It was a lame answer but he couldn't argue with it, not when it was probably the truth. "Which one's mine?"

"Yours?" Hannah glanced at him, down at the fish, then back at him. "I don't know. Why?"

"Because I'd rather have mine seasoned on the grill. Depending on what kind of seasonings you have."

Hannah raised the spatula and pointed toward a small cabinet mounted on the wall next to the refrigerator. "Everything we have is in there. And since when do you know anything about cooking?"

"Since I had to learn as a matter of survival." He opened the cabinet, studied the scattered bottles of spices, then grabbed a few of them. He moved back to the grill. "So which one is mine?"

"I don't know. Pick one."

He bit back a grin at the irritation in her voice then nudged her out of the way and quickly seasoned two of the filets.

"You only get one—"

"The other is for Ninja."

"Who?"

"Ninja. Colter." He swallowed back a chuckle at the confusion marring Hannah's face. "My buddy? The one I dragged down here for the life-and-death situation?"

"Oh. I didn't know his name."

"Well, now you do." He took the spatula from her and turned each filet, then added more seasoning to the two he had picked out for Ninja and him.

"That wasn't my idea."

"What wasn't?"

"Calling you. I told Allison it wasn't a good idea."

"Yeah?" Ryder turned, caught Hannah's gaze with his own and lowered his voice. "Because you don't think there's anything to it? Or because you didn't want me to come down here?"

A small flush stained her cheeks and she quickly looked away. "No, there's definitely something to it."

Yeah, she definitely put him in his place with *that* answer. Ryder clenched his jaw and turned back to the grill. "Do you have plates anywhere? These are ready to go."

"Already? I thought they had to cook longer."

"Not unless you want them dried out. Plates?"

Hannah moved toward the low row of cabinets that made up a makeshift island bar behind her and pulled out a stack of plates. "The rice and vegetable mix probably isn't done yet. I put them on late—"

"Is that what's in the pot?"

Hannah nodded. "It's only been boiling for ten minutes or so."

"Then it's probably done." Ryder grabbed the stack of plates and slid a filet on each one before handing it to Hannah so she could place them on the makeshift bar. Then he moved to the pot, removed the lid, and stared at the contents. What the hell was that mess even supposed to be? It was a mix of overcooked rice, peas, and something red. Peppers? Something else?

He had no idea and part of him was afraid to ask.

He grabbed the two potholders and pulled the pot from the burner, then looked around for someplace to drain all the water. Hannah pointed to the large double sink off to the side. "I already put the colander in there. You just—"

"Yeah, I know." Ryder dumped the mess into the colander, waited until it was completely drained, then emptied the contents back into the pot. "And that takes care of that. Dinner's ready."

And why the hell was Hannah looking at him that way? With her brows furrowed and that full mouth pursed like she'd just gotten a taste of something sour? Not angry. Not irritated. Just...baffled. Like she was trying to figure out the punchline of a joke someone just told.

He started to ask her what was wrong but she

turned away from him and called out to everyone. Yeah, like they hadn't all been standing there watching for the last ten minutes and couldn't tell that dinner was ready. Instead of rushing toward the food like he'd expected, everyone hung back, waiting. For what, he didn't know. He caught Ninja's gaze, shrugged, then reached for his plate—only to be stopped by Hannah's hand on his arm.

Heat rushed through him, the sudden awareness of her touch sharp and biting and holy fucking hell, what was that about? It was just her hand, for fuck's sake. On his *arm*. It wasn't like she just shoved her hand down his pants and wrapped her fingers around his cock and started stroking.

And fuck, he didn't need that image. He didn't need *any* image, not of Hannah. Not of sex. Especially not of sex *with* Hannah.

Shit. Too late. The image was there, crystal clear in vivid color, complete with scent and sound and touch. Not a memory of what they'd done before, all those years ago—although the memory certainly added to it. No, this was a vivid image of what he wanted *now*.

Hannah's body under his, her legs wrapped high around his waist as he plunged his cock inside her. Deep. Hard. Fast. Hannah's hands clutching him, nails scoring his bare flesh. Her soft voice, calling his name as she splintered apart with the force of her orgasm, her pussy clenching his cock over and over as she came.

Holy.

Fucking.

Shit.

His balls drew tight with the image and for a horrifying second, he thought he'd made a sound, a low groan or even a grunt as he recalled in excruciating detail exactly how it felt to drive his cock deep inside her. How it felt to lose himself in her tight pussy.

Maybe he *did* make a sound because everyone was staring at him. No, not everyone. Just Ninja, who didn't miss a damn thing, and Hannah—

She jerked her hand from his arm and looked away, a blush staining her cheeks as she focused on the crowd—and on the weasel who was talking, droning on and on about something stupid.

Completely ignoring the fact that Ryder had just mind-fucked Hannah to completion in thirty seconds flat, damn near exploding himself with nothing more than the image of her naked body, lush and willing, under his.

Fuck.

He grabbed his plate before the weasel finished talking and stormed toward the furthest of the three tables, Ninja right behind him. That seemed to be all the invitation anyone else needed because the small crowd converged on the food, chattering amongst themselves.

Ryder tuned them out, cut off a piece of the fish and popped it into his mouth—and had to force himself not to spit it right back out. He looked around, searching for beer or *something* but there was only bottled water. He grabbed one, uncapped it, and took three long swallows.

Shit.

He forced himself not to choke then sat there, waiting to see if his stomach was going to rebel or not. Allison dropped into the chair next to him, frowned, then nudged him in the arm.

"Get that expression off your face before Hannah

sees it."

Ryder froze. Shit. Did he still look guilty about his mind-fucking episode? Or embarrassed, maybe? Because yeah, he was, but he sure as hell didn't think anyone would be able to tell, not just by looking at him. Especially not his sister. And Christ, how fucking mortifying was that? To be caught—

"She's very self-conscious."

"Uh—"

"So don't say anything. Just pretend you enjoy it."

"What?" Maybe the question came out louder than he planned it to because Ninja kicked him under the table. Ryder ignored him, his gaze focused on Allison—on the brows pulled low over her eyes and the slight purse of her lips as she frowned at him. She leaned closer and lowered her voice.

"That's what everyone else does."

Ryder blinked, raised one hand and rubbed his knuckles against his mouth. Looked around to see whose ass he needed to kick.

Finally realized that no way in hell was Allison talking about what he *thought* she was talking about. At least, he hoped to hell she wasn't.

"You, uh, want to clue me in here?"

"About what?"

"About whatever the hell you're talking about. *What* does everyone pretend they're enjoying?"

"Hannah's cooking. What did you think I was talking about?"

Her *cooking*. Yeah. Of course.

Ryder looked down at the plate filled with unappetizing food and had to force himself not to push it away. "This isn't cooking."

Allison laughed, the sound whisper-soft. "No

kidding. Welcome to my hell for the last six months. But don't say anything because Hannah's self-conscious about it. Just eat it as fast as you can—you don't really taste it much that way." She forked a small bit of fish into her mouth, chewed once, and swallowed. "See?"

"It's not that bad."

Ryder shot a disbelieving look at Ninja. "Are you for real?"

"Compared to other things I've had to eat? Yeah, I'm for real."

The man had a point. And while Ryder hadn't expected a gourmet meal—hell, he hadn't expected *any* meal—the chewy fish and soggy rice were a far cry from what he'd call edible.

He forced himself to eat a few more bites then placed the fork down. "Does Hannah cook every night?"

"No, everyone takes turns. You guys will, too, if you stay past Monday."

"Yeah, not happening." The cooking *or* staying. His gaze drifted to the other two tables a few feet away. Hannah was sitting at the furthest one, along with the elderly couple—and the weasel. "So what's that guy's story?"

Allison took a long swallow from her water bottle, capped the lid, then followed the direction of his gaze. "You mean Kevin?"

"Yeah. The weasel."

"Don't be an ass. He's the project coordinator."

"Anything going on with him and Hannah?" Ryder tried to infuse his voice with nonchalant curiosity. From the knowing look Allison shot his way, he had failed miserably.

"No, not like you're thinking. She acts more or less like his assistant."

"Assistant? I thought you said you guys were volunteering."

"We are, for the most part. But we're part of the organization so there's a small stipend."

There was something about the way she said it that made Ryder's brows shoot up. "How small?"

"Um—" Allison shifted in the chair, her gaze focused on the plate of food in front of her as she mumbled her answer. Ryder leaned closer.

"What was that?"

"I said a few hundred."

"A week?"

"Um, no. A month."

"A month."

"Yes, a month. But we don't have any expenses—at least, not many, just anything personal we might need while we're here so I'm able to save all of it."

"Christ." Ryder shook his head, glanced at the people sitting at the other tables and swallowed back a curse. "So everyone here works for the same organization?"

"No, we're the only staff. Kevin, Hannah, and me. Everyone else has paid to come here to help out."

"Wait. What do you mean, *paid*? They're not volunteers?"

"No, they are. But they pay to come here. It helps cover the cost of materials and food and other expenses." Allison nodded toward the table where Hannah was. "The Millers came down for four weeks with their granddaughter, Katie. She's the younger girl at the other table. They're retired and go on a few volunteer trips each year. Next week is their last week here."

Allison paused long enough to take a few more bites of food. She washed it down with more water then nodded toward the second table. "This is the first time for the two women. Cindy Mitchell and Darla Brooks. They only came for a week and leave on Saturday. I, uh, I don't think this is exactly what they were expecting."

"Yeah, can't imagine why." Ryder looked over at Ninja, frowned at the man's empty plate, then pushed his own toward him. Hell, if Ninja could choke the food down, then he might as well have Ryder's, too.

"So what about Casanova? What's his story?"

"Who?" Allison looked over, frowned then sat back in the chair. "Oh, you mean Tim Keaton. I'm not really sure what his story is. He's been here for a little more than a month already and he's staying until we head home for the holidays. I think he comes from money or something."

Ryder grunted. "More dollars than sense, then."

Allison smacked his arm. "You know, you don't have to be so cynical all the time."

"How the hell was that cynical?"

"It was the way you said it. So what if he flirts with everyone? He isn't afraid to work and right now, we're really short on help so stop being such an ass."

"Why the hell are you getting so upset?"

"Because of you and your attitude." Allison pushed her chair away from the table and grabbed her plate. "There's more to saving the world than killing the bad guys, you know."

Ryder watched in surprise as his sister walked away. He turned to Ninja, who looked just as surprised as he did. "What the fuck did I say wrong?"

"No idea." Ninja motioned to the plate Ryder had pushed his way. "You sure you don't want the rest of this?"

"Yeah. Positive." Ryder tossed his napkin down and pushed away from the table. "I'm going back to our room. Hut. Bungalow. Whatever the fuck they're calling it. Do me a favor and find out what we're supposed to be doing tomorrow."

"You still planning on staying?"

Ryder clenched his jaw, shot a look at the people gathered around the other two tables, laughing and talking. At his sister, her shoulders rigid as she worked on cleaning up the night's meal.

At Hannah, whose gaze moved from Allison to him. She tilted her head to the side and frowned, concern mixing with censure in her warm eyes.

Ryder pulled his gaze from hers and stood. "Yeah, we're still staying."

For now.

But he didn't say that out loud. From the look Ninja gave him, he didn't have to.

CHAPTER FIVE

Kevin was monopolizing the conversation—again. Excitement laced his accented voice as he regaled the table with a story from a trip he'd taken last year to Egypt. The Millers seemed genuinely interested, leaning forward to absorb every single word coming from the man's mouth.

To Hannah, the words were nothing more than a low drone. Annoying background noise that created a ringing in her ears and a dull throbbing at the base of her skull. She didn't care about Kevin's stories, thought they were probably just that: stories. Carefully constructed tales woven to paint a picture of an adventurer. A seasoned world-traveler. An experienced humanitarian who had seen it all and done it all.

His leg brushed hers under the table, a touch that was probably anything but accidental. She moved her leg and shifted away but didn't bother looking at him, staring instead at the spot where Ryder had disappeared into the darkness only a few minutes ago.

She hadn't missed the tension in the set of his broad shoulders or the way the muscle jumped in his clenched jaw. Similar tension tightened Allison's shoulders as she worked on cleaning up the kitchen area. Had the two argued about something?

Possibly, although Hannah hadn't heard any raised voices. She hadn't heard *anything*, period, mostly because Kevin's accented voice drowned out everything else. Like right now, when he was leaning toward her, his leg once again nudging hers under the table.

She turned toward him, frowned, then pushed away from the table. "Excuse me, I just remembered something I have to do."

She didn't, of course. It was nothing more than a weak excuse to escape—and do something that would probably rank right up there as one of the stupidest things she'd ever done. Mr. Miller slowly rose to his feet, a gesture of manners from bygone days. Kevin simply sputtered his objections. Hannah almost laughed at the surprised dismay on his face as she walked away—almost. She simply didn't have the patience to deal with his self-absorption, not anymore. Not for the last few months.

She paused a few feet outside the pavilion, letting her eyes adjust to the darkness. Nighttime was so absolute here, the darkness unmarred by the light pollution she had never really noticed back home—not until coming down here. For the most part, she was used to the darkness now, knew the layout of their small compound well enough to walk it blindfolded if she needed to.

Not that they didn't have lights—they did. Cindy and Darla had left the small light in their bungalow on every single night since their arrival. Not just until they retired, but *all* night, even when they were asleep. Probably during the day as well, even though they'd been asked not to.

Would the soft glow of the light from their bungalow serve as a point of reference for Ryder? Would he even need it, or was he able to maneuver through the dark without assistance? Hannah thought he probably could, that he would have been trained to move in the dark to do...well, whatever it was he was trained to do.

Almost as if she had willed it, the light from his bungalow came on, another soft glow ten yards away. A beacon of sorts, calling her. Tempting her. Hannah hesitated, indecision pulling at her.

Indecision? No, not even close. She already knew what she was going to do—just as she knew that it was a mistake in the making.

She ignored the hum of conversation behind her, ignored the sound of her name as Kevin called her. Ignored everything as she placed one foot in front of the other, moving closer to Ryder's bungalow. Closer still, until she stood outside the door. Raised her hand. Took a deep breath meant to fortify her courage—

And finally knocked.

Sixteen seconds went by—she knew because she counted every single one—before the door opened. Her eyes widened at the sight of the man standing in front of her: bare-chested, wearing nothing but a pair of dark boxer briefs that hugged his hips and thighs and clung to...well, *everything*. Holy hell, how had he undressed so quickly?

Not that she was complaining because she wasn't. And yes, he had definitely filled out during the years.

Everywhere.

Her palms itched with a sudden need to run her hands over that broad chest, to feel the dark hair under her palms, to trace that line of dark hair down the washboard abs, down lower to where it disappeared—

She slammed her eyes closed and spun around, but not before she saw the way his full mouth curled into a teasing grin. "Can you, um, maybe put on some clothes?"

Ryder muttered something under his breath—or maybe that was a strangled laugh, she couldn't really tell. She heard a rustling sound, followed by the soft whisper of a zipper being pulled up. Irrational disappointment swirled through her and really, how stupid was that? He was only doing what she asked, there was absolutely no reason to be disappointed—

"You can turn around now."

She nodded, pulled in another fortifying breath, turned around—and nearly choked when she exhaled. "You, uh, you forgot your shirt."

Ryder raised one brow as he eased his weight onto the edge of the mattress. "The sight of a bare chest offends you?"

"No. Of course not." *Offend?* Oh boy, not even close. That was such the wrong word. *Tempt* would be a much better choice—but she wasn't about to admit that, especially not to the man who was watching her with the slightest hint of a smile on his face, like he knew exactly what she was thinking.

Damn him.

She yanked her gaze from the chest in question and focused on a spot on the wall just over his shoulder. A minute went by, then another, the silence finally broken by the sound of Ryder clearing his throat.

"Was there something you needed, Hannah?"

Needed? Talk about a loaded question—

Hannah gave herself a mental shake, met his amused gaze, quickly looked away. "I, um, just wanted to make sure everything was okay. With you and Allison, I mean."

"You mean other than the fact that she called me down here under false pretenses?"

Hannah swallowed her spurt of anger. "It wasn't false pretenses—"

"Bullshit."

"Did she tell you what happened?"

"Yeah—and it's not exactly a life-or-death situation like she said on the phone."

Her eyes snapped to his. "You don't think the dead guy covers the *or death* part?"

"Since I seriously doubt either one of you are in any danger, no, it doesn't."

A tingle of warmth filled her. That feeling was quickly followed by irritation. The last thing she needed to do was read into his comment. Just because he happened to include her in it meant absolutely nothing. She was here with his sister so of course he'd include her, that's just part of who he was and what he did. The big brother, looking out for his kid sister and her best friend.

Except Ryder hadn't been a big brother to her, not since the night she'd given him her virginity—and her heart.

She pushed those thoughts away and forced herself to focus on why she had come here in the first place. At least, on the pretense of why.

"Is that what you two were arguing about at dinner?"

Ryder frowned and shifted on the bed so he was leaning against the cheap headboard. He stretched one leg out in front of him then raised his arms and clasped his hands behind his head. "We weren't arguing."

Was he deliberately trying to distract her? Probably.

She ignored the broad expanse of that sculpted chest and forced herself to meet his gaze. "If you weren't arguing, why did you storm off? And why did Allison look pissed?"

He shrugged, the nonchalant gesture at direct odds with the brief clenching of his jaw. "I don't know. You'll have to ask her."

"I'm asking *you*."

"And again, I don't know. One minute we were talking and the next, she was accusing me of being a cynical ass."

"Why? What did you say to her?"

A flash of annoyance lit his dark eyes. "Because I'm automatically to blame, right?"

"That's not what I said—"

"Isn't it?"

There was something about the way Ryder was watching her that made her think he was no longer talking about Allison. And how foolish was that? Of course he was talking about Allison. What else could he be talking about?

The way he had left with no warning and no explanation, leaving her with nothing but hurtful words all those years ago.

The way she had blamed him for her broken heart—a heart that was still mending, even after all this time.

No, of course not. That was silly. Yes, she had blamed him—back then. She'd been young and foolish and in love. Had thought, at the ripe old age of almost-seventeen, that she had met her soulmate. That they'd be together forever.

But that was a long time ago. A lifetime ago. She'd grown up in the years since then, knew there was no such thing as *soulmates* and that *forever* was nothing more than a fairytale. Ryder had been her first love—maybe her only love—but certainly not her last encounter. What she felt for him now was nothing more than nostalgia.

And attraction.

And a healthy dose of lust.

And she really needed to stop thinking like that because now so wasn't the time. Or the place. And she wouldn't be standing here trying to reign in her wayward thoughts if he had put on a damn shirt like she had asked—

She yanked her gaze from the expanse of his hairy chest—again—and forced her mind back to their conversation. "Allison doesn't get angry for no reason at all. Are you sure you didn't say anything to her?"

"Positive. I just made some crack about Casanova having more dollars than sense, that was it."

"Casanova?" Hannah frowned—until she figured out who he was talking about. Tim. He had to be talking about Tim. "Oh. Well, that would explain it."

"Explain what?"

"Why Allison got angry."

"Yeah? Care to enlighten me?"

"She, um, she may have a little crush on him." Maybe more than a little crush, but no way was Hannah going to tell him that. Maybe she didn't need to because he jumped to his feet, a dark scowl on his face.

"Did he sleep with her?"

Hannah was going to tell him *no*—it was the truth, as far as she knew, because she didn't think Allison had gone quite that far with him. Not that she didn't want to, even if he was slime.

Ryder was already moving past her before she could get the word out—and that expression on his face was *not* a good sign. In another fifteen seconds, he'd be ripping the door from its hinges and storming outside. Poor Tim wouldn't stand a chance.

Hannah couldn't let that happen. Not that Tim didn't deserve it because he *was* slime, but because it would only cause additional problems. Kevin wasn't thrilled with Ryder or his friend being here in the first place—he'd made that very clear to her earlier. It wouldn't take much for him to force them both to leave. It might even put Hannah's position in jeopardy. Not to mention the negative impact it would have on the organization as a whole if one of their volunteers had his ass kicked.

Hannah reached for Ryder, her hand closing around his steely bicep. Heat from his bare flesh scalded her palm, made her fingers tingle. The muscle under her hand bunched and tensed and she held her breath, waiting for him to brush her hold off. She looked up, caught his gaze and held it.

"Ryder, don't."

The muscle in his jaw clenched and released. Clenched and released. He dropped his gaze from hers and glanced at her hand, at the way her fingers still gripped his arm. An odd expression crossed his face, much like the one she noticed earlier, when she had placed her hand on his arm just before dinner. She hadn't understood the expression then—

But she thought she understood it now.

If she were smart, she'd release his arm and leave. Run out the door and lock herself in her bungalow while he ran out and went all big-brother on Tim's worthless ass.

Except Ryder didn't look like he was in a hurry to avenge his sister's honor. Not anymore.

His gaze moved back to hers, his eyes dark with

need. Hannah's hand tightened around his arm, nothing more than a reflex from being studied so intently. Yes, she should move. Drop her hand. Step away from him.

Run like hell.

Instead of moving away, she stepped closer. The swell of her breast brushed against his arm, the nipple tightening almost painfully. He shifted, one of his legs moving between hers. Mere inches separated them and it would easy, so easy, to rise up on her toes and brush her mouth against his—

Why shouldn't she? She wanted him—she had never stopped wanting him, even after all these years. What *wasn't* there to want? Tall. Broad. Defined muscle and hot flesh. A solid wall of pure male perfection. She wasn't the only who wanted, she could see the truth of his own desire in the smoldering eyes that held hers.

One kiss. That was all she wanted. One kiss, just to see if he could still make her stomach clench and her toes curl. To see if he could make her body come alive the way he had all those years ago.

No, she didn't need a kiss for that, not when her body was already yearning for his touch. Not when damp heat was already spreading between her legs, readying herself for him. Needing his touch, begging for a release it knew only he could give.

One kiss.

Only a single kiss wouldn't be enough. It never was, not with Ryder. And if that single kiss led to more?

She didn't care. She wanted him. *Needed* him.

Hannah leaned up on her toes, let her eyes drift shut as she brushed her mouth against his—

And felt him stiffen in response.

She hesitated, slowly leaned back and carefully

opened one eye. Ryder was scowling down at her, the desire she had seen in his eyes mere seconds ago nothing more than a shadow now.

She closed her eye, stepped back as the heat of mortification filled her, quickly dousing the flames of need that had threatened to consume her. God, she was such a fool. Should that surprise her? Was that really anything new? No, not when it came to the man in front of her.

She opened her eyes and took another step back. Started to apologize only to be stopped by Ryder's own voice, deep and husky and rough. "What are you doing, Hannah?"

She blinked, almost laughed in surprise—would have laughed if she hadn't noticed the burning desire that flared in Ryder's eyes one more time for a brief second before he hid it. He wasn't a stupid man, not even close—he knew exactly what she had been doing. And he wouldn't ask unless he was trying to throw her off-base. Make her doubt herself and what she wanted. What *he* wanted.

Filled with renewed confidence, she leaned closer, pressing her chest against his and silently cursing the thin barrier of her shirt. What would he do if she suddenly reached down and peeled it and her sports bra off? If she pressed her half-naked body to his? Would he take advantage of what she was offering?

Or would he stutter in surprise at her boldness?

Yes, he'd definitely be surprised—she wasn't the shy, awkward girl she'd been all those years ago. And he wasn't the only one who had filled out, either. But he wouldn't let her see even a hint of surprise. Ryder kept his emotions—and his reactions—carefully guarded. He'd always been that way, even back when they were growing up.

It was one of the things that had hurt the most during their oh-so-brief time together.

She pushed the past away and focused on the present. Here. *Now*, with her body pressed against his. That dark gaze of his focused on her with an intensity that sent shivers racing through her—not shivers of fear or anxiety, but shivers of excitement.

Because no matter how hard he tried to hide it now, she didn't miss the desire smoldering in the depths of those dark eyes.

She pressed her lips against the base of his throat. Tasted the heat of his skin, the slight muskiness of pure male. Felt the way his body tightened, the way his arms pulled her the tiniest bit closer before he tried to step back.

"Hannah, what are you doing?" His voice was even lower now. Huskier, edged with a roughness that pebbled her skin. She bit back her smile and looked up, caught his gaze.

"Kissing you."

"Why?"

"Why not?"

The muscles in his throat silently worked as he swallowed. His hands closed over her arms but he didn't push her away as she feared he would.

"This isn't a good idea."

He was probably right but— "I don't care."

Heat flashed in his eyes, igniting an answering heat deep inside her. Then he blinked and the heat was gone. No, not gone—it was merely hidden behind a carefully constructed mask designed to push her away.

"You want me to fuck you? Is that what this is about?"

The callous words almost did what they were intended to do: push her away. Make her run out the door and never look back. But it was too late because she saw what Ryder was trying to hide with those words:

Need.

Desire.

And beyond that, a yearning so deep and complete that it nearly took her breath away.

She leaned up on her toes and pressed her mouth against the corner of his, heard the sharp hitch in his breath before he could hide it. Then she lifted her head and caught his gaze, let him see the answer in her eyes.

Let him hear it in the single whispered word that fell from her mouth.

"Yes."

CHAPTER SIX

You want me to fuck you?

He'd spit the question with as much ice in his voice as possible—a damn hard thing to do when he was fucking burning up inside. His cock was already straining for release, hard and rigid, begging for just a taste of Hannah's sweet heat.

The question should have frightened her. She should have pushed him away and run for the door. And if it didn't frighten her, it should have pissed her off.

It sure as hell shouldn't have created that flame of need burning deep in her eyes as she stared up at him.

Yes.

Christ, had she really said that? Yeah, she had. Everything about her was saying *yes*, from that slow burn in her eyes to the way her body pressed against his to the way her tongue darted out and gently slid against her lower lip. And holy fuck, it was so fucking easy to picture that tongue sliding along something else. Picture, hell—he *remembered* what it felt like. Hannah straddling him, one hand gently cupping his balls as her eager tongue darted out and ran along the length of his cock. Swirled around the head and back down, those shining eyes never leaving his as she gave him a blowjob for the very first time. *Her* first, not his. But holy shit, it had been the best one ever.

And *fuck*! He had to stop thinking like that. Had to stop those fucking—damn, wrong word—

memories from coming back. Especially now, when her warm body was pressed against his, when her hips gently rocked against the hard length of his cock.

When she stared up at him with those wide eyes filled with need and desire.

It would be easy, so fucking easy, to peel off her clothes and toss her on the bed and sink his cock into her welcoming heat. But he couldn't—she deserved better than he could ever give her. She wanted commitment—happily-ever-after and a house full of kids. Ryder couldn't give that to her.

And he'd be damned if he took advantage of her knowing that. He'd done that once. Nothing could make him do it again.

He tightened his hold on her arms and stepped back. Waited to make sure she wouldn't close that distance between them before finally dropping his hands. "This is a bad idea, Hannah."

She didn't move—thank God. But he couldn't understand why the barest hint of a smile curled her full mouth, or why she tilted her head to the side and slowly raked her gaze from his head to his bare feet and back again—with a long pause at his chest. And Christ, just that look was enough to make his cock twitch with desperate need.

"Why? We're both consenting adults."

What. The. Fuck.

He hadn't expected her to say that. Not in his wildest imaginings. He folded his arms over his chest and took another step back. Shook his head. Refused to meet her gaze. If he did, he'd be lost. This whole acting honorable thing wasn't his gig. He didn't do relationships—because they didn't last. He'd learned that a long time ago. And it worked for him. Worked for his partners, too. Well, mostly. One or two had thought they could change him, even when he'd been honest and upfront from the very get-go.

No relationships—because the one time he'd tried it, he'd broken the girl's heart.

And lost his own heart in the process.

And yeah, fuck, wasn't that a real kick in the fucking balls because that one time had been with the woman currently eyeing him up like a starving man at an all-you-can-eat buffet.

He took another step back and bumped up against the warped dresser. "I don't do relationships."

The words—blurted out with a desperation he didn't quite understand—had the exact opposite effect he'd hoped. Instead of turning for the door, Hannah simply shrugged, one sculpted brow arching high over laughing eyes.

"Who said anything about wanting a relationship?

"I—you—" Ryder snapped his mouth closed and frowned. "Hannah, you fucking *proposed* to me the last time we were together!"

She shrugged and dropped her gaze, but not before he saw the palest blush fan across her cheeks. That blush was gone when she raised her head a few seconds later. "I was young and foolish. You were my first love. I didn't know any better."

"And you do now?" It was a shitty thing to say—which was exactly why he said it. But the words didn't have the effect he'd thought they would because instead of looking upset, Hannah just shrugged again and moved a little closer.

"I'm not young *or* foolish anymore. And I'm certainly not in love."

The casual words flew through the air and

punched him dead-center in the chest. And fuck, that made no sense. He shouldn't feel like he'd just been sucker-punched. Shouldn't be upset that she had so readily admitted she wasn't in love. Dammit, that was a *good* thing.

Ryder was still mentally floundering, trying to make sense of his asinine reaction, when Hannah closed the distance between them. He uncrossed his arms and started to reach for her—to push her away, because that was the only smart thing to do—but she shook her head and grabbed the hem of her shirt—

And yanked it over her head. The sports bra went next, the soft pink material landing somewhere near her feet. He thought. Hell, for all he knew, she'd tossed the damn thing across the room. He didn't care, could barely form a string of coherent thoughts in his mind because holy fuck, Hannah was standing in front of him, naked from the waist up. He stared at her full breasts, the delicate skin paler than her arms and shoulders. His mouth dried and his cock stiffened almost painfully as the rosy nipples tightened into hard peaks just begging to be touched. To be licked. To be sucked.

Holy.

Fuck.

All he wanted to do was reach out and mold his hands around those firm breasts. To flick each nipple with the tip of his thumb. To close his mouth around each one and lose himself in all that delicious skin.

But he couldn't move. Hell, he could barely fucking breathe. But his mind—just a tiny sane portion that hadn't completely deserted him—told him to back off. Warned him that touching her was a mistake. This was *Hannah*, dammit—and no matter what she said, she deserved more than a casual romp.

That's what his *mind* said. The look in Hannah's eyes, in the way her body moved toward his, said something completely different. And when she finally spoke, he knew he was doomed.

"We're just two consenting adults, Ryder." She trailed the tip of her finger through the hair on his chest. Down along his sternum, his abdomen. Lower, to the waistband of his pants. Then she leaned forward, the tight points of her nipples pressing against the heated skin of his chest. Her lips brushed against the base of his throat, igniting a fire deep inside that threatened to consume him.

"Please."

It was that final word, so low and throaty and filled with need, that snapped his tenuous control. He cupped her face between his hands and tilted her head back, captured her mouth in a deep kiss meant to conquer. But was it really a conquering when she surrendered so willingly?

He didn't know.

He didn't care.

Not when her hands closed over his shoulders. Not when she dragged those hands down along his arms, fingers kneading and digging into flesh and muscle until they closed over his wrists.

Not when she guided his hands from her face to her own breasts then sighed in delight when he cupped their heavy weight in his palms.

He deepened the kiss, caught her moan in his mouth, answered with one of his own. Then he broke the kiss, dragged his mouth along the column of her throat, nipping and licking. Down further, across the line of her collarbone, down until his mouth closed over one tight peak and pulled it into his mouth.

She sighed again, her back arching to give him fuller access to those beautiful breasts. Her fingers tangled in his hair, holding him in place as he sucked and nipped. And Christ, she tasted so good. So fucking sweet.

But he wanted more. So much more.

He reached between them, undid the button of her shorts and slid the zipper down then dipped his hand inside. Fuck, she was so fucking wet. He pressed one finger against her clit, teased the sensitive flesh. Heard her low moan as her hips rocked against his hand. Slow at first, then faster, each breathy sigh growing louder. She reached between them, pushing at her shorts and underwear until they slid down her legs. She untangled one foot from the bunched material then spread her legs, opening herself more fully to his touch. Hands closed over his shoulders for balance, fingers digging into bare flesh. No, not balance—she was pushing against him.

Not away, but *down*.

Fuck, yes.

Ryder dropped to his knees, wrapped one arm around her hips, and closed his mouth over her heated flesh. How. Wet. Sweet. So fucking sweet. He used the fingers of his free hand to spread her lips, flicked the point of his tongue against her clit. Again. Over and over as he slid one finger inside her tight pussy. In. Out. Gentle. Slow at first then faster, matching the needy rhythm of her rocking hips.

He released his hold on her, reached down and undid his own pants, pushed them past his hips and closed his hand around his throbbing cock. Stroked, hard and fast, his tongue and finger still teasing her clit.

Her pussy. Bringing her closer. Closer still.

Fuck.

He released his cock, dug into his pants for his wallet. Opened it one-handed and searched for a condom, damn near dropped the fucking thing in his hurry. He lifted his mouth from her pussy, her low moan unleashing something almost desperate inside him. This is what it was like with Hannah, what it had always been like.

Desperate. Hungry. Out of control.

No, fuck that. He was older now, had one hell of a lot more control than before.

Yeah, right. Sure he did. That's why his hand was shaking, why his balls were already drawing tight against his straining cock.

He swore softly, finally tore open the wrapper with his teeth and quickly sheathed himself before closing his mouth on Hannah's sweet pussy one more time. Her hands closed over his shoulders again, nails biting into flesh as he licked and stroked and teased. Harder. Faster. Faster still as her inner muscles clenched around his fingers. Gripping. Squeezing. Tight. Tighter. So fucking tight—until her orgasm exploded.

She called his name, the sound hoarse with need as she came undone. He tugged her down, sat back on his heels as she straddled his legs. He caught her mouth with his, swallowed each groan and cry as he guided his cock to her wet entrance.

As he drove deep inside her with one long push.

She cried again, broke the kiss and arched her back, meeting each desperate thrust with her own. And God. Fuck. Holy shit. She was so fucking tight. So fucking hot. So fucking wet.

He grabbed her hips, thrust his cock even deeper. Harder. Faster. And fuck, he was close. *Too* fucking close. He'd never lost himself like this before, not since—

Not since Hannah.

He stilled his hips. Tilted his head back and swallowed a groan as her inner muscles clamped around him. Squeezing. Milking.

Tempting him into paradise.

Ryder groaned, raised his head and felt the breath rush from constricted lungs as watched Hannah. Her head was tilted back, her back arched, her lower lip caught between her teeth as she rode him. Her skin glowed with a deep flush; her nipples puckered into two tight peaks. He looked down, swallowed another groan at the sight of her sweet wet pussy sliding along the hard length of his thick cock.

And *fuck*. It was too much. Too hard. Too fast. Sensation and pleasure and need coiled low in his gut, pushing him closer and closer—

He reached up, fisted his hand in Hannah's silky hair and dragged her face toward his. Caught her mouth in a searing kiss. Drove his hips up. Hard. Fast. Faster, until his own orgasm crashed over him with blinding strength, robbing him of air. Of thought. Of reason.

Of everything except pleasure so sharp, he'd thought his fucking skin would split from keeping it contained.

Mindless minutes went by. He slowed the kiss, finally dragged his mouth from Hannah's and rested his forehead against her chest. Her own breathing was as ragged and harsh as his, the sound filling the still air of the small bungalow.

The Defender: RYDER

Ryder closed his eyes. Sucked in a few more deep breaths. Tried to calm his racing heart. He needed to get up, dispose of the condom. Hell, they both needed to get up, they were on the floor and—

Fuck.

He opened his eyes, looked around as shame washed over him. Hannah's shorts and underwear were tangled around one ankle, her rugged sandals still on her feet. His own fucking pants were still on, pushed down to his thighs and bunched under Hannah's spread legs. What the fuck was wrong with him? The bed was right behind him, less than a foot away, and they were on the fucking *floor*.

He needed his fucking head examined. What the fuck had he been thinking?

He hadn't been, that was the problem.

And he probably shouldn't start thinking now. Thinking would be bad. Real bad.

He looked at Hannah. At the way her hand drifted back and forth along his arm. At the dreamy smile that curled the corners of her mouth—a mouth swollen from his punishing kisses. God, she was so fucking beautiful. She always had been. He could sit here all night and just fucking watch her.

Except he couldn't. He needed to get up. Clean up. They both did. And then they needed to talk.

Probably.

Maybe.

He started to nudge her, froze when he heard the doorknob rattle. Started to call out, to warn Ninja not to come in—

Except it was too late.

Hannah's eyes shot open and the blood drained from her face as Ninja opened the door. The man took one look at them, grinned, and quickly backed out of the room.

"I'll come back later."

Ryder waited for the door to click shut then softly swore. Tightened his hold around Hannah's waist when she started to move. "He, uh, he won't say anything."

"I know." She pushed against him and he finally released her, swallowed back a groan when she stood and turned her back on him.

He wanted to tell her again not to worry, to reassure her—but it was already too late. He'd seen the emotion on her pale face, in her wide eyes, before she had turned away.

Not embarrassment.

Regret.

Fuck.

CHAPTER SEVEN

"You're swinging that hammer like you'd rather hit me than the nails."

Ryder paused mid-swing, tossed a dark look at Ninja, then went back to pounding nails. "Don't fucking tempt me."

"I left."

"I know."

"I apologized."

"I know."

"About twenty times."

Ryder grabbed another nail from the small bag by his knee and drove it into the plywood with two hard hits. "Yeah. I know."

Silence. Finally. Ryder grabbed one more nail, held it against the plywood between his thumb and forefinger and started to swing.

"You should have gone after her when she ran off."

Ryder misjudged his aim. Pain exploded along his thumb, deep and throbbing. He tossed the hammer to the side and pulled his hand toward his chest, his jaw clenched until the pain finally ebbed to a dull ache. "Son-of-a-*bitch*!"

"Did you break it?"

He scowled at Ninja, at the glint of amusement dancing in the man's eyes and the hint of a smile curling his mouth. Ryder released his breath in a sharp hiss and reached for the hammer, briefly considered slamming it into Ninja's head. No, that would be too easy. Too quick. Ninja deserved something much worse.

Maybe he could throw the other man from the roof. It was a good thirty-foot drop, with nothing but gravel and construction materials to break his fall. If Ryder aimed just right, he could make sure Ninja hit the stack of concrete blocks.

Nah, still too easy. Ninja would probably land on his feet like a fucking cat before laughing at him. The cliff—yeah, there was an idea. He could throw him off the cliff. No way would Ninja land on his feet then.

No, even *that* was too easy.

Voices drifted up to them. One voice in particular caught his attention—it was a little too sharp, a little too shrill. And just like that, Ryder had the perfect revenge. His mouth curled in a slow smile and he turned toward Ninja. Satisfaction warmed him when he saw the other man's eyes widen in horror.

"No way, man. No fucking way. You wouldn't."

"The hell I wouldn't."

Ninja's face paled. He glanced over the edge of the half-finished roof. A small group gathered below: Cindy and Darla, Katie—and Mrs. Miller. It was the older woman's voice that could be heard above the others, chattering away about the best ways to spread the paint. Yeah, because rolling paint required an engineering degree. But directing the younger women seemed to make her happy and nobody else was complaining.

Nobody except Ninja.

The woman seemed to be taken with him. She'd latched onto his side at breakfast and would probably still be attached to his hip if they weren't up here on the roof, nailing plywood sheets to the uneven joists.

The woman's fascination with Ninja had been amusing for the first five minutes, right up until Ryder realized that Allison hadn't been joking yesterday when she'd said breakfast was fresh fruit.

A small bowl of fresh fruit and a single cup of coffee, to be exact. That was it.

Ryder's mood hadn't been the greatest to start out, considering he'd tossed and turned all night, trying not to think about Hannah. About the way she had looked at him. Touched him. The tiny little sounds and whimpers she'd made as he plunged deep inside her. The way she'd come apart in his arms.

The way he'd lost all control when he'd been inside her.

And the way she'd fled from the bungalow, her loose hair flying behind her, refusing to look at him, not even hesitating when he called after her.

Fuck.

He should have never touched her. Should have never let it go as far as it had.

Who the fuck was he kidding? Hannah was his weakness, always had been. That's why he'd left the way he did all those years ago. Yeah, he'd been leaving anyway—he'd already enlisted, had already planned on leaving. But he'd never told Hannah *when* he was going. How could he, when he was worried that one look from her would make him forget everything and decide to stay? That wouldn't have been fair—to either one of them.

Especially not when he knew she was already talking about forever.

But she had found out anyway. Had tracked him down. And instead of telling her how he felt, he'd thrown those hurtful words at her, severing their connection forever.

Until last night.

Yeah, he could have gone after her last night. But why? What would that have accomplished? Not a damn thing except make this whole fucking trip even more awkward and uncomfortable than it was turning out to be.

Yes, he wanted her. He'd *always* wanted her. Would probably want her until the fucking day he died. But wanting and having were two different things. Being with her was a mistake. He'd sworn, years ago, that he'd never hurt her again—yet that's exactly what happened last night. Despite all that bullshit she'd spouted about not being in love and being two consenting adults, Hannah was made for commitment. For settling down and getting married and raising a family.

He wasn't.

It was as simple as that.

So no, Ryder's mood hadn't been the greatest to begin with this morning. The lack of two mandatory morning staples—caffeine and protein—had transformed his piss-poor mood from annoyed to downright surly. Ninja's teasing—interspersed with an apology here and there—hadn't helped.

The other man deserved a little payback.

Ryder opened his mouth, ready to call down to Mrs. Miller, but a scream split the air. Long, sharp, the sound sending a chill of pure fright down his spine.

Hannah!

Ryder hit the ladder at full speed, his hands gripping the rails and his feet barely touching the rungs as he slid down it. The scream had come from the other side of the building, near the cliff. Ryder took off at a run, Ninja right behind him—

Then slid to a stop as cold fear washed over him.

Hannah was hanging over the edge, her left hand scrambling for something to hold onto. Her eyes were wide with fear, her face red from panic. She kicked her feet, the toes of her work boots digging for purchase in the loose soil and sand. Instead of anchoring her, the motion caused her to slide another few inches, dangerously close to plummeting over the edge.

Ryder dove for her, his hands closing around her ankles with the force of a vice grip. "I've got you—"

"It's not me!" Panic sharpened her voice; desperation made it nothing more than a whisper. Tears shone in her eyes as their gazes met. "Ryder, please. I can't hold her much longer."

Her? What the fuck?

Ryder crawled over Hannah, anchoring her against the soft ground with the weight of his own body. He heard Ninja behind him, felt the other man's hands close over his legs for added support. Then he leaned over the edge—

And his heart catapulted into his throat.

Hannah's hand was twisted in the thin shirt of a little girl, maybe seven or eight-years-old. The child was swinging mid-air, her legs thrashing in panic, her hands clawing the air in front of her. Seventy feet below her, clear blue surf crashed against jagged rocks and sand. Stark fear twisted the delicate features of the girl's face. Brown eyes, wide with terror, met his a second before she screamed, the hoarse sound carried away by the breeze—but not before it was drowned out by the sound of fabric tearing.

"Ryder!"

He ignored Hannah's strangled cry. Ignored

Ninja's low voice and the frightened murmurs coming from the small crowd behind him. His entire focus was on the little girl—and Hannah's precarious grip on her tearing shirt.

He scrambled over Hannah, stretching as he reached for the girl. One hand closed over her bony wrist, the other around her slender arm. The girl screamed again, her legs kicking wildly as she struggled against Ryder's hold. The motion was enough to pull him forward, until the entire top half of his body was hanging from the ledge—with Hannah right under him.

If he went over, he'd take Hannah with him.

No! No way in hell would he allow that to happen. "Grab Hannah! Now!"

Voices erupted behind him—a cacophony of excited mutterings overlaid by Ninja's calmer one, issuing orders to the people standing there. Below that was Hannah's voice, nothing more than a whisper as she said his name. He glanced over his shoulder, met her frightened gaze. Could she see the lifetime of regret in his eyes? His secret wish that things had been different?

Or was she merely focused on his determination to see her safe? To make sure that if he went over, he wouldn't take her with him?

She started to say something but he looked away, focused solely on his grip on the little girl who seemed determined to fight him, to take them both over the edge. A second later, Hannah was pulled from underneath him. The girl screamed again, twisting in his hold until he lost his grip on her arm.

Fuck!

Ryder stretched as far as he dared, caught her

loose arm with his free hand and yelled over his shoulder. "Pull me back. Now, dammit!"

Hands closed over his ankles. His legs. Grabbed the waistband of his pants. Pulling. Slowly at first, then faster, until he was no longer in danger of plummeting over the edge.

Until the little girl was safe beside him, tears streaking her dusty face. He pushed to a sitting position and folded his arms around the little girl. She clung to him, tears soaking his shirt as she buried her face against his shoulder and cried. He rubbed gentle circles along her thin back, whispering words of reassurance in her ear. Then Hannah was beside him, her arms wrapped around both of them, her own tears mingling with the little girl's.

Ryder sat there, momentarily stunned, not knowing how to act. The little girl's tears he could handle—she was nothing more than a child, one who had just gone through a terrifying experience. Hannah's tears were another matter altogether. They sliced through him, ripping away every defensive barrier he had erected in the last ten years.

And he had no idea how to handle that.

It was his sister who came to his rescue, although she probably didn't realize it. She shoved two bottles of water at them, a trembling smile on her pale face. Ryder gently extricated himself from the two sets of arms threatening to strangle him and took one bottle. Uncapped it and held it for the little girl. She closed both hands around the bottle and cautiously raised it to her mouth, her brown gaze never leaving his—

Until a woman's shriek split the air, making Ryder—and the little girl—jump. The girl dropped the bottle in Ryder's lap and launched herself at the woman, fresh tears streaming down her face. The girl—and the woman—were both talking too fast, their musical voices rising and falling in a rapid melody of island dialect he didn't even pretend to understand.

"That's her mother."

"Yeah, figured that much." Ryder grabbed the half-empty bottle, mentally wincing when he saw the puddle spreading between his legs. Water seeped through his pants, soaking his legs—and his ass.

Perfect. Just fucking perfect.

He pushed to his feet, extended his hand to Hannah. She hesitated then finally placed her hand in his, her firm grip surprising him. She jumped to her feet then quickly dropped her hand, her gaze sliding past him.

Ryder spun around, narrowed his eyes at the small crowd of people watching them. Mrs. Miller and Katie. Cindy and Darla.

Allison and Ninja.

The weasel.

And, coming up the path that wound down the cliffside, Casanova. The man stopped, guilt deepening the flush of exertion coloring his cheeks, then smiled and made his way toward them.

"Is it lunchtime already?"

One of the two women—Darla—hurried toward him and snaked a possessive arm around his waist. The woman's eyes raked over Ryder as a broad smile wreathed her face. "I can't believe you missed it!"

"Missed what?"

"Our action hero, saving the day!"

Ryder choked back a groan, exchanged a knowing look with Ninja and barely refrained from rolling his eyes. But it was the weasel who spoke, his voice clipped and chilly.

"No need for exaggeration, Darla. It was just a little mishap, nothing more." The weasel shot a cool look at Ryder—and at Hannah, standing so close next to him. His thin mouth pursed, irritation and something else Ryder couldn't make out flashing in his cold blue eyes. "What happened, Hannah? You were working on that side. How did she get past you?"

"I—I'm not sure."

"Really?" The weasel's voice lowered. His gaze darted to Ryder then shot back to Hannah. "Are you sure you weren't distracted? Because if you'd been paying attention, this wouldn't have happened."

Anger shot through Ryder. He expected Hannah to say something, to verbally tear into the other man, but she just stood there, her head lowered, her eyes wet with unshed tears. What the hell? Why wasn't she saying anything?

Ryder stepped forward, ready to defend her by ramming his fist into the weasel's smug little face. Ninja's hand shot out and wrapped around his arm, stopping him. Hannah finally spoke up, her voice hoarse and strained, as if she'd spent the last two hours at a rock concert, screaming along with the band.

"She was chasing a ball. I didn't see her until it was too late. I chased after her but..." Hannah's voice trailed off and she just stood there, her shoulders sagging, those unspent tears still glittering in her eyes.

Why the hell was the weasel blaming Hannah? She deserved to be commended for what she'd done. If she hadn't reacted as fast as she had, if she hadn't caught that little girl's shirt—Ryder hid his shudder at the image. Hannah didn't deserve the accusation the weasel was throwing at her. He started to say as much but the asshole kept talking, his voice dripping with condescension.

"I guess it's just a good thing Allison's *brother* was able to reach you so quickly, hm?" His cool gaze moved to Ryder, drifted down to his wet pants and back up to meet his gaze. A smirk accompanied the condescension that was still clear in his voice when he spoke. "It's unfortunate about your accident. I'm sure everyone would understand if you went back to camp for the rest of the day."

Allison stepped forward, her fingers curled against her palms. Not quite a fist, but close. "It's water. Naomi spilled the bottle—"

"No need to make excuses for your brother—"

"It's not an excuse! If you'd been doing *your* job instead of disappearing—"

"Enough. We still have work to do." The weasel clapped his hands together. "And since everyone has already started their break, we may as well have lunch. Hannah, if you'll come with me and help me get everything set up." It was an order, not a suggestion. Hannah stood there, unmoving for a long minute. Then she cast a look at Ryder, her expression a mixture of apology and gratitude. He didn't understand the reason for either one.

And he didn't understand why she moved forward to follow the weasel instead of telling him where to go. Even Allison turned to follow them, along with everyone else. Casanova was the last one. He paused in front of Ryder and Ninja, his glassy gaze slightly unfocused.

"Sounds like you're a good man to have around in an emergency."

"Yeah. Sure." Ryder's words were short and

clipped. If Casanova even noticed, he showed no signs of it. He just offered both men a big grin and turned toward the small building, leaving Ryder and Ninja outside. Alone.

"Son-of-a-*bitch*. I've never wanted to hit someone as much as I want to hit him."

"Which one?"

"Both of them, but I was referring to the weasel. What the fuck is his problem?"

Ninja rubbed his knuckles across his mouth then shrugged. "No idea. He doesn't like you, though. At all."

"Yeah, no shit. The feeling is entirely mutual." Ryder stared at the door everyone had disappeared through. Allison's words came back to him and he tilted his head to the side, frowning. "What was that Allison said? Something about doing his job instead of disappearing?"

"Yeah, something like that. Why?"

"Because I thought I saw someone down on the beach."

"When?"

"When I was hanging over the ledge, playing Superman. I thought it was Casanova at first but now I'm wondering."

"You think it was the project manager?"

"Maybe. I only caught a brief glimpse. Male. Light hair." Maybe. Or maybe he'd just been seeing things. It wasn't like he hadn't been preoccupied, trying to hold onto the little girl. Worrying about Hannah.

Christ. He never wanted to feel that way again. Never wanted to experience that bone-chilling sense of helplessness he'd felt in that one brief second when he'd been convinced he was going to slide completely over the edge—and take Hannah with him. It wasn't *his* life he'd been worried about—it had been the girl's. And Hannah's. The mere thought of anything happening to her—

"I don't think it was him."

Ryder shook off the memory's chill and turned to Ninja. "Why not?"

"Think about it. That path down to the beach is, what? A half-mile? Maybe a little more? Plus it's all uphill. I don't think your buddy would have been able to make it back up here in time."

What Ninja said made sense—and if he'd been thinking clearly, Ryder would have realized it before opening his own mouth. Neither one of the men—the weasel *or* Casanova—would have been able to make it back that quickly. Which meant whoever he'd seen—if he'd seen anyone at all—didn't belong to Hannah's little group.

And even if he *had* seen someone, it didn't necessarily mean they were up to no good.

Ryder might even believe that—if his gut wasn't screaming otherwise.

He turned to Ninja, clapped him on the shoulder and started heading toward the building. "We're taking a hike tonight."

"Is that so?"

"Yeah. It's time to figure out what the hell Allison and Hannah really saw."

"And if it's what we think it is?"

"Fuck if I know. Call the authorities, I guess—whoever that might be down here."

"And if it's not?"

Ryder shrugged. "Then we catch the next ferry back and enjoy a few days on the beach before our flight out on Monday."

Yeah, it sounded good. But Ryder knew it wouldn't be that easy or simple.

Hell, it never was.

CHAPTER EIGHT

Dinner was much the same as it had been the night before: everyone mingling and chatting as one person did most of the cooking. The weasel was the one in the kitchen this time, which surprised the hell out of Ryder—he'd gotten the impression that the weasel was the kind of person who gave orders instead of leading by example.

The man's focus was split between the fish on the grill and the small crowd. Despite the chatting, the conversation was more subdued tonight, maybe even a little strained.

A direct result from the weasel's steely gaze, no doubt. As soon as any one conversation showed signs of becoming animated, the man would turn around and scowl until everyone quieted back down. Then he turned that scowl on Ryder, his eyes narrowing until they were nothing more than pale slits in his face.

Subtlety definitely wasn't the man's strongest suit. The hell of it was, Ryder had no idea what he'd done to piss the man off. Then again, the weasel hadn't done much to piss *him* off, so he figured it was a fair trade.

He made his way over to where Hannah was standing with the Millers and the young girl, Katie. She looked up at him, offered him a weak smile, then quickly looked away. Ryder ground his back teeth together, drew in a sharp breath, then dipped his head toward her.

"Let's take a walk."

Hannah's eyes widened in surprise. She glanced around like she was seeking help—or trying to figure out the best way to turn him down without causing a scene. He didn't wait for her to come up with an answer, just grabbed her hand and tugged.

For five seconds, he seriously thought she was going to literally dig her heels in and refuse. Her fingers were chilled against the warmth of his own flesh. Uneasiness thrummed through her, evident in the way she tensed, in the way her hand stiffened in his. She must have seen the determination in his gaze because her hand finally relaxed a second before she quietly excused herself and allowed him to tug her away from the curious trio.

Ryder remained silent as he led her out of the pavilion and into the soft shadows of descending twilight. He didn't go too far—he wanted to keep an eye out on the weasel, certain the man would follow them if they disappeared from view. Just far enough to give them some privacy, far enough that they wouldn't be overheard by the small crowd that had watched them leave.

He dropped Hannah's hand then spun so he was facing her. She kept her gaze averted, focused on the ground at her feet as she quickly wrapped her arms around her middle.

Ryder shifted his weight, glanced behind her at the curious gazes being tossed their way. They were in no danger of being interrupted, at least not yet. Not with Ninja playing pseudo-guard by diverting everyone's attention.

Satisfied that they'd have at least a few minutes of uninterrupted time, Ryder turned his gaze back to Hannah. She looked so forlorn, so...lost. He wanted to pull her into his arms and hold her. Reassure her.

Carry her back to his bungalow and spend the next ten hours fucking her, until she forgot everything except his name.

Shit. He had to stop thinking like that. Nothing else was going to happen between them, especially after last night. It couldn't, not when he knew she wanted so much more than what he could give.

He ran a hand through his hair, blew out a quick sigh. Shoved that same hand into his pocket. "You doing okay?"

Her head darted up, surprise flashing in her eyes. She blinked, lowered her gaze, quickly nodded. "Yeah. Fine."

"You sure about that?"

"Of course. Why wouldn't I be?"

Because of the way you flew out of the bungalow last night. Because of the way I hurt you again.

But he couldn't say that, couldn't bring himself to even mention it. Ryder swallowed back his irritation and forced himself to speak quietly. "It was an exciting afternoon."

Her head darted up again. "Exciting? Is that what you call it? Naomi almost died."

"But she didn't, thanks to your quick thinking."

"I'm not the one—"

"The hell you weren't. If you hadn't caught her, she would have—"

"Please don't say it."

Ryder slammed his mouth shut before the words tumbled out. He didn't need to say them, not when Hannah already knew the truth. Her face paled and she pressed a fist against her stomach, inhaled deeply and shook her head.

"If you weren't there—when I think about what almost happened to *you*—" She shook her head again. "And it was my fault. I should have been paying closer attention."

He ignored her whispered comment about what almost happened to him—he couldn't read into it, had to pretend he didn't even hear it. He focused instead on everything else she said, on the way she was so readily taking the blame. "Were you in charge of watching the kids?"

"No. But I—"

"Then it wasn't your fault. It wasn't anyone's fault, so stop it."

"But it was. You heard Kevin—"

"He's an asshole." Anger crept into Ryder's voice, adding an extra bite to the sharp words. "I don't know even know why you listen to him."

"Because he's the project manager."

"That doesn't give him the right to belittle anyone the way he did you."

"He was just upset—"

"Bullshit. Why are you making excuses for him?"

"I'm not."

"Then what the hell do you call it?"

"It's not an excuse when he's right." Hannah hugged her arms more tightly around her middle and started pacing in a small circle. "We haven't had time to get the fence up yet—Kevin wanted to finish the roof first. So everyone keeps an eye out on the kids, just in case. I—I should have been paying closer attention. I wasn't, and look what happened."

Ryder reached for her arm to stop her dizzying pacing, spun her around to face him. "You're telling me the fence was supposed to go up first?"

"No, not really. I mean, maybe. I'm not sure. But you saw the old building. The way it's practically falling down around the kids. They can't be expected to learn like that. If we can finish the roof, they can start to use the new building. At least, parts of it. That's why Kevin decided to put off building the fence. That's why everyone keeps an eye out when the kids are playing."

Unfuckingbelievable. No, what was unbelievable was the fact that Hannah actually *believed* what she was saying. That she was defending the weasel even now. After what happened. After the way he spoke to her.

Ryder stepped back, laced his fingers together behind his neck, and closed his eyes with a small growl. He needed to walk away. To just turn around and walk away. Walk, hell. If he were smart, he'd run.

But he'd never been smart when it came to Hannah. Not all those years ago when they were growing up together. Not eleven years ago when he gave in to the desire that had been his constant companion whenever he thought about Hannah—which was damn near every second of every day.

Now was no different. Just looking at her was enough to drive him over the edge—only it was ten times worse than what he'd felt all those years ago because now he knew what it was like to be with her. To hold her. To hear her call his name as she exploded around him. To feel her warm breath on his skin and the touch of her hands against his body.

That didn't stop the insane urge to reach out and grab her. To shake her until some of the common sense he knew she possessed reasserted itself. Why was she being so damn pigheaded about this? Why did she keep defending the weasel and making excuses for him?

That's what didn't make sense. The Hannah he remembered would have never tolerated such high-handed behavior. She would have gotten right in his face and given him a piece of her mind. Would have read him the riot act and quickly set him straight.

"Are you sleeping with him?" The words fell from his mouth before his brain had time to engage. And fuck, it was the wrong question to ask. Hannah's face reddened—not with embarrassment, but with anger. He braced himself, wondering if maybe she'd slap him. He sure as hell deserved it, wouldn't blame if her she did.

But she didn't, despite that small fist hanging by her side.

She stepped toward him, her head tilted back, their bodies separated by mere inches of humid air. Those warm brown eyes of hers flashed with anger as she impaled him with nothing more than a simple look. Simple, hell. That look alone was enough to singe his flesh.

"How dare you even ask me that! Especially after last night. Who do you think you are, coming down here and disrupting everything, then asking me something like that? You have no right—"

"If it's going to affect me doing what you two asked me to come down here for, then yeah, I do." Which was a total fucking lie. Who Hannah slept with didn't concern him—at least, it shouldn't. And it sure as hell didn't affect his ability to look around. It wasn't his business—had never been his business.

That didn't stop the burning need to hear her answer.

Ryder held her angry gaze, refused to look away as his lungs ached with the need to breathe. He could no more do that than he could look away, not until she answered.

If she answered.

The small muscle along the side of her jaw jumped, telling him that she was grounding her teeth as hard as he was. The breath left her with a small hiss as she leaned even closer, anger still flashing in her eyes.

"No, I'm not sleeping with him. Not that it's any of your business."

Relief fell over him. The tension gripping his shoulders eased and he inhaled, filling lungs that had been close to bursting with their need for air. "Good."

Hannah blinked, stepped back and shook her head. "Oh God, Allison was totally right. You really are an—"

"Yeah, I know. I always have been. I thought you would have figured that out by now."

Astonishment crossed her face. She started to move toward him, hesitated and took another step back instead. "You don't honestly believe that, do you? I never thought that, not even after—"

"I didn't ask you out here to stroll down memory lane, Hannah." Hell no, that was the last thing he wanted—or needed. He was having a hard enough time forgetting the past, felt himself being tugged back to their time together every single time he looked at her. He sure as hell didn't want to dive into the memories head-first.

"Then why *did* you bring me out here? It wasn't just to make sure I'm okay."

Ryder thought about denying it—for two seconds. He shook his head, slid his gaze back to the pavilion. The weasel flipped the fish on the flat grill then reached behind him for the plates. They had a few more minutes—plenty of time to ask her the other question that had been burning inside since this afternoon.

He caught Hannah's gaze with his own, watching for the slightest change in her expression. "Why did you let him talk to you like that?"

Her gaze slid from his, just as he knew it would. Her cheeks paled and she absently kicked at a small patch of weeds with the toe of her hiking sandal. A second went by, then another, before she carelessly shrugged.

"I don't know what you're talking about."

"Yeah, you do. Why didn't you rip him a new one like you just did to me?"

"I didn't—"

Ryder waved his hand, cutting her off. "Close enough. That's what you should have done to the weasel when he talked to you that way."

"Stop calling him 'the weasel'. He has a name. *Kevin*."

"He's still a weasel. And you haven't answered my question: why did you let him get away with it?"

"Because he's my boss—"

"Bullshit. That doesn't excuse what he did."

"He's not usually like that—"

"That still isn't an answer."

Hannah started her pacing again, around and around, wearing another small circular pattern in the sandy dirt beneath her feet. She finally stopped, crossed her arms in front of her, and blew out a quick breath. "I don't know why. I—I guess I was still upset about what happened. What *almost* happened. I think he was, too."

Ryder wanted to argue with her. Tell her that

being upset didn't excuse behavior like that. Tell her that bowing down to behavior like that only made it worse. The weasel was nothing more than a bully. A little man who had to demean others to make himself feel more important. And no way in hell was he buying her comment that he usually wasn't like that, that he had simply lashed out because he was *upset*.

He didn't say any of that, though. Now wasn't the time. It would probably never be the right time. Ryder and Ninja would be leaving this island in a few days, would never see most of these people ever again. He sure as hell wouldn't be working with them.

But Hannah would be. Her and Allison both. It wouldn't do anyone a damn bit of good if he stirred up shit and left the two of them to deal with it. But God help the weasel if he stepped out of line one more time while Ryder was here. If he did, all bets would be off.

"Dinner's ready." The weasel's voice drifted through the evening air, the sound of it grating on Ryder's nerves and making his jaw clench. Hannah glanced over her shoulder then back at him.

"Was that all you wanted?" She was already turning away, ready to do the weasel's bidding when Ryder spoke.

"No." He reached for her arm, tugged her further away from the pavilion—a move that didn't go unnoticed. The weasel was standing near the edge of the pavilion, a frown on his face as he watched them. Fuck him. Let him watch. Let him think whatever the hell he wanted to.

Ryder dipped his head toward Hannah and lowered his voice. "Ninja and I are going to look around that cave of yours later tonight. I need to know what everyone's routine is for later. I don't want anyone to see us."

"We'll go with you—"

"That wasn't an invitation, Hannah." And fuck, he should have seen that one coming. The last thing he needed was Hannah and Allison tagging along.

"You'll never find it without us."

"I said *no*. We're going to be hiking—"

"But that's more than three miles away!"

"Yeah?" Three miles was a cakewalk, nothing more than a quick stroll.

"In the dark. Along roads you're not familiar with."

"And you're point is?"

"My point is, you won't find it. Not without our help."

"Hannah, the only help I need from you is what everyone's routine is. What time everyone turns in. If anyone stays up late or is likely to come outside at the wrong time—"

"Are you two going to join us?"

Ryder looked over Hannah's shoulder, clenched his jaw when he saw the weasel heading toward them, his stride filled with purpose. Yeah, because God forbid someone didn't jump to do his bidding right away.

Hannah twisted to the side, a bright smile on her face. "We'll be right there, Kev." She turned back to him and the smile faded—but the flash in her eyes was just as bright as her smile had been. Maybe even brighter.

With a sinking feeling, Ryder realized that flash dancing in her eyes wasn't a remnant of the phony smile she had given the weasel. Hell no, that would be too much to ask. The sparkle was due to excitement—

and he knew exactly why it was there.

He shook his head, started to tell her *no*. No way, no how. Not just *no*, but *hell no*.

He never got the words out. Hannah's hand dropped to his arm, her touch scalding him as she leaned closer and lowered her voice to a whisper. "Meet us behind our bungalow at ten. Everyone should be in bed by then."

"Hannah—"

But it was too late because she was already walking away, a spring in her step that hadn't been there fifteen minutes ago. Hell, it hadn't been there yesterday, either.

What kind of an ass was he that he was actually entertaining the idea of letting them tag along? That more than anything told him he needed to have his head examined. Bringing them along was a stupid idea. Beyond stupid. So stupid that it bordered on lunacy.

But he was going to do it anyway—which was a sure sign that he was in over his head. Then again, with Hannah, he always had been.

"Fuck."

CHAPTER NINE

He watched the newcomer pull Hannah off to the side. What were they talking about?

Probably nothing. The stupid woman was still upset from this afternoon. Just look at her, standing there with her arms wrapped around her middle, her face pale in twilight's shadows. Her reaction disappointed him. The emotion and the crying she'd done earlier. So the little brat had almost fallen off the cliff. There was no need for all the drama and overreaction.

He'd given her credit for being smarter than all the other naive twits here. Still naive, yes, but—

He sighed. As much as he hated to admit it, it was probably a good thing she'd reacted so quickly and saved the girl. If she hadn't, people might have stumbled across the cave—and what was in it—when they went down to scoop up the girl's remains.

That in itself was enough to worry him. What worried him even more was the sudden appearance of the two newcomers. The timing was suspicious—in his line of work, *everything* was suspicious.

The other woman—Allison—had claimed the man talking to Hannah was her brother. What was his name? Something weird. Unusual. He frowned, thinking...

Ryder. Yes, that was it.

What a stupid, stupid name.

A stupid name, yes—but he wouldn't make the

mistake of thinking the man himself was stupid. Far from it.

Why was he here?

He nonchalantly made his way over to sniveling bastard, secretly smiled when the pathetic man jumped at his approach. So, he was nervous. Good. Maybe he'd learned his lesson last week.

He casually nodded toward Hannah and her friend. "How long will the newcomers be staying with us?"

"Until Sunday."

"Sunday." His suspicion grew a little more. The timing was inconvenient—very inconvenient. Anything that had the potential to disrupt his plans was inconvenient.

"What do you know about them?"

"Nothing. He's Allison's brother. They're here on vacation and came to see her."

He inclined his head to the two women looking their way, offered them a warm smile that betrayed none of his disdain, then turned back to his unwilling partner. "And you believe that?"

"I have no reason not to."

"Then you're an even bigger idiot than I first thought." He took a careful sip of his water. "Get rid of them. Tomorrow."

"And how do you suggest I do that?"

"How you do it doesn't concern me, as long as you get it done." He leaned closer and lowered his voice. "Or you may find yourself going for a nice long swim like our other friend."

The color drained from the man's face but—as expected—he said nothing.

He turned away from the sniveling bastard, his

pleasant smile still in place. He'd have to come up with an alternate plan—he didn't trust the bastard to follow-through with his orders. He was too weak, too incompetent.

And expendable. Definitely expendable.

Did he realize his time was already drawing near? Probably not. He had apparently convinced himself that he was needed, when nothing could be further from the truth.

But not yet. There was still use for him.

For a few more days, at least. After that...

Well, after that, it was just a matter of taking care of business.

He hadn't quite decided how he'd dispose of the man. Something fitting, of that he was certain. The different scenarios lifted his spirits and placed an even bigger smile on his face.

And, as always, stroked his appetite. Just in time for dinner, too. How convenient.

Dinner first. And then...dessert.

He looked around at the small crowd gathered under the pavilion, his gaze settling on the girl. Yes, definitely dessert.

He was looking forward to it.

CHAPTER TEN

Hannah had always considered herself to be in shape. Not athletic—she didn't go to the gym to work out or lift weights or jog several miles every day. But she did eat healthy—down here, there was no other choice—didn't shy away from hard work, enjoyed an occasional hike, and generally kept herself fit. Again, being down here, doing what they did, certainly helped with all of that.

That's why she hadn't balked when Ryder said they'd be walking. It was only three miles. Yes, they usually drove back and forth from their little compound to the building site each day, but that was because there were so many of them. Not to mention they were usually hauling everything they needed for the day.

It was only three miles. It wasn't *that* far. She was sure she'd been on hikes that were longer.

Except she'd never been on hikes at night.

In the dark.

Along uneven terrain.

Without a flashlight.

And why had she never noticed how damn *hilly* this route was? They were walking along the same road they took every day but the inclines seemed much sharper than she remembered—and definitely longer than the downhill portions. How was that even possible?

Her only consolation was that she wasn't the only

one unable to keep up with the pace the two men set. Allison was right beside her, her breath coming in slightly labored gasps that matched Hannah's.

And neither one of them was carrying a pack, like Ryder and his friend were.

Hannah squinted her eyes and peered ahead, searching for the two large shadows somewhere in front of them. They were there, she knew they were. But she couldn't really see them, not through the thick darkness that cloaked everything around her, not when they were both dressed in black: black t-shirts, black cargo pants. And she certainly couldn't *hear* them. How could two men as big as they were move so silently?

It was creepy. Creepier even than the shadows moving all around her. Hannah had always felt safe down here, had readily embraced the slower pace and the open friendliness of the people who called the remote island home. Had quickly adapted to the change in routine, her day governed by the rising and setting of the sun.

The absolute darkness that settled over the island while the sun slept had never bothered her, had never given her pause before—until now. The shadows had taken on an ominous cast, their mere presence somehow threatening. Anything—or anyone—could be lurking just to her right, waiting to jump out at her, and she would never know it until it was too late.

The mere thought was enough to make her jumpy. She veered to the left, moving away from the lush vegetation lining what passed for a road. Her foot hit something and she stumbled, her arms flailing out to the side as she frantically tried to regain her balance. A hand closed over her arm and she swallowed back a scream—only she must not have done a very good job at it because a warm chuckle washed over her.

Ryder.

How sad was it that her body recognized the touch of his hand long before her mind caught up? How sad was it that just the sound of his chuckle, low and warm and a little husky, was enough to weaken her knees?

To weaken her resolve. Last night had been proof of that.

She brushed his hand off and straightened, then wiped at the strands of hair that had fallen into her face when she stumbled. "I'm fine. I'm good."

"You sure about that?"

"Yes, I'm sure." The words came out a little sharper than she intended, filled with the same embarrassment heating her face. At least the darkness was good for hiding *something*—unless he had a cat's vision and could see through the dark with no problem.

"How much farther do we have to go?" Allison asked the question before she could.

"We're about halfway."

Hannah and Allison groaned in unison. "Halfway? Seriously?"

"No, I'm teasing. We're almost there. I figure a half-mile at the most." She heard Ryder rummage through his pack—at least, that's what she thought he was doing. A few seconds later, something cold and wet was placed into her hand. She almost jerked back with a sharp gasp and caught herself in time.

It was nothing more sinister than a bottle of water. She uncapped it and raised it to her mouth, gulped half of it down then lowered it and recapped it.

"Are you sure that's all?"

"Yeah, give or take, from what I remember of the drive. Look around. Can't you tell?"

No, she couldn't tell. The darkness had completely disoriented her. They could be ready to walk off a cliff and she wouldn't know it.

A shudder raced over her, prickling her skin. She tried to push the thought away but it was already there, right in front of her, the memory as clear as the horror from this afternoon.

Naomi, scrambling for something to hold as she slid toward the cliff edge. Brown eyes wide with fear, her mouth opened in a silent scream.

Hannah running, nearly tripping as she dove for Naomi, her own scream piercing the air.

The feel of soft cotton against her palm as her hand closed around the young girl's shirt. The horrible sound of fabric tearing and the deathly certainty that she'd lose her grip. The cold fear that paralyzed her when the girl's slight weight dragged her forward.

Fear of another kind—slick and oily and nauseating—when Ryder had started sliding off the ledge. She'd seen the expression in his eyes, the complete disregard for his own life as he demanded that they pull her back first. She'd been so certain she'd never see him again. So sure that her last glimpse of him would be his face as he fell seventy feet to the surf below—

Hannah shuddered again and forced the memory away. Ignored the cold sweat beading on her forehead and along her hairline as she uncapped the bottle and tilted it up, draining its contents in two long swallows. Could the other three see the way her hand shook? Hear her short gasps as she struggled to pull air into her lungs? Sense her fear simply by the way she had momentarily stiffened?

No, of course not. It was too dark, they couldn't

see anything. Even if they could, they weren't paying attention to her. Ryder and Ninja were standing off to the side, their shadows slightly darker than the night, their voices too low to make out the words as they spoke. And Allison was right next to her, too busy downing her own water in thirsty gulps to notice anything else.

"You two ready?" Ryder's voice, still pitched low but clear. Hannah nodded, realized he probably couldn't see her, then started to answer with a *yes*.

"Not really." The answer came from Allison, a hint of irritation in her voice. Ryder laughed, just a breath of sound that washed over Hannah. And damn him, how had he gotten so close to her without her realizing it?

His fingers brushed hers a second before he took the bottle from her hand. She heard the sound of a zipper sliding, the crinkle of plastic as he shoved the empty bottle into his pack. "Too bad. You should have stayed back."

"This wasn't *my* idea." Allison's grumble was meant for Hannah's ears only but Ryder laughed again, the sound already drifting away as he moved ahead of them. Hannah sighed and followed, Allison right beside her.

"This really was a stupid idea."

"I know."

"We could be sleeping right now."

"I know."

"Kevin is going to have a fit if he finds out."

"The weasel isn't going to find out. And if he does, I'll deal with him." Ryder's voice drifted back to them, filled with the barest hint of amusement. Allison grumbled then quickened her steps.

"You're not supposed to be eavesdropping."

"Then stop being so loud."

"I wasn't being loud! I was whispering. You just have ears like an elephant. And is there a reason we aren't using a flashlight? I can't see anything."

"A light would make us a target."

Hannah stumbled, caught herself and hurried forward. "A target for who?"

"The bad guys."

"There are no—" She was going to say *bad guys* but stopped at the last second. She couldn't say that, not with any certainty. If there were no bad guys, they wouldn't be out here walking in the middle of the night. They wouldn't be hiking to a cave to spy on whatever treasure might be lurking in that damn chest they had found.

And suddenly, everything became real. *Too* real. Her heart slammed against her chest and more sweat beaded along her hairline—sweat that had nothing to do with the still, humid air clinging to her. Up until a few minutes ago, this had been nothing more than an adventure. Even when they'd learned about the dead man, Hannah hadn't really considered the ramifications, had thought it nothing more than a coincidence even if Allison had tried to convince her otherwise. She'd been thriving on the make-believe, wrapped up in the romance of pirates and buried treasure.

Words like *target* and *bad guys* had never entered her mind. Those words didn't exist in her world, not unless it was a fictional world in a book she was reading.

But they very much existed in Ryder's world. The casual way he had tossed them over his shoulder, as if they were part of his everyday vocabulary, told her that much. The realization chilled her, made her wonder exactly what it was he did now. She knew he'd been in the Army, doing some kind of specialized stuff, but she had no idea what. And she knew he worked for a private company now, doing...she didn't know what he did. She'd never bothered to ask, had always tuned Allison out whenever she talked about her brother because it was easier to do that than to remember the way he'd broken her heart when he'd left all those years ago.

The toe of her shoe caught on something and she tumbled forward, came to a stop against the brick wall of Ryder's back. No, not his back—his chest. His arms came around her, steadying her, and for one second, she allowed herself to think about last night. To remember the way he'd held her, grounding her even as she flew apart. Big, strong, his size and presence almost overwhelming. Their lovemaking hadn't been gentle but he hadn't hurt her. Not last night, not all those years ago. At least, not physically. He'd always been so careful, almost like he was afraid of hurting her—

Except for now. He quickly dropped his arms and stepped back, fast enough that she nearly lost her balance again. And oh God, how stupid could she be? She wasn't that forlorn teenager who fancied herself in love anymore and last night meant absolutely nothing. She couldn't *let* it mean anything. She needed to get over it. Over *him*. Their history was just that: history. She had moved on and she had no doubt he'd done the same. She needed to remember that.

And she really needed to pay attention because Ryder was talking, his voice pitched so low she could barely hear it.

"—stay close. If I tell you to do something, do it. Don't ask questions. Don't argue. Just do it."

There was an edge to his voice that caused her skin to pebble. Did he really think they might be in danger? No. He was just being cautious. If he honestly thought they might be in danger, he would have never let them tag along.

She felt his gaze on her, somehow knew when that dark gaze slid to Allison.

"Is that understood?"

Hannah nodded, knew Allison—for once—was doing the same. She heard a low noise, the sound reminding her of a growl, and realized it was coming from Ryder. That had to be a good sign, right? He wouldn't be growling his impatience if he was leading them into danger, would he?

Hannah didn't bother to ask—there wasn't time because he was already walking away, leading them down the narrow, winding path that would take them to the beach. She sensed something behind her and whirled, swallowed a gasp when she saw Ninja's pale smile. How had he gotten behind her? She didn't know, didn't ask, just turned and kept going, each step hesitant, feeling for purchase before setting her weight down. Again and again, the minutes stretching as the sound of the surf grew louder. Until her feet finally sank into the soft sand of the beach.

She started to step around Allison, to lead the way to the cave, but Ryder was already heading in that direction. How was that even possible? He couldn't know where it was, hadn't had time to come here before. Unless Allison had told him. Yes, that must be it. But he'd still need help finding the opening—

He stopped a few yards from the cave, turned

back to them. Hannah realized she could see him a little easier now, had no trouble making out the slight frown on his face. "I'm going to check it out. Stay here."

Ryder was gone before she could say anything—not that she knew what words might have tumbled from her mouth. What was she going to do? Tell him not to go? No, not after Allison had made him come all the way down here to the remotes island to do exactly this.

Tell him to be careful? Yes. Yes, she wanted him to be careful, didn't want anything to happen to him. Couldn't bear the thought of anything happening to him. Not now. Not ever.

She opened her mouth, ready to call him back. What if someone was inside the cave? What if those bad guys Ryder had referred to were in there, doing whatever stuff bad guys did? It was too risky. Ryder was going in alone, had no way to protect himself, nobody to watch his back in case anything happened, not with Ninja standing guard *here*, watching her and Allison.

A low sound, not quite a whistle, drifted over the gentle pounding of the surf. A hand touched her back and she jumped, a scream lodged in her throat. Nothing but air escaped her mouth, soundless and pathetic and unhelpful.

But there was no need for help—the hand belonged to Ninja. The touch was gentle, nudging her forward. Not just her, but Allison, too.

"Let's go." Ninja's voice, low and steady—which meant that other sound must have come from Ryder, signaling the all-clear. They moved toward the cave, their steps silent, any noise masked by the sound of the waves to their left.

And then they were inside, engulfed in total blackness. Hannah reached for Allison's arm, not just for comfort but to anchor herself in the disorienting darkness, to ground her confused senses and calm her racing heart.

The air was cooler here, cool enough that her skin prickled with the temperature change. A chill raced over her but she wasn't sure if that was from the air—or the sudden fear that gripped her. And how silly was that? There was nothing to be afraid of. She knew what was in here, had been in here only last week to look around.

Maybe that was what lay behind the irrational fear. Last week, when she'd come here with Allison, they'd been able to see. Sunlight had filtered into the opening, chasing away any ominous shadows that might have been lurking around them.

There were no shadows now. There was nothing but darkness. Complete. Absolute. Swallowing her whole, wreaking havoc with her senses until she lost track of where the opening was. She could get lost in here forever, stumbling around in the darkness, never finding her way out, never knowing where the exit was.

Hannah pushed back the panic, forced herself to take a deep breath and calm down. There was no need to panic, no excuse for the sudden urge to flee the darkness swallowing her whole—

"Watch your eyes." Ryder's voice, steady and confident. A small click echoed in the cavernous room, the sound immediately accompanied by a pinprick of light—not bright, but still enough to make her blink.

Relief surged through Hannah as the dim light pushed back the wall of suffocating darkness. She pulled in a deep breath and exchanged a small smile with Allison. Funny, how just that tiny bit of light was enough to ease the tightness in her chest. She turned, ready to make a small joke at her own expense, and gasped in surprise instead. The single chest she and Allison found last week had been joined by two more. Large. Metal. Dark green.

And locked.

Ninja knelt in front of one, reached into the side pocket of his black pants and removed something small. Hannah moved closer, watching as Ryder aimed that small light around the heavy lock.

"What are you doing?" The question was too loud, bouncing off the rough walls as if she had shouted the question instead of whispered it. She winced, wondered if Ryder would remind her to keep her voice down, but he didn't even turn toward her when he answered.

"We're opening it."

"But it's locked—" Only it wasn't, not anymore, because Ninja had done something and the lock opened with a small click. He pulled it from the clasp and Hannah moved forward, eager to see what was inside.

"Stay back. Both of you." There was an edge to Ryder's voice that left no room for argument—not that she would have, anyway. Hannah moved several feet back, tugging Allison with her.

The two men exchanged a silent look. Ninja turned the small clasp then reached out and eased the lid open with a low creak of hinges. Hannah stiffened, her breath held, waiting for...something. But nothing happened, nothing except another quiet exchange of looks between the two men.

Only there was something different about this

look. Something…she wasn't sure what. Harder? Edgier? She didn't know how to describe it, only knew that it sent a shiver of apprehension along her spine—a sensation made worse by Ryder's low oath.

"What? What is it?" Allison moved forward, Hannah right next to her. Ryder jumped to his feet, his arms spread out to the side to block their view as Ninja silently closed the lid. It was too late. Hannah's blood chilled as her mind tried to process what her eyes had seen.

Guns. A lot of guns. Big. Long, like the machine guns she'd seen in all those different war movies her father loved to watch while she was growing up.

Oh, God. What had they stumbled on? To think she and Allison had thought this was nothing more than buried treasure. That she had been swept away by the romantic fantasy that those metal chests contained gold or jewels or something equally improbable.

"Time to go." Ryder's calm voice cut through her astonishment. She looked over at him, saw the worry in his gaze before he blinked it away. She started to ask him what they should do now—because they *had* to do something, they couldn't just leave the guns here—when his entire demeanor changed. His body tensed, his weight shifting as he went instantly alert in the blink of an eye. It was fascinating to watch—until Hannah realized what it meant.

Until that small, reassuring light blinked out.

Until Ryder spoke, his voice nothing more than a whisper of breath in the darkness.

"Someone's coming."

CHAPTER ELEVEN

Ryder swore to himself, calling himself a fool—and worse—for letting Hannah and Allison tag along. For thinking that this whole fiasco was nothing more than his sister's wild imagination run amok. The weapons in that fucking crate said this was anything *but* Allison's imagination.

And now his lack of belief in his sister's story had put both women in danger.

He'd almost missed the sound. Nothing more than a shifting of sand, a scrape of a shoe and a whispered oath. Close. *Too* close.

There was nowhere for them to go except deeper into the cave—which was the last place he wanted to take them. He had no idea what was back there, no idea how deep it went. But he didn't have a choice—going out the front was out of the question.

What the *fuck* had he been thinking?

He moved toward both women, Ninja right beside him. Allison and Hannah were visible targets, the pale skin of their bared arms and legs dangerously visible in the cave's darkness. He should have made them wear long pants. No, he should have made them both stay back at the pathetic compound they called their base of operations.

It was too fucking late for that.

He grabbed Hannah's hand, pushed her in front of him and nudged her forward. Thank Christ she didn't fight him or ask him what he was doing. He just

The Defender: RYDER

hoped she stayed silent, that both women would stay silent and not ask questions because they needed to move, *now*.

Maybe they sensed his urgency because they moved with very little prodding. And thank God for small favors because he couldn't spare even a fraction of his attention on them right now, not when he was focused on getting them out of sight. There had been a small bend a few yards back that veered to the left and that's where he headed now, his hand trailing soundlessly along the wall for guidance. Yeah, his night vision was pretty damn good and he could see enough—barely—but it was still fucking dark. For all he knew, the damn ground would drop away in front of them as soon as they moved around the bend—

That thought was enough to make him stop. He eased around Hannah so that he was in front, placing the two women between him and Ninja. If the ground dropped away, *he* would be the one to find out first. Although, with Hannah's death grip on the waistband of his pants, he'd probably take her with him.

He slowed his pace, reached behind him and took Hannah's hand in his—just in case something *did* happen, he'd be able to release his hold on her in time. Her fingers tightened around his, the grip surprisingly strong. He gave those chilled fingers a brief squeeze and moved forward, reaching out with the toe of his boot before each step. They were behind that bend now, but was it far enough? If whoever he'd heard came in and lit the place up with light, would they be able to see them, or their shadows?

Ryder moved a few more feet ahead then stopped, unwilling to go any further without knowing what was ahead of them. He reached past the women, tapped

Ninja's shoulder three times. *Tap*. Pause. *Tap, tap*. He felt an answering tap on his arm, felt the briefest whisper of air brush against him as Ninja moved ahead of him, Allison glued to his side.

Ryder tugged on Hannah's hand, repositioning her so she was to his right. Then he lowered himself to a crouch, pulling Hannah down with him. Her body stiffened and for a brief second, he thought she was going to balk and ask him what the hell he was doing. The second passed and she finally lowered herself next to him, the cool air thick with her unasked questions.

They'd have to remain unasked—and unanswered, at least for now. At least until he figured out what the fuck was going on.

He eased to the side, blocking Hannah's body with his own, then reached into his boot for the knife he'd grabbed from the make-shift kitchen earlier. It was a shitty knife, the blade only a few inches long and nowhere near as sharp as it should be, the handle too light and insubstantial. It made an even shittier weapon because he figured the fucking thing would probably break the first time he tried using it.

Damn. He wished he had his fucking K-bar. And his Smith & Wesson M&P 380 Shield. Bringing either one had been out of the question because they'd flown commercial to get down here.

Just one of the many reasons he fucking hated flying commercial.

He readjusted his grip around the lightweight handle of the shitty-ass knife. Fuck it. It was better than nothing.

He leaned forward, tilted his head to the side and strained his ears, listening. The only sound he heard was the faint wash of the surf lapping against the shoreline—and the raspy sound of Hannah's breathing. He reached behind him, closed his hand over her arm and gave it a reassuring squeeze. The only thing his touch did was make her gasp in surprise. He whirled, raised his hand and pressed it over her mouth, leaned forward so his mouth was against her ear. Soft hair teased his lips; the faint scent of tropical flowers and salty air and pure woman teased his nostrils. He closed his eyes, forced himself to concentrate on the here-and-now.

"Quiet."

Had she heard the word in his soft breath? She must have because her breathing quieted as she stilled beneath his touch. He released his hand and turned away from her, his attention once more focused on the dark interior of the cave and the sounds drifting back to their location.

Footsteps, faltering and uneven. A quiet thud, followed by a small grunt and a swallowed oath. Whoever was out there obviously wasn't worried about being heard. Was it one person, or two?

Ryder dipped his head and closed his eyes, concentrating. Picking out each tiny sound, mentally sorting them into what belonged—and what didn't.

Another step, this one lighter but just as hesitant. The scrape of a shoe against rock, followed by the rustle of fabric. Distant, the sounds nearly lost in the rhythmic crash of the waves.

A murmur. A soft sigh. A small groan. Another rustle of fabric, followed by an impatient whimper.

"Uh-uh. Not yet."

"C'mon, baby. Let me taste them."

A giggle, followed by another rustle of fabric, this one longer. "You can look but no touching. Are you going to light that or not?"

An impatient sigh then a muted metallic scratch. A lighter? Possibly. Ryder's suspicion was confirmed when he heard a deep inhale, followed by an even slower exhale.

"My turn." The woman's voice, filled with eagerness. A few seconds later, Ryder caught the pungent odor of cheap marijuana. Christ. Was that what this was about?

"Hmm. Not yet. Not until you show me everything." Another deep inhale.

"No." The word was pouty, laced with the barest touch of teasing. "I'm too shy."

Laughter, loud and obnoxious. "Sure you are. We, uh, we could always go into the cave."

A long pause. "No. It's too dark."

"But there's nothing in there."

"Have you been in there before?"

"No."

"Then how do you know there's nothing in there?"

"I dunno. Just do."

"No, I don't think so." The woman's voice was a little sharper now, showing the first hint of impatience. "I don't even know why we had to come all the way down here when we could have stayed at the camp."

"Somebody might've seen us."

"I don't care. This was stupid."

"Babe, no, don't. They're too pretty to cover up."

"I don't care. I want to go back. Coming here was a stupid idea."

"Then here, take it." Desperation laced the man's voice. The woman said something, the words to low to make out—but Ryder understood the tone well enough. It was the sound of someone who'd gotten their way.

"Ooo, this is good."

"Yeah? You like it?"

"Mm-hm."

"Enough to take everything off?"

A giggle, followed by another long exhale that ended in a cough. "Maybe. I want to see your party favor first, make sure it's worth it."

Party favor? Fucking shit. And fuck, Ryder was losing patience. He knew who it was—had known the second he heard the voices: Casanova and Darla. Had they come down here just for the sake of getting high and getting laid? Maybe. He didn't want to give the asshole enough credit for anything more but he didn't believe in coincidences—and their timing was one hell of a big, inconvenient coincidence.

No matter what their reasons for being here, Ryder sure as hell didn't want to wait for them to get their game on. And he sure as fuck didn't want to hang out here until they were finished, not with Hannah and Allison here.

Allison.

Fuck! If his sister really did have a thing for the asshole, what was going on at the entrance of the cave must be tearing her apart. She must be fighting against Ninja, ready to tear out of their hiding space so she could go after the man.

No, there was nothing but silence coming from his right—for now. But for how long?

Ryder didn't plan on waiting to find out. Yes, what he was about to do was risky—but he weighed the risks with the odds and decided it was a chance he had to take.

He slipped the knife back into his boot then dropped to his stomach and belly crawled toward the edge of the wall that formed the bend. His left hand swept in front of him then out to the side, back and forth, back and forth, until it closed over a rock. Not a big one—not that he wouldn't be able to bash the asshole's head in with it if he wanted to—but big enough for what he needed.

He slid forward, his progress silent as he eased around the bend. He drew his hand back and threw the rock, heard a satisfying thud as it hit the wall near the cave entrance.

Even more satisfying was the startled oath and muffled scream coming from the couple outside.

"What was that?"

"I dunno. Probably nothing." Fear laced Casanova's voice, only to be replaced by a wail of disappointment. "Darla—Darla, where are you going?"

The sound of running footsteps sliding in loose sand drifted toward Ryder. He waited, breath held, listening—

"Dammit. Darla, wait up!" Another set of hurried footsteps, heavier than the first, fading as they disappeared up the beach.

Silence settled in the wake of the steps. Ryder remained where he was for several long minutes, his ears attuned to the slightest noise, waiting to see if the pair would come back. He moved forward on his belly, drawing closer to the entrance, still listening.

All he heard was the sound of the waves drifting in from the beach.

He pushed to his feet and quickly brushed the front of his shirt and pants, then called over his shoulder. Ninja appeared a few seconds later, guiding the two women in front of him. Ryder aimed the penlight toward the ground and quickly turned it on, just long enough to get a glimpse of their faces, to make sure both women were okay.

Hannah looked worried, maybe even a little confused, but there was no sign of the fright he had felt running through her earlier. He turned to Allison, trying to figure out what to say to her—he sucked at consolation, always had because whatever he tried to say always came out the wrong fucking way and made things worse. But he didn't have to say anything because she didn't look upset.

She looked...stunned. Not in a shell-shocked kind of way, at least not what he'd been expecting. Maybe *dazed* was a better word. Or distracted. Or...hell, he didn't know. He was just glad she wasn't upset and on the verge of tears like he had expected.

He turned the small light off and dropped it into the side pocket of his pants. "Come on, let's get out of here."

Hannah's hand closed over his arm, stopping him. "What about the guns? You can't just leave them here!"

"For right now, we can."

"But—"

"I'll take care of it tomorrow." How, he had no fucking clue—he'd figure it out then. Right now, his priority was getting Hannah and Allison back, before any more late-night visitors showed up.

Because he had a feeling they wouldn't be as lucky the next time.

CHAPTER TWELVE

Hannah absently sipped at her coffee, barely tasting the bitter brew as she watched the four people sitting at the other table. Cindy was hunched over her bowl of fruit, her shoulders pulled up around her ears. Katie was absently stirring her tea, the spoon moving around and around and around in a slow circle, her vacant gaze focused on something nobody else could see.

And the other two...Hannah wanted to roll her eyes and make gagging noises at the way Tim and Darla were acting. Their arms would brush and they'd move away from each other, only to slide closer a minute later and repeat the whole process. Snippets of the overheard conversation from last night played in her mind and she had to tamp down the urge to go over and knock both of their heads together.

What the hell had they been thinking, sneaking out and borrowing the van to take them to the beach? Not just any beach, but the strip just outside the cave. Couldn't they have found someplace closer for their own little private party?

Did Kevin know they'd taken the van? Probably not—he'd be on a rampage if he knew. Hannah herself would have never known—the van was in the same exact spot it had been in when she'd parked it yesterday afternoon. Ryder was the one who had thought to check it by pressing his hand against the hood when they finally got back last night. He didn't say anything—he didn't have to, not when the scowl that crossed his face spoke volumes.

Was this the first time Tim had taken it? Hannah doubted it—which only made her wonder what else had been going on right under her own nose this entire time. What else had she blindly missed—

"Ouch!" She jerked her leg back, reached down to rub the sore spot on her ankle where Allison had just kicked her. "What was that for?"

"Stop staring before they notice."

"I wasn't staring."

"Yeah, you were."

Hannah sighed then leaned back in the chair. "Okay, fine. I was—but not deliberately. I was just thinking."

"About?"

"Everything. What we found down there. The fact that Tim and Darla just happened to show up the way they did." Hannah paused, studying Allison's face, waiting for some sign that her friend was more upset about last night's events than she was letting on. The only emotion she saw in Allison's eyes was irritation, and even that was brief.

Hannah rested her elbows on the table and leaned forward, her voice pitched just above a whisper. "And wondering why you don't seem as upset as I thought you'd be."

"Upset? Why would I be upset?"

"Because, you know—you had a thing or whatever for Tim."

Allison popped a chunk of fruit into her mouth, chewed it, then swallowed. Her gaze didn't quite meet Hannah's when she spoke. "Maybe. I guess I had an epiphany of sorts last night."

"An epiphany?"

"Yeah."

Hannah waited three seconds then nudged her friend's leg under the table. "Well? What was it?"

"My brother was right: Tim's an idiot and not worth my time." She leaned forward and wagged her finger in Hannah's direction. "And don't you dare tell Ryder I said that!"

"I won't." Hannah reached for the coffee, took another sip and forced herself not to stare at the foursome. "Do you think last night was the first night he's snuck out like that?"

"Who? Tim?"

"Yeah. Or anyone else, for that matter. I mean, think about it: we don't really know anyone here. We get these groups coming in for a week or two or three but what do we really know about them? They have background checks done but we never see the reports. The only thing we know about them is what they tell us and who's to say they're telling us the truth?"

Allison frowned, glanced around the pavilion, then shrugged. "I guess. I never thought of it that way before."

Neither had Hannah—she'd simply taken everyone at their word, trusted what they'd said and moved on. But now, looking around, she wondered. Katie, for example. The young woman had just turned eighteen and was down here with her grandparents—but she never seemed to want to be with them, had been hanging around Cindy and Darla and Tim for most of the last week, even though she never really socialized with them.

And even though it was obvious she didn't want to be *with* her grandparents, she was always looking over at them, silently seeking permission for...something. Hannah hadn't thought anything about it—the girl was young, of course she'd want to hang around people closer to her own age. But something about the whole thing suddenly struck her as *off* somehow.

Or maybe she was just jumping to the wrong conclusions because of last night. Thinking that some unknown bad guys were going to find them inside the cave had scared her. The only reason she hadn't completely freaked out had been because of Ryder, knowing he was there, knowing he'd protect her.

And the sight of all those guns had rattled her, as well, maybe even more than the thought that someone was going to walk in on them. Who had put them there? And why? How long had they been there? Was this something totally new, or had she and Allison stumbled onto something that had been going on for a while?

Hannah took another sip of coffee and casually studied everyone around her. Another thought pushed its way to the front of her mind. She placed the cup down then leaned toward Allison.

"You don't think any of them are involved, do you?"

"What? No, of course not." A frown creased her face as she looked around. Shook her head. Frowned even deeper. "No. They couldn't be. We'd know somehow. We'd be able to tell—"

"Like we could tell Tim's been sneaking out?"

Allison's mouth snapped shut. Her gaze darted over to the man in question then shot back to Hannah. She shook her head again, but there was no conviction in it—or in her voice when she spoke.

"It's not him."

"We don't know that. It could be. It could be any of them."

"Would you listen to what you're saying? Do you actually think anyone here is capable of murder? Because that's what you're saying."

"Murder? I didn't—"

"Yes, *murder*. Or are you forgetting about the body they found the other day? The one who just happened to be the same guy we saw on the beach with those other two men?"

No, she hadn't forgotten—but she *had* conveniently put it out of her mind, at least in connection to the group of people around her.

Murder.

The word sent a cold chill dancing across her skin, put an entirely new perspective on the way she viewed everyone around her. *Could* any of them be capable of murder?

Hannah didn't want to think they could but the truth of the matter was, she simply didn't know.

She couldn't know, because she didn't *know* any of them.

Funny how that had never bothered her before. How it had never even really crossed her mind before. She'd been too wrapped up in the day-to-day, worried about completing their small list of projects down here, knowing how important each one was. Worried about their lack of resources and manpower. Frustrated at Kevin's lack of direction and constant changing of priorities. But she'd plugged away, her and Allison both, doing what they could with each group that came down to help. Some weeks, they had more help than they knew what to do with. Other weeks, they were scrambling to accomplish even the smallest tasks. The next few weeks would be like that, as the holidays approached and fewer and fewer people signed on to help. Even Hannah and Allison would both be going home for a small break before signing on for another six-month commitment. At least, Hannah would be—Allison hadn't really decided yet.

And now, for the first time in three years, Hannah herself was starting to question if she wanted to come back.

Anger shot through her, brief and totally unexpected. Of course she'd be coming back. She loved what she did. Loved the people. The culture. Loved knowing that she was making a difference. No, she wasn't going to get rich doing it—but she didn't care about the money. That wasn't why she had chosen this calling. She'd chosen it because she believed in what she was doing, believed in helping others.

Now someone was threatening to take that away from her—and it could be someone who was here with her right now.

She curled her hands into fists and shoved them into her lap. No! No, she was *not* going to start thinking that way. That wasn't who she was. She wasn't the suspicious type, always suspecting those around her, always questioning other's motives. She trusted people. Not blindly—she wasn't quite *that* foolish. Whatever was going on wouldn't change that. She couldn't let it, *refused* to let it.

Hannah took a deep breath and pushed the possibility that she could be breathing the same air as a murderer from her mind. The entire idea was ludicrous.

A sharp clap made her jump, startling her more

than it should have. She looked around, swallowed back a nervous laugh when she noticed Kevin standing in the middle of the pavilion, his hands braced on lean hips as he looked around him.

A lord, surveying his fiefdom.

And oh, good God, where did *that* thought come from? She swallowed back another nervous laugh, her face heating from embarrassment when Kevin looked over at her, his eyes narrowed in irritation.

"Time to clean up. We leave in ten minutes."

Chairs scraped against the concrete floor as everyone pushed away from their tables, chatting quietly as they started the process of cleaning up. It wouldn't take long—it never did because there wasn't much to clean up. Allison had already placed the fruit back in the refrigerator and the coffee pots had been emptied and cleaned before Hannah sat down. That left mugs, bowls, and silverware, all quickly washed and dried and put away.

Hannah dried her hands on a towel then looked around, finally asking Allison the question that she'd been wanting to ask all morning. "Where's your brother?"

"I'm not sure. Colter was here earlier, just long enough to grab two cups of coffee, but I haven't seen him since."

"Who?"

"Colter." Allison tilted her head to the side then rolled her eyes. "His friend? The guy who came down with him?"

"Oh. Ninja." His real name was *Colter*? Why didn't she know that? She mentally brushed the question away and looked around. "So where are they now?"

"No idea but wherever they are, they better hurry.

Kevin isn't going to want to wait for them."

No, he wouldn't. In fact, he'd probably leave them behind and take great delight in doing so. Hannah quickly folded the small towel and placed it on the chipped counter. "They're probably in their bungalow. I'll go get them."

"I'll go with you."

"You don't need to."

"Maybe not, but at least this way I know you won't get, um, distracted."

Hannah stumbled to a stop and whirled toward Allison. "What is that supposed to mean?"

"Just what I said." Allison grinned then gave her a teasing nudge in the arm. "I'm not blind, you know. I know you were with him the other night."

"But I—he—" Hannah clamped her mouth shut, inhaled through her nose and quickly exhaled. "It's not what you think."

"Did I say anything? No, I didn't. And I'm not judging, either." Allison grinned again. "I've always thought you two were destined to be together."

Hannah shook her head. No, it definitely wasn't what her friend thought. And she had to stop Allison from even thinking that way. God forbid if she slipped and accidentally said something in front of anyone—especially Ryder. "It's not like that. And we're not together. We never were, so don't even go there."

"You're in denial."

"No, I'm not. Trust me, I'm really, really not." She hurried away from Allison before she could say anything else, before her friend could comment on the way Hannah's face had turned red or the way the words had hitched in her chest when she spoke. She'd knock on Ryder's bungalow and let them know they were getting ready to leave, and that would be that.

Hannah was several feet away, Allison right behind her, when the bungalow door opened. Ryder stepped out, wearing the same tan cargo pants he'd had on yesterday. A dark t-shirt pulled tight across his chest, the sleeves stretched around his thick biceps. His damp hair was tousled, as if he'd done nothing more than run his hands through it when he stepped out of the shower. Dark stubble covered his jaw, which only made the scowl on his face more menacing.

His gaze met hers and that scowl deepened. No, this was more than a scowl—this was anger like she'd never seen before. Hannah started to back away, froze when he pointed at her—at both of them.

"We need to talk. *Now.*"

CHAPTER THIRTEEN

The color drained from Hannah's face. Her eyes widened as she glanced over her shoulder, then narrowed when she turned back to him. Ryder expected her to spin around and take off in the other direction. Hell, he'd probably do the same damn thing if anyone barked at him the way he'd just barked at her.

Fuck it. He'd apologize later but right now he was pissed. No, *pissed* didn't even begin to cover it—he was fucking livid. After what he'd just learned, they were lucky he wasn't tearing the weasel's head from his neck.

Hell, he still might do that.

Ryder pointed at Hannah again. "We need to talk. *Now*. Get in here."

She started to shake her head, actually took a single step back, but Allison nudged her forward. His gaze shot to his sister, freezing her in place before she could make her own escape. "That means you, too, so don't even think about it."

"Me? What did I do?"

Ryder stepped to the side and motioned toward them. "Get inside. Now."

The two women looked at each other, some kind of silent communication passing between them. They both hesitated, until Hannah finally straightened her shoulders and stepped toward him. He thought she'd move right past him and head into the bungalow but no, that would have been asking for too much. She stopped, tilted her head back to meet his gaze, and frowned. "What is your problem?"

His *problem*? Fuck, where did he start? Thanks to that fucking phone call, he had a list at least a mile long. But he couldn't explain that, not right now, not with the weasel heading their way.

He stepped around Hannah, using his body to push her inside. Then he grabbed Allison's arm and tugged her toward him, dipped his head and whispered in her ear. "Get rid of him. I don't care how you do it, just do it. Now."

And thank God Allison finally picked up on the fact that something was wrong. She quickly nodded and turned toward the weasel, a bright smile on her face. "We'll be right there, Kevin."

"We're leaving—"

"I know. It'll only be a few minutes."

Ryder ground his teeth together. They were going to be more than a few minutes. A hell of a lot more—as in never.

"Tell him you'll catch up later."

Allison turned back, frowning. She started to open her mouth, quickly closed it at the dark look he gave her. She took a deep breath, turned back toward the weasel. "Um, you should probably just go now, Kev. We'll catch up later."

The weasel hesitated then started forward again, his stride a little longer. "Catch up? How? What's going on?"

"Um—" Panic crossed Allison's face then just as quickly disappeared. "Colter's sick. We're, uh, we're just going to, um, make sure he's okay then we'll walk to the school."

"Sick?" The weasel stopped. "Sick, how?"

"I'm not sure. Maybe something he ate. He, uh, he

has a weak stomach so..." Allison's voice trailed off with an apologetic shrug. The weasel's face paled and he actually took a step back, caught himself then took another step forward.

"If he's sick, maybe I should—"

"No, I wouldn't." Allison forced a small laugh and waved her hand under her nose. "It's, um, it's not pretty. Coming out both ends, if you know what I mean."

"Oh." The weasel stopped. Pale eyes slid to Ryder, met his gaze then quickly darted away. "I'll take everyone down to the school and get them started then come back for you—"

"We can walk."

"I said I'll come back."

Allison tossed a helpless glance at Ryder then turned back. "Sure, no problem. Just, um, just give us an hour. We should have everything, you know, um, cleaned up by then."

"An hour. Sure, no problem—"

Ryder pulled his sister inside and slammed the door before the weasel could finish talking. He leaned to the side and peered out the small louvered slats in the door, watching. Would the man change his mind and decide to come after them, or would he just turn around and leave?

A minute went by, then another. The weasel muttered something, ran one hand through his hair, then turned and walked away. Ryder watched as he made his way over to the van, climbed in and started it up. Two minutes later, the van was making its way out of camp, a small cloud of sandy dust trailing in its wake.

Ryder turned around, not surprised to see two sets of eyes staring at him. Their combined anger didn't surprise him, either, although Allison's, at least, was offset by curiosity.

"Nice work, sis. Not sure Ninja would appreciate it, though."

"What's going on? And where *is* Colter?"

"He's doing a little recon."

"Recon? What—"

"Later. Both of you, sit."

"Dammit, Ryder, we aren't dogs. Or men under your command. Or whatever you call them. You can't just order us around—"

"Sit." He paused, forced the next word from between clenched teeth. "Please."

Allison narrowed her eyes then finally sat on the edge of Colter's bed. Hannah hesitated but only for a second before she, too, took a seat. Both women stared up at him, impatience clear in their glares.

Ryder folded his arms in front of him, dug his fingers into his biceps and inhaled. Held it for a count of five and slowly exhaled. Again, only longer this time because if he didn't, there was a real good chance he'd fucking explode.

Hell, he might do that anyway.

"Are you going to tell us what's going on or—"

"How long have you two been down here?" Ryder forced the words from between his teeth. Allison and Hannah exchanged a quick glance then both of them shrugged. It was Allison who answered, even though he had directed the question at Hannah.

"Six months. I told you that the other day. Why?"

Six months. Six fucking months. And they didn't know, had no clue. Shit. How was that even possible? They weren't stupid. Far from it. Maybe a little naive but hell, Ryder thought *everyone* was naive. If people in general had even the tiniest clue of the shit that went on around them, they'd be afraid to get out of bed in the morning. How the hell could they not know?

Because they didn't have his resources, that was why.

The answer didn't do anything to settle the anger and rage that had been seething inside him since his call with Derrick "Chaos" Biggs. Chaos was Cover Six Security's master hacker—which was only one of a myriad of other shady talents the man possessed that Ryder could only guess at. Considering the man's background, those talents probably numbered in the high double-digits—and that was a conservative estimate. Chaos could discover anything, usually with dizzying speed.

"Ryder—"

"What do you know about your project manager?"

Hannah and Allison exchanged another long look, this one filled with confusion more than anything else. Hannah finally met his gaze with a shrug.

"Not much. He's from Australia. He's been working for VRA for a few years. He was placed in charge of this project nine months ago."

Ryder watched her as she spoke. Studied her facial expressions, the way she gestured with her hands. Even the quizzical look in her eyes as she held his gaze.

She didn't know. She really didn't know. And fuck, it was up to him to tell her.

To tell both of them.

"Why are you asking all these questions? What's going on? And what did you mean when you said Colter was doing recon? What does that even mean?" Allison barraged him with questions, each one a little more impatient than the last. Ryder answered with one of his own.

"Who did you work for before coming here?"

"It was a place called—"

"No. Wait." Hannah silenced his sister with a quick touch to her arm. Then she tilted her head to the side, her eyes narrowing as she studied him for a long minute. "How do you know we worked for someone else? What makes you think we haven't been working for VRA all this time?"

Ryder met her gaze, held it for a long time. Knew exactly when she suspected what he was going to say, saw the realization in the way her pupils flared. It didn't make what he was about to say any easier.

And if she didn't hate him now, she would when he finished.

"It's a con. The organization. Your project manager. All of it is just one big con."

Silence descended on the room. Heavy. Oppressive. Thick with suspicion. With denial. Long minutes went by, each one stretching out before them, pulling tighter until finally reaching their breaking point.

It was Hannah who spoke first. She jumped to her feet, her head shaking so fast that her long ponytail flew from side-to-side. She pressed her hands against her waist and started pacing in small circles between the two beds.

"No. No, it can't be. This—" She stopped, waved her hand around to encompass the small bungalow and everything in it. "This isn't a con. The work we've been doing. Rebuilding the school—it's not a con. It can't be. Kevin's made sure—"

"His name isn't Kevin."

Hannah stopped her pacing, whirled to face him.

"What? Yes, it is. He's—"

"His name is Samuel Bannister and he's from Phoenix. He's already served time for embezzlement and he's currently wanted for fraud."

"No. I don't believe it. His name is Kevin Wright."

Ryder took a step toward Hannah, stopped when she waved him off. "I'm sorry, Hannah, but it's not. The real Kevin Wright *is* from Australia. He was seventy-six when he died—two years ago."

"No. You're wrong. This isn't a con. The school, all the work we've been doing. The people who have come here to help." Hannah stopped, hugged herself tighter and blinked. Shook her head and blinked again. She inhaled, lifted her chin in sheer stubbornness and shook her head. "It's *not* a con. Look at what we've done! None of that would have happened if this was a con!"

Ryder started toward her again, stopped. All he wanted to do was pull her into his arms and hold her. Reassure her. But he couldn't. He didn't need to be an expert in body language to know touching her right now was the last thing she wanted. "Hannah, I'm sorry."

She shook her head again, anger in her eyes—anger that was directed at *him*. "It's not a con. I don't know where you got your information from but it's wrong."

He gentled his voice, silently urged her to see the truth in his eyes when he spoke. "Sweetheart, my information is never wrong."

It was the wrong thing to say. Ryder wasn't sure if it was his tone of voice—which he'd tried like hell to soften—or if it was the words he'd used, but Hannah stiffened as if she'd been slapped. She moved toward him, placed both hands against his chest and pushed him out of the way. Then she was tearing open the door and racing outside before he could do anything more than call her name.

"Fuck!"

"You, uh, you probably shouldn't have called her *sweetheart*."

Allison's forlorn voice stopped him from chasing after Hannah. He turned, swallowed back a sigh at the expression in his sister's damp eyes. She was still sitting on the bed, her hands curled around the edge of the thin mattress, staring up at him with an expression of defeat on her face.

"Is it true? This is really a con?"

He watched her for a few long seconds, knew the question was for nothing more than verification. He sighed, finally nodded.

"Yeah, it is. I'm sorry."

Allison nodded, lowered her gaze to the cracked tile floor and released a long breath. Ryder heard steps behind him, turned as Ninja walked inside. He glanced at Allison, something like sympathy flashing in his eyes, then turned to Ryder.

"Find anything?"

"Yeah." Ninja grinned and held up a flash drive. "Got everything right here. And Chaos was able to get into his accounts, too."

"Yeah? And?"

"Let's just say he's in for a big surprise. I wouldn't mind hanging around to see his expression when he finds out he just made several sizable donations to a few different charities."

"Yeah, I don't think so. As much fun as that would be, we're not hanging around."

"What do you mean?"

Ryder glanced at Allison. "I mean we're leaving."

"But—"

"No *buts*, Allison. We're going down to catch the next ferry then getting on a plane and heading home."

She pushed to her feet, worry dancing in her eyes. "But what about those guns? You can't just leave without—"

"Already handled. The authorities are being notified."

"So that's it? They're just going to come and take care of it? You don't have to wait around and do, I don't know, whatever it is you do for something like this? Make a statement or whatever?"

"It doesn't work that way, Allison. Especially not when they receive an anonymous tip." At least, that's what Ryder was counting on. If they were back home, things would be handled differently. Daryl Anderson, the head of CSS, had contacts who dealt with that shit. Hell, even Ryder had contacts. But down here? No, things down here worked differently. The island was remote and, as far as he knew, didn't even have its own police force or military or whatever passed for law enforcement nearby. He wasn't about to tell Allison that, though, not on top of everything else she'd been dealt this morning.

"What about Kevin? What's going to happen to him?"

"I wouldn't be surprised if he's in custody by this weekend."

"This weekend? But that's only two days away. Can't we—"

"No, we can't. Now go pack so we can get the hell out of here."

She looked like she wanted to argue, actually opened her mouth. Then she quickly shut it on a small sigh. "I'll find Hannah—"

"No, I'll find her. You go pack."

"But—"

"No *buts*." He didn't wait for another objection, just turned and walked out. He'd didn't need any more arguments from his sister, not when he'd be catching an earful from Hannah when he found her.

As soon as he figured out where the hell she went.

CHAPTER
FOURTEEN

Hannah wasn't in her bungalow.

Or in the pavilion.

Or in the small office that had been left unlocked. *That* surprised him—not that Hannah wasn't in there, but that the place was unlocked so that anyone could get in and access the files. Not that they contained much of anything—Ryder took a few minutes to flip through the dented filing cabinet, browsed through a few folders here and there.

Waivers. Signed contracts. One file with a few overdue bills stuffed inside.

There wasn't a damn thing that would implicate the weasel in either the filing cabinet or the computer—which was probably why the office door wasn't locked.

The door leading back to the weasel's private quarters was a different story. Is that where Ninja had found everything? Probably. Ryder tried the knob one more time but it did nothing more than wiggle in his hand. Definitely locked. Maybe the weasel wasn't as stupid as Ryder first thought.

He pressed his ear to the door and listened, just in case Hannah was inside, but there was nothing but silence. He ignored the relief that shot through him. Tried like hell to ignore the sharp slice of jealousy that ripped through him at the same time. Hannah said there was nothing going on between the two of them and he believed her—not that he had any claim on her.

Uh-huh. Sure. Maybe if he told himself he had no claim on her enough times, he'd actually fucking believe it.

Fuck. He should have never had sex with her, knew it had been a mistake before they even started. But he'd kicked his common sense to the curb and gave in to the one thing he wanted that he couldn't have: Hannah.

The image of her face the other night flashed in front of him. The expression of shock on her face, the flare of regret in her eyes. He should have never believed all her talk of being two consenting adults and it just being sex, should have stepped away and said he was interested.

Yeah, he should have—but he hadn't. And her immediate regret had been more than obvious. Would she have been able to hide her feelings if Ninja hadn't walked in on them? Would she have pretended it was no big deal, just like she'd said it was before they got started? Maybe. In the end, it didn't matter. He should have known better but he'd acted on his desires anyway and now it was too late.

And if she didn't hate him for that, she sure as hell hated him for the fucking bombshell he dropped in her lap a few minutes ago.

Could he blame her?

No, not really.

Fine. If she hated him, she hated him. He'd deal with it now the same way he had eleven years ago—by ignoring it and letting time take care of the rest. The only problem was, he didn't have time. If they wanted to catch that morning ferry, they needed to get out of here *now*.

He stepped out of the office, pulled the door

closed behind him, then looked around. Where the hell was she? There weren't that many places she could go, at least not in the immediate area. She probably wanted to be alone, so she'd find a spot that was secluded—

Yeah. *That* really narrowed it down.

Ryder turned to the left and started his search again, checking behind each bungalow, stopping to listen every few feet. He'd walk the perimeter then extend the search in an ever-widening circle until he found her. And he *would* find her—it was just a question of when.

He glanced at his watch then bit back a growl of frustration. *When* needed to be *now* because they didn't have much time left.

Dammit. Where the hell was she?

He moved past the pavilion, even looked inside the old storage shed he hadn't noticed before. No sign of Hannah—just some rusty tools and old paint cans and a worn-out tarp tossed in the corner, all of it overlaid with a lingering odor of marijuana.

He finally found her fifteen minutes later, on his third pass around the small camp. She was sitting on the ground, her back against the trunk of a thick tree, her knees drawn up to her chest. She didn't look at him when he approached but Ryder knew she was aware of his presence, could see that awareness in the way her entire body stiffened.

He stood there for a long minute, waiting for her to look up. Waiting for her to say something. Waiting for...something. Hell, he'd even settle for a *go to hell* or a *get lost* but there was nothing.

He sighed then crouched down next to her, braced his arms against his thighs and clasped his hands together. If he didn't, he might do something completely foolish, like reach for her.

"We need to get going, Hannah."

Silence greeted his words. Great. Was she planning on just completely ignoring him? Apparently. He didn't want to drag her back to the bungalow and force her to pack but he would if he had to, consequences be damned. He'd save that as a last resort because this would be a hell of a lot easier if she cooperated.

Yeah, because dragging Hannah onto the ferry kicking and screaming was sure to attract unwanted attention.

He gentled his voice as much as he could and tried again. "We need to get to the ferry—"

"I'm not going."

Her hoarse words hung in the air between them. Certain. Defiant. And shit, he so didn't have time for this.

"You don't have a choice—"

"Yeah, I do. And I'm not going. I came here to do a job and I'm going to finish it—"

"What job? Hannah, it's a fucking con. Can't you see that?"

She finally looked at him. Brown eyes filled with anger and determination stared back at him. But under those two emotions lay something else—something she was doing her best to hide: acceptance of the truth cloaked in a healthy dose of denial.

"It's not a con. We wouldn't be here if it was. We wouldn't have started rebuilding the school or—or—" She paused, frowned, shook her head. "Or anything else we've done. We wouldn't be here now, still working, if it was a con."

"I know this is a lot to take in—"

"There's nothing to take in because your information is wrong." She blinked against the moisture welling in her eyes and looked away.

Ryder glanced at his watch, swallowed his frustration and decided to try reasoning with her one more time. If that failed, he'd simply drag her with him—he didn't have any other choice.

"Hannah, stop and think, will you? How long have you been doing sh—" She stiffened and Ryder immediately picked another word. "—stuff like this? Two years? Three? You can't seriously tell me it's always this unorganized. Hell, even *I* can tell and I've only been here a couple of days."

She shook her head again, still in denial, once again refusing to look at him. "Kevin just gets a little distracted. Overwhelmed. He—he's not used to being in charge—"

"Bullshit. Stop making excuses and open your eyes and see what the hell is really going on. He's not distracted or overwhelmed, he's running a carefully constructed con—"

"No! No, he's not. If this was a con, he'd have taken off already. He wouldn't still be down here working—"

"Working on what? Because I sure as hell didn't see him do a damn thing yesterday—"

"He's in charge, he has other things to take care of, too."

Ryder reached up and pinched the bridge of his nose. Took a deep breath and quickly released it. Why was she being so damn stubborn? Why was she refusing to admit the truth when he could clearly see it in her eyes? Instead of admitting it, she was making one excuse after another, almost like she was trying to cover for the asshole.

He dropped his hand and frowned. "Hannah, you're not stupid—"

"Which is how I know this isn't a con." She bit down on her lower lip, blinked several times and sucked in a deep breath. "It's not a con, Ryder. I'm *not* stupid. We checked, Allison and I both did. We did research. Looked into references and reviews—"

"Which can all be faked."

"No." She shook her head, spoke a little louder. "No. I refuse to believe that. I'm *not* stupid."

"I didn't say you were."

"But that's *exactly* what you're saying. It must be, because only stupid, gullible people fall for a con."

Ryder reached for her. "Sweetheart, that's not—"

She flung his hand from her arm and jumped to her feet. "Don't call me that. And stop talking to me like I'm two. I'm not an idiot and you don't need to be so damned condescending."

The last of Ryder's patience snapped. He pushed to his feet, closed the distance between them. Hannah's eyes narrowed in anger as she backed away from him, stopping only when she collided with the tree behind her. He kept moving, pinning her in place with his body—and his hard gaze.

"I'm trying to be considerate, not condescending. And I don't understand why you won't admit the truth when it's staring you straight in the face." He reached down and grabbed her hand. "We don't have time for this bullshit, we need to leave—"

"I'm not leaving."

"You don't have a choice."

"The hell I don't. I came here to do a job and I'm not leaving until it's done." She ripped her hand from his and pushed past him.

"Hannah, dammit—"

She spun around, pointed at him with one trembling finger. And dammit, moisture filled her gaze despite all the blinking she was doing to stop it. "People are counting on me, Ryder. You keep saying it's a con but we actually started something here. We're doing something good here. I can't just walk away. I'm not like that." She paused, took a shuddering breath and lowered her voice. "I'm not like *you*."

The accusation slammed into him, freezing him in place, robbing his lungs of air. Spots danced in front of his eyes and he blinked, pushed back the grayness that hovered at the edge of his vision.

Told himself he was hearing things. Told himself that Hannah hadn't meant the words hanging in the air between them the way he was taking them.

One look at her face said otherwise. Yes, she meant them the way they'd come out. And yes, the guilt shining in her eyes let him know she regretted saying them and wished she could take them back—but she couldn't.

No more than he could take back the awful words he'd said to her eleven years ago.

"I don't understand how you can just walk away, Ryder."

He didn't look up from packing his bag. He couldn't, not when he knew what he'd see. Not when he knew how much harder that would make things. "I signed up to do this. You know that."

"But you can change your mind. It's not too late."

"No, Hannah, I can't. Uncle Sam doesn't work that way."

A long pause. A muffled sniffle.

The floor creaked beneath her slight weight when she moved toward him. Close. Close enough that he felt her right behind him. Close enough so that all he had to do was turn around and she'd be right there. He'd pull her into his arms and—

No. That was the last thing he could do. This was hard enough as it was. But he couldn't tell her that. If he did, she'd think there was hope. Think he'd be coming back.

And he wouldn't be. Not any time soon. Not with what he'd already obligated himself to do.

"*You could stay. I know you could...if you really wanted to.*"

And there it was, the accusation that had been simmering for the last few weeks as the date of his departure moved closer.

If he wanted to.

And fuck, this was all his fault. He should have never touched her. Never gotten involved with her, not when he knew he was leaving. But he'd been stupid, had let himself believe she could handle the brief relationship. Hell, he'd let himself believe it, too.

And now he had nobody to blame but himself.

He wished he could drag out the packing because he didn't want to turn and face her, didn't want the temptation that was Hannah to lure him into doing something they'd both regret— and if he stayed, they would *regret it. Maybe he was still young but even he knew that.*

He zipped the small duffel—he didn't need to pack much, not for where he was going—then slowly turned. He kept his gaze focused on the wall behind Hannah, refused to even look at her. She was going to hate him before this was over and he didn't think he could handle seeing that hate in her eyes when she left.

Because she would *leave. He was going to make sure of it.*

"*I don't want to stay, Hannah.*"

"*But—*"

"*You knew going into this how it would end. You knew it was just a...a thing.*"

Tears filled her eyes but she didn't move away. Didn't turn on her heel and run like he expected her to.

"You said you loved me."

Yeah, he had. He'd blurted the declaration out the first time they'd had sex because he'd been too stupid to keep his mouth shut. It didn't matter that he'd meant it then, and every single time he'd said it in the three months since. And it didn't matter that he still meant it now. She couldn't know that.

Ever.

He forced himself to laugh, the sound cold and impersonal. "Sweetheart, don't you know guys will say anything to get fucked?"

There it was, the shock he'd been expecting. The color drained from her face, only to replaced by two bright spots of red on her cheeks. She blinked but it wasn't enough to stop the tears from finally falling. The sight of those tears trailing down her splotched cheeks made him physically sick. He wanted to reach for her, pull her into his arms and tell her he didn't mean it.

But he couldn't. If he did, she'd hold out hope that there could be something more between them. She'd put her own life on hold and wait for him to come back. He couldn't do that to her, not when an entire world of possibility was stretched out in front of her. He couldn't make her wait for something that was never going to happen.

"Y-you don't mean that."

Dammit, why was she still here? Why wouldn't she believe him? She should have turned and left as soon as the words left his mouth. No, she should have slapped him first then *left.*

Ryder dug down deep for the strength he needed to push her away for good—and prayed that he could hide his real emotions while he forced the biggest lie he'd ever told from his mouth.

"Yeah, sweetheart, I do. It was fun for a while but it's over. Fucking you was nothing more than a distraction. A way to kill time until I left."

The hurt spreading across her face tore him apart inside—but he didn't move. Didn't say anything to ease the harsh sting of the lie. Seconds stretched into minutes before the hurt in her watery gaze morphed into hate. Cold. Sharp. Biting.

He clenched his jaw. Held his breath against the pain slicing through him. Another minute went by before Hannah blinked away the last of her tears. She lifted her chin a notch, those brown eyes focusing on him with a coldness that chilled his heart. Then she turned and walked away.

Out of his room.

Out of his life.

Ryder pushed the painful memories away, ignored the taste of bile building in the back of his throat. This wasn't about him—it had never been about him. Let Hannah hate him—it was, after all, what he'd aimed for all those years ago. She could hate him all she wanted—

As long as she'd go pack her things so they could get off this fucking island before the weasel came back.

"Hannah, you can hate me all you want for what I did to you eleven years ago. Fuck, hate me for what I did the other night. I don't care. What I care about is getting you out of here—"

"I'm not leaving."

"You don't get it, do you? The money your friend conned out of all those people is gone."

"Because it's been spent on supplies and—"

"No. It's gone because Chaos moved it from his account. And when the weasel finds out, there's going to be hell to pay. I don't think you want to be here when that happens. And you sure as hell don't want to be here when they come pick his ass up."

"You're lying." There was no conviction in the words, not this time. But the stubbornness didn't leave her eyes. She shook her head, backed up a step. "And even if you aren't, I don't care. There's still work that needs to be done. The school. The fence—"

"Hannah, stop and *think*. You saw the materials up there. That's not enough to do anything."

"Yes, it is. We can—" She stopped, took a deep breath. "We can work with what we have, do as much as we can until the rest of the supplies get here."

"Hannah—"

"I'm not leaving, Ryder. I came here to do a job and that's what I'm going to do." She spun on her heel and stormed away. Ryder started after her then stopped.

Fuck. Why was she being so damn stubborn about this? Why couldn't she see the truth? What the hell did he have to do to prove it to her?

He had no fucking idea—but whatever it was, he needed to figure it out. Fast. They didn't have much time, not if they were going to catch that morning ferry.

He looked down at his watch and swore.

They didn't have time, period.

CHAPTER FIFTEEN

It was a con.
He's served time for embezzlement...wanted for fraud.
All of it is just one big con.

The words swirled through her mind, faster and faster as she hurried away from Ryder. Was he coming after her? She didn't think so, prayed that he wasn't. Prayed that he'd just leave her alone. She didn't want him to see her like this. Didn't want him to see the tears that she was trying so hard to blink back.

Didn't want him to see the heat of embarrassment flushing her face.

Because—no matter what she'd told him—she believed him.

It was a con.

And oh God, how could she have been so stupid? So naive? How could she have allowed herself to be so easily drawn into Kevin's scheme?

Because she had wanted to believe they were doing something good. Because she believed in what they were trying to do here. That belief—and her own naivety—had completely blinded her to the signs she should have seen.

Hannah stumbled, caught herself and quickened her steps.

No, she'd seen the signs—but she had refused to accept them, had made excuses for every single one of them. The delays in receiving supplies. The way Kevin constantly changed priorities, switching to a new project before one was finished, or making excuses for why something couldn't be done right away. He'd done that so many times that even she couldn't keep up, had no idea what they were even supposed to be working on anymore.

She should have pressed the issue harder. Should have demanded answers months ago when she first noticed things were slipping. But she hadn't. Instead of questioning Kevin, she'd given him the benefit of the doubt. She assumed he was overwhelmed and tried to do more herself to help him out, to take some of the pressure off his shoulders so he could focus on the priorities.

But even that hadn't helped—and she had blamed herself for not doing enough.

It was a con, all of it—and she had played right into his hands.

How much money had he taken in? She knew how much the weekly fee was for each person who came to help. At least, she thought she knew. It could be even more but she had no way of knowing for sure. And she knew exactly how much was spent each week for expenses—which wasn't much. Was he pocketing the rest? Yes, he must be—that's what made it a con, right?

She did the math in her head and stumbled to a stop. The figure was staggering. So staggering that she doubled over and nearly threw up. Oh God, all that money. Money that could be put to use *here*, where it was needed.

Money that would never be seen again because of one man's disgusting greed.

How long was he planning on keeping the con going? Weeks? Months? Years? No, definitely not years. Then how long?

She knew the answer as soon as the question came to her: until the holiday break. Nobody was scheduled to come in for those two weeks. Hannah and Allison would be going home. And when the holidays were over and they returned, Kevin would be gone—along with the money.

No, the money was gone. What was it Ryder had said? Somebody had moved it. But moved it where? It didn't matter because it wasn't *here*, wasn't going to be used to do what needed to be finished *here*.

And she was partly to blame. She'd actually *helped* Kevin. For the last six months, she'd stood by his side and allowed herself to be caught up in his visions for improvements—then made excuses when none of those visions made it to fruition.

That made her just as guilty.

Nausea rolled over her and she squeezed her eyes closed, fought against it as she pulled in several deep breaths. God, how could she have been so stupid? So naive? So damned *trusting*? Ryder must be laughing at her, seeing how easily she had been drawn into the web of lies.

Except he hadn't looked like he wanted to laugh. Not earlier when he'd first told them. Not a few minutes ago when he had tried to convince her to leave. Convince? No, he'd flat out *told* her they were leaving, making it a command and acting like he expected her to immediately obey. Acting like *he* was in charge and knew what was best for her.

Well she sure showed him, didn't she? Just like she'd shown him eleven years ago when she stormed out of his room the day he left to join the Army. The day he'd lied to her and said all those hurtful things just to push her away.

Because he thought he knew what was best for her.

And God, why was she even thinking of that day right now? Didn't she have more important things to worry about? Yes, she did—but that didn't stop the memories from flooding back, not when she had just thrown them in his face ten minutes ago. Memories of that day *still* hurt, the pain as raw now as it had been back then. It didn't matter that she now knew he'd been lying—she hadn't known it *then*, had believed every hurtful word he'd said to her. It wasn't until years later, when she was older and able to think back on that day with wisdom she hadn't possessed when she was younger, that she realized what he'd done—and why. But knowing didn't ease the pain she'd felt, not even now.

Laughing? No, Ryder wouldn't laugh at her. He'd lie through his teeth if he thought it would protect her, but he would never laugh at her.

She opened her eyes, brushed the back of her hand across her forehead and looked behind her, expecting to see Ryder catching up with her. All she saw was empty road. Funny, she didn't even remember reaching the road, but here she was, standing in the middle of it, maybe a quarter-mile from their tiny compound.

A chill prickled her skin. *Compound?* Odd how the word carried a more sinister meaning now that she knew what had been going on. Now that she knew everything had been nothing but one big con.

She should turn and go back. Pack her things like Ryder had said and just leave. There was nothing here for her to do, not now. He'd been right about that, too. As much as she wanted to, she couldn't just walk to the work site and try to finish what they'd started. They didn't have enough supplies. They didn't have enough people, not when everyone except Tim would be leaving soon. A new group would be arriving on Monday but that wouldn't help, not now.

Even if they had the people and the supplies, they didn't have enough time. If Ryder was right—and there was no reason to think he wasn't—everything would come to a screeching halt and they'd all be leaving in a few days anyway. The authorities were coming for Kevin, would pick him up and haul his sorry ass off so he could face justice somewhere. As much as she wanted to be here when that happened, Ryder was right—it would be better if they left. Better to let the authorities handle everything.

She turned, ready to head back, when the sound of an engine approached from behind. Soft at first, then growing louder as it neared. She recognized the sound, had listened to it several times a day each day for the last six months.

The van. The worn-out, beat-up van.

Hannah almost darted into the dense brush lining the road. She didn't want Kevin to see her, and she certainly didn't want to see him. How could she even look at him without showing her disgust? Acting wasn't one of her strong suits, not when almost everything she felt showed on her face. One look at her and he'd know something was wrong.

But it was too late. The van was in sight, which meant Kevin must have already seen her. Yes, he had, because the van was slowing down. There was no way she could hide, not now.

Think. Think. Think.

She was still thinking when the van stopped next

The Defender: RYDER

to her. Kevin rolled the passenger window down and leaned across the seat, a frown creasing his otherwise smooth face. "Why are you walking? I told you I was coming back to get you."

The phony accent—the same one she had once thought so charming—grated on her nerves. "Oh. Um, yeah. I know. I just thought..." Her voice trailed off, every possible excuse in the back of her mind dying before she could grasp it. Kevin just rolled his eyes.

"No worries. Hop in and we'll head back." He unlocked the door then looked up the road with another frown. "Where's Allison? And her brother and his friend?"

Hannah glanced over her shoulder, breath held as she willed for them—any of them—to suddenly appear. But the road remained empty. She searched for another excuse, anything to bide some time because she did *not* want to get in the van with Kevin. She didn't want to be anywhere near him, especially not by herself.

"They, um—Colter still isn't feeling well. In fact, that's what I was doing. I was just coming to tell you that we wouldn't be coming." She mentally winced, wondered if the excuse sounded as idiotic as she thought it did.

Kevin's brows shot up and an amused smile teased the corners of his mouth. "You were going to walk all that way to tell me that?"

"Oh. No. No, of course not." She forced a laugh and waved her hand, as if to say she'd meant it was a joke. "I just figured I'd save you some time because I thought I'd run into you and I did. So, yeah. Um, Colter's still sick so we're not going to make it. I'll just head back to camp and—"

"It takes three of you to care for one sick man?" Impatience laced Kevin's voice and flashed in his blue eyes. "Don't be ridiculous. Now get in so we can get back."

He stretched across the passenger seat and opened the door. She shook her head, wanting to say *no*. Searched her mind for another excuse, one that wouldn't sound so ridiculous and superficial. "Let me get Allison—"

"No. Just get in. I wanted to talk to you anyway and it's better if Allison isn't here."

Oh God, now what? She couldn't keep putting him off, not without making him suspicious. She glanced over her shoulder one more time, hoping she'd see Allison or Ryder or Colter, but the road was still empty.

"Hannah."

"Okay, I'm coming." She was careful not to meet his gaze as she climbed into the van and carefully closed the door behind her. Kevin turned the van around then headed back the way he'd come. A few awkward minutes passed before Kevin sighed, the sound loud enough to be heard over every creak and groan of the van as it bounced over ruts and bumps.

"Is there something going on between you and Allison's brother?"

Hannah choked back a surprised gasp and made the mistake of looking at Kevin. Thank God he wasn't looking at her—if he was, he might see the heat filling her face. "What? No, of course not. Why would you even say something like that?"

"It just seems as if you two know each other."

"Well, we do. We grew up together. All three of us."

"I didn't mean it that way."

Anger shot through her. How dare he ask her something so personal? Even if she didn't know what he'd done, she'd still be angry. Her personal life was none of his business. She started to tell him that but he stopped her with a sharp wave of his hand.

"I'm only asking because I sensed some tension there. I can't afford to have any disruptions. You know that. And reputation is everything. I can't afford for word to get out that this is anything but a family-oriented program."

Hannah stared at him, unable to hide her disbelief. "There's nothing—"

He silenced her with another sharp wave. "I believe you. Irregardless, I think it's better if they leave."

"*Regardless*."

"What?"

"It's *regardless*, not *irregardless*." And oh God, was she really correcting his language? He frowned at her, his disbelief as real as her own.

"Either way, I think it would be best if they left. I know Allison said they were only here until Sunday but I'm going to tell her tonight that I want them gone in the morning. This afternoon would be better but I'm not sure if we'll be back in time to get them down to the dock before the last ferry leaves."

Hannah opened her mouth to argue with him then quickly snapped it shut before she could say a single word. Why would she argue? He was giving them the perfect excuse. Now they wouldn't have to come up with another story about how they had to stay back. They could just leave.

All four of them, because Hannah planned on

going with them.

"Okay. I'll tell them when we get back."

"Just like that? No arguments?"

"No arguments."

"Hm. I expected more of a fight from you."

"Why? It's only a few days. And you're right, you can't afford—"

"Shit!"

Kevin slammed the brakes and Hannah was thrown forward, the seat belt catching her around the neck before she hit the dash. Momentum stopped and she was jerked back, the force pushing a surprised gasp from her. She turned toward Kevin, ready to ask him what he was doing, stopped when her eyes focused on the figure standing in the middle of the road.

Ryder.

She blinked. Blinked again, certain she was hallucinating.

But it wasn't a hallucination—Ryder really was standing in the middle of the road. How was that even possible? The last time she'd seen him, he'd been standing by the tree fifty yards outside their small compound. No way could he have gotten that far ahead of her—ahead of *them*.

But he had—which meant he must have run the entire way. Not just run. For him to have caught up to them—to *pass* them—he must have been doing an all-out sprint.

"I thought you said he was back at the camp."

"I—he—" She was saved from answering by Ryder himself. He approached the van, a careless smile on his face, and opened the rear sliding door. Hannah twisted in her seat, frowning as he climbed in.

"Thanks for stopping. I really didn't feel like

walking all that way." He pulled the t-shirt away from his chest a few times, fanning himself with the damp material. "It's already hot. No idea how you guys deal with it down here."

Confusion crossed Kevin's face. "But—I didn't pass you on the way up."

"You did."

"No, I would have seen you."

Ryder shrugged, leaned toward Kevin with one of those man-to-man grins like he was ready to share some kind of raunchy joke. "I was taking a leak. You know how it is."

Kevin swore beneath his breath, the words too low for Hannah to hear, then started the van forward again. Whatever he'd said didn't matter because she wasn't paying attention to him. How could she, when she was so focused on Ryder?

On the way his pulse beat heavy in his strong throat.

On the way the slightly damp shirt clung to his broad chest and arms.

On the faintest sheen of sweat covering his face.

And on the dark anger simmering in the deep brown eyes staring back at her.

CHAPTER SIXTEEN

Ryder slammed the post into the ground. Once. Twice. Harder. Vibrations ran through the post and into his arm, spread through him until his entire body hummed with them.

Vibrations, hell. That was anger thrumming through his body. Anger—

And the tiniest sliver of fear.

He slammed the post again, ramming it deeper into the ground. The sun beat down on him, the warmth fighting the chill that had overtaken him when he saw Hannah climb into the creep's van a few hours ago.

What the *fuck* had she been thinking? It was one thing to verbally deny everything Ryder had told her. She didn't want to admit she'd been duped, was convinced it meant she was stupid—which it didn't, but at least he understood *why* she was so reluctant to accept the truth. He understood it, no problem. It was a lot to take in, he got that. But to actually *go* with that asshole when she *knew*, deep down, what he'd done?

Fuck.

His damn heart had literally stilled for a few seconds when he saw her get into that van. As he watched it drive away. A dozen different scenarios played through his mind, none of them good. He couldn't take the chance nothing would happen, couldn't risk the chance that Hannah might actually *ask* the fucking weasel about the money—because yeah, he could totally see her doing that. Could totally see her confronting him and demanding answers. God only knew how the man would react if she did something like that. At best, he'd kick her out and run and hide. At worst—

Yeah, it was that *at worst* that propelled him into action. He'd taken off after them, running like hell, his long stride eating up the distance between them. He couldn't just jump on the back bumper—well, he *could*, but that would create a hell of a lot of questions he didn't want to answer—so he'd veered off the road for a little cross-country sprint until he got ahead of them. The expression on the weasel's face when he saw him standing in the middle of the road had been fucking priceless.

And yeah, he was shallow enough to admit that the look on Hannah's face had been pretty damn rewarding, too, because she'd looked at him like he was some kind of damn superhero. Only for a few seconds but yeah, it had been worth it.

Until she realized how angry he was.

He grabbed the stained rag from his back pocket and mopped the sweat from his face then finished setting the post. It wasn't the greatest job he'd ever done but considering what he had to work with, it would do. It didn't have to look pretty as long as it did what it was supposed to do, which was support the rails for the fence.

He looked behind him and studied the other posts he'd already put in during the last couple of hours. They were set back fifteen feet from the edge of the damn cliff, a staggered line of pale wood sentinels marking a buffered safety zone. Ryder was under no assumption that the damn fence would keep anyone from venturing too close, and it sure as hell wouldn't stop a full-grown man from breaking through, not if they hit it running. But it might—stress on the *might*—stop a kid from getting too close and getting into trouble.

That's all he cared about.

Of course, there were no guarantees that he'd even finish the damn thing today—which meant it wouldn't get finished at all. There weren't enough supplies to line the entire perimeter so he'd marked off what he thought was the most vulnerable area, then paced off the distance between each post. The lack of supplies wasn't the only thing hampering him—he was working by himself because everyone else was doing something different. The weasel had thrown a damn fit when Ryder told him he'd be working on the fence. His face had gone all red and his eyes had damn near popped out of their sockets. But it wasn't like he could say no, not without giving a damn good reason—and he didn't have one. Not after the near-accident the other day. Not when Hannah had immediately jumped in and said what a great idea it was.

No, the weasel couldn't tell him no, not without looking like a total ass—but he made damn sure Ryder didn't have any help doing it.

He shoved the rag back into his pocket then pulled the damp shirt away from his chest. At this rate, he wouldn't have any more clean clothes. Not that he needed them because they were leaving in the morning. They'd get a room at one of the resorts on the other island and he'd send his clothes out to be cleaned. Or hell, maybe he'd even buy some new ones, he didn't give a shit. They'd have two days to just kick back and relax, a mini-vacation of sorts. Clear blue water. Sandy beaches. Tropical drinks.

Him. Ninja. Allison.

And Hannah.

Because she was coming with them, even if he had to carry her kicking and screaming.

He would have preferred to leave this morning but that hadn't happened. Hell, even this afternoon would be better than waiting until tomorrow—he was starting to get that little tingle at the back of his neck that warned shit was about to get real. But this afternoon probably wasn't going to happen, either, so he'd have to settle for tomorrow morning.

Sixteen hours shouldn't make much difference, not in this situation.

Yeah, sure. So why the hell was his internal warning system starting to kick into gear?

He moved closer to the edge of the cliff and looked at the deserted beach below. He couldn't see the cave from here but he knew it was down there—along with that cache of weapons.

Those weapons still bothered him. Not just their presence—that was bad enough. Shouldn't the authorities be storming the beach by now? Surrounding the cave and removing the weapons, searching for whoever in hell had put them there? At least five hours had gone by since the call was made, surely that was enough time for somebody to do something. He'd heard of island time but Christ, surely that didn't apply to gun smuggling.

Ryder would keep an eye on things while he worked on the fence and if he didn't see any movement by the time they left, he'd call Mac when they got back. Between him and Chaos, they should be able to light a fire under someone somewhere and get it taken care of.

He heard hesitant footsteps behind him, followed by the sound of a throat being cleared. He knew who it was without looking, had sensed her approach long before hearing her.

Hannah.

He glanced over his shoulder but didn't bother turning around. "If you were going to push me off, you lost your chance."

Her eyes widened then quickly narrowed as she glared at him. "That's not even funny."

"Wasn't saying it to be funny."

"Then why say it all?"

"Because I know you're still pissed at me." He turned his head away from her, went back to staring at the beach below. At the clear blue water and the white-capped waves crashing against the sand and rocks.

Hannah moved next to him, close enough that their arms brushed when she held out a bottle of water. "I thought you might be thirsty."

He nodded, accepted the water and took several long gulps.

"Lunch is going to be ready in a few minutes."

"I'll pass. I want to get as much done as I can."

"Ryder, you need to eat. You skipped breakfast and—"

"I had a protein bar." A high-calorie, nutrient-dense, protein-laden slab of cardboard was a more accurate description but what the hell, it served its purpose.

"Where did you get a protein bar?"

"My pack. I always carry some with me." Along with a bunch of other goodies that she didn't need to know about. Not that he had most of those goodies with him on this trip—another downside of flying commercial.

"Well, you should still eat."

"We'll see."

They stood in silence for several minutes, staring out over the water below. Not talking. Not touching. Just...being. For a few precious moments, it was just the two of them. No history. No anger. No regrets. No tension.

Of course, it was nothing more than an illusion, one that ended when Hannah shifted beside him.

"I—" She hesitated. Cleared her throat. Jammed her hands into the front pockets of her khaki shorts and rocked back on her heels. "I owe you an apology."

That surprised him enough that he looked over at her. But she was still staring straight ahead, her gaze focused on something only she could see.

"An apology for what?"

"For overreacting this morning. For storming off the way I did."

"For getting into the van with that asshole when you knew what he'd done?" Despite his attempts at keeping his voice calm, the words carried an edge that hinted at his anger. He expected Hannah to storm off again, or at least lash out at him, but she did neither.

"Yeah, that too." She sighed, glanced at him from the corner of her eye, then stared straight ahead. "What's going to happen with the—with what's down there?"

Ryder frowned at the question, then remembered she had already stormed out of the bungalow when he relayed that information to Allison this morning. "The authorities were called this morning and given an anonymous tip."

"Called? How? Cell service—"

"We have a sat phone. I called back home and they relayed the intel."

"Is that how you found out about—"

"Yeah."

Hannah nodded. "Have they come to get them yet? Whoever it was you called, I mean."

"Not yet, no. Not that I've seen." Was it possible the authorities had shown up earlier, before he got here? Maybe—but Ryder doubted it. If that was the case, there should still be activity on the beach. At least, there would be if they were back home. The beach would be a solid wall of black as officials combed every nook and cranny and turned over every grain of sand.

"Do you think Kevin is involved at all? With what's down there, I mean."

Ryder didn't answer right away. He couldn't, because he didn't know *how* to answer. The weasel—aka Kevin, aka Samuel Bannister—was a real piece of shit, there was no doubt about that. But was he actually involved in smuggling guns? Ryder didn't want to give him credit for being smart enough—or ruthless enough—to run an operation like that but he also wasn't foolish enough to discount the possibility. It took a degree of intelligence—or sheer stupidity—to execute a con like the one he had going on down here. Had he branched out into gun smuggling?

Maybe.

Maybe not.

And his gut was totally undecided, which didn't help matters.

"I don't know. It's possible. But whether or not it's likely is a different story. That's a big leap to take, from running a con to running guns."

Hannah nodded, a frown creasing her face as she studied the water below. She tilted her head to the side, her voice a little distracted when she spoke. "Do you think it could be anyone else here?"

"Like who?"

"I don't know. Any of the volunteers. Could any of them be responsible?"

Ryder turned and studied the small group spread out behind him.

The weasel, standing off to the side with his hands on his hips, frowning at nothing in particular. At least, nothing that Ryder could see. A con man, yes. But was he guilty of anything else?

Katie Miller. Young. Quiet. Ryder didn't think he'd heard her talk once since he'd been here. She was talking now, though, her expression distracted and fearful as she slapped paint on the concrete walls of the half-finished building under the direction of her grandmother, Eva Miller.

The older woman seemed nice enough, not that Ryder had spent much time talking to her, either. She had certainly taken a liking to Ninja, though, had even asked about him earlier when Ryder got here. Was she nothing more than a happy-humanitarian-retiree or was that simply a cover for something else?

Her husband, George Miller. The older man was standing under the shade provided by the lush vegetation near the start of the trail leading down to the beach. As Ryder watched, he fanned himself with his hand and drank greedily from a bottle of water. He'd no doubt overexerted himself doing...Ryder had no idea what he'd been doing. It could have been nothing more strenuous than carrying paint cans back and forth, evidenced by the paint that was smudged on his sleeve and the hem of his shirt.

Cindy and Darla, two college women who seemed more interested in partying than working. Why they had signed up for a week of volunteering—and paid for the opportunity on top of it—was beyond Ryder. They'd done more bickering than anything else in the time he'd been here. Even now, the paint brushes in their hands were forgotten as they bent their heads together. Tension radiated from each woman as they quietly argued about something. If he had to guess, it was about Casanova.

Casanova, the typical party dude. He was—Ryder frowned, searching the small crowd. Casanova was nowhere to be found.

Ryder turned back to Hannah, ready to ask where Tim was. He never got the words out because Hannah's hand clamped down on his arm, fingers biting into his flesh as she pointed with her free hand.

"Ryder, what's that?"

He ignored the sudden chalkiness of her complexion, ignored the tremor in her voice and the trembling of her hand as she pointed. He quickly scanned the horizon, his gaze landing on the debris floating in the surf. It looked like a log, drifting in with each wave before being pulled farther out by the current.

Except it wasn't a log.

It was a body.

Ryder took off at a run, shouting for someone to get help as he hit the trail and started his way down to the beach. Someone screamed, the shrill noise drowned out by shouts—confused at first, then surprised, then horrified. Pounding footsteps echoed behind him, fading as he outran whoever was following him.

His boots sank into the sand at the end of the trail but he kept going, hitting the surf at a dead run. Waves pulled at his feet, threatening to throw him off-balance as he surged deeper into the water. He dove in, salt stinging his eyes, arms slicing through clear blue water. Closer, fighting for each inch of distance until he reached the body. His hand closed onto an arm, fisted in the soggy shirt as he pulled the body into his chest and turned toward the shoreline. Kicking. Pulling. Letting the waves push him closer, using his powerful legs and free arm to fight the current trying to pull him back out. Close. Closer, until his feet touched sand and he was able to stand. To walk out, dragging the body closer until hands reached for him, trying to help.

Hannah, her pale face twisted into an expression of horror.

He pushed her away, dragged the body onto the sand and knelt beside it. Did a quick triage then leaned back on his heels. His gaze met Hannah's and he shook his head. Denial flashed in her eyes. She shook her head. Moved closer.

"Ryder, do something. CPR. Mouth-to-mouth. Maybe it's not too late—" She started to kneel, reached out to touch the body. Ryder pushed to his feet and wrapped one arm around her waist, pulling her away.

"There's nothing we can do, Hannah."

"But—"

He turned her away from the body, looked down into her eyes and slowly shook his head. "There's nothing we can do."

It was too late. Tim would never party again.

Whoever had crushed the back of his skull in had made sure of it.

CHAPTER
SEVENTEEN

The activity on the beach was fading as quickly as the heat of the day beneath the clouds moving in from the east. Three people had shown up more than twenty minutes after the call for help had been placed—which had been a good fifteen minutes after Ryder had shouted for someone to make that call.

Three people.

Two men who Ryder figured must be the equivalent of paramedics and a police officer.

One single police officer.

The onlookers outnumbered the officials two-to-one. Not surprising, considering everyone from Hannah's small volunteer group was here. And nobody seemed inclined to leave, not when the officials were still huddled around the shroud-draped body, talking in low tones so they wouldn't be overheard. A preliminary investigation had been completed—which consisted of the officer looking at the back of Tim's head and snapping a few pictures with a digital camera. He'd taken a brief statement from Hannah and Ryder then returned to the two men standing by the body.

The screams and cries had died down, fading to nothing more than an occasional sniffle. A brief wail of disbelief, a subdued whisper of speculation. The sounds were caught by the growing breeze and carried away, dying under the angry waves pounding the shoreline.

Hannah remained silent, saying nothing since

giving her brief statement to the officer. Yes, she had been the first one to spot the body. Had pointed it out to Ryder, who took off toward the beach. No, she didn't know who it was first. No, she couldn't remember the last time she'd seen Tim.

She'd turned to Ryder as soon as the officer left, had wrapped her arms around his waist and buried her head in his chest, heedless of his wet clothes. He didn't say anything, just folded her into his arms and held her as he watched the men talk.

As he watched the small group around him. Listened to snippets of their muted conversations. Studied each face, looking for something—anything—that didn't belong. All he saw was a mixture of emotions, ranging from shock to disbelief to sorrow. If anyone from their small group had been involved, they were doing a good job of hiding it.

And none of them had even glanced toward the cave, its entrance hidden fifty yards away. Not even Darla, who had just been there. She was huddled against Cindy, the two women comforting each other, their differences forgotten in the face of Tim's death.

Had it been an accident? Maybe. Tim could have come down here for a 'smoke' break. He could have waded into the water and slipped. Could have hit the back of his head on something and been knocked unconscious.

Maybe...but Ryder wasn't buying it. He knew what a head looked like when it had been bashed in with something big and heavy. An injury like the one on the back of Tim's head didn't come from simply slipping and falling in the surf. If he'd fallen from a distance and landed on his head then yeah, he might have sustained an injury like that. But there were no other visible bruises on the body. No scrapes or cuts or contusions. Nothing marred his clothes except for a few smudges of paint. No rips. No tears. Nothing.

As far as Ryder was concerned, this hadn't been an accident.

A cool gust of wind blew over them. Hannah shivered and he tightened his arms around her, looked up at the sky. A storm was coming in. The surf was getting rougher, the blue changing to an angry gray under the darkening sky. Some time within the next half-hour, give or take a few minutes, they'd all be drenched.

The three men must have realized the same thing because they stopped talking and started moving. The paramedics secured the body to the stretcher then picked it up, balancing the weight between them before moving to the trail that would take them back up. The officer led the way, stepping to the side when they reached the path then falling in behind them. One by one, the onlookers followed, a somber funeral procession winding its way up the narrow trail.

He tried to step back but Hannah's arms tightened around his waist, holding him in place. He didn't stop to think, just pressed a quick kiss against the top of her head before looking down at her. "We need to go."

"I know. I just—" Her words trailed off in a sigh, the sound muffled against his chest.

He ignored the sensation of her breath, and the way it warmed his skin through the damp shirt. Tightened his arms briefly then stepped back. He didn't miss her sigh, or the fleeting expression of loss that shadowed her eyes. Loss at his hold—or loss of an acquaintance?

And what kind of ass did that make him, to even

wonder about such a thing? She'd probably never seen a body before, not one recently killed and certainly not one of someone she knew. Tim's body hadn't been disemboweled or decapitated or otherwise mutilated except for the injury to the back of this head but that wouldn't make it any easier for her to see. Violent death was ugly, no matter how it happened. If she wasn't in shock, then she most certainly must be stunned. Her silence the last half hour was testament to that. Hell, the fact that she had stepped into his arms with a silent plea to be held told him she was stunned.

He looked at her now. At her pale face and wide eyes. Her thick hair had come loose from the ponytail she always wore, the wind blowing strands of it into her face. She brushed them away then shivered as another gust blew in off the water.

"We need to catch up with the others before you freeze."

"I'm fine."

"You're cold."

"Not really. And I'm not the one who's wet."

"Don't worry about me, I've been through a hell of a lot worse." He reached for her hand then led her toward the trail, shortening his stride so she wouldn't have to walk fast to keep up.

"You don't think it was an accident, do you?" Her question was hesitant, her subdued voice quiet enough that it wouldn't be overheard by the group several yards in front of them. Ryder hesitated—not because he didn't know what to tell her, but because he didn't want to talk about it *here*. Not when there was a chance they might be overheard.

"We'll talk about it later."

"Okay."

"Then we're going to talk about leaving."

She nodded, without even the slightest indication that she wanted to argue. Ryder almost made a joke about her quick agreement, about the entire situation, but bit the words off before they tumbled from his mouth.

If they were on a mission somewhere, or running an op, the dark humor would have already been flying. But they weren't—and Hannah wasn't exactly one his men. Now wasn't the time for gallows humor.

They reached the van as the first drops of rain fell from the sky. Big, fat drops that hit the dry ground with heavy plops. Slow at first, just a small tease of the downpour that was to come. He helped Hannah inside then started to climb in after her, only to stop when the weasel's arm shot across the open door, blocking him.

"You're wet."

Ryder stared at the man, wondering if he'd heard correctly. Wondering if he'd interpreted the outstretched arm correctly. Yeah, he had. The stupid fucker was actually trying to stop him from getting inside.

"Yeah, I am. I'm going to get wetter the longer I stand out here." Ryder's voice was low. Even. Deadly. But the fucker was too damn stupid to realize he was seconds away from being dragged out because he just sat there, shaking his head.

"I'm sorry but I can't let you ride with us. The seat would never dry, not in this weather—"

"Kevin! You can't be serious."

The weasel turned toward Hannah, the smirk he'd been wearing morphing into a small smile. "You know the rules, Hannah. This is the only transportation we have. I'm responsible for it and—"

"Fine. I'll stay with Ryder." Hannah slid across the seat and started to climb out but the weasel grabbed her arm, stopping her. Ryder was moving before Hannah's surprised gasp even left her. He grabbed the asshole's hand and twisted it back, stopping before bones snapped. A high-pitched scream filled the interior of the van, drowning out the surprised gasps of everyone else already seated. Ryder ignored the pathetic sound, ignored the looks being directed at him, and leaned forward.

"Don't ever touch her again. Is that understood?"

Sweat broke out on the weasel's pale face. He tried to yank his hand from Ryder's hold then gasped in surprised pain once more before finally nodding. Only after he stuttered a weak answer in the affirmative did Ryder release him.

The other man pulled his hand against his chest, cradling it while his breathing evened out. Anger turned his pale face red and he leveled an icy glare of hatred at Ryder.

"I want you gone. You and your friend both. You're no longer welcome here. I want you both on the ferry first thing tomorrow morning."

Ryder almost laughed. Was the man actually *threatening* him? He was clueless. Absolutely clueless—but Ryder didn't care. He climbed into the van, closed the door behind him, then met the weasel's cold stare with one of his own.

"Not a problem."

Maybe the man had finally seen something in Ryder's gaze that let him know he was flirting with danger. The color drained from his face and he quickly turned away, starting the van and putting it in gear without another word.

The ride back was quiet, the only sound that of the rain battering the roof over their heads. Minutes stretched as they bounced over ruts and rocked side-to-side, the bald tires spinning in the wet sand and dirt before gaining traction and lurching them forward. More than once, Ryder thought they might have to get out and push, but the aging vehicle finally made it back to the camp. He opened the door and helped Hannah out, did the same for the women and Mr. Miller. Then he placed his hand in the middle of Hannah's back and guided her toward his bungalow, not saying a word as they walked away.

Knowing that the weasel's gaze was focused on his back the entire time. Fine, let him send death glares. Not like the man had the balls—or the skill—to do anything about it.

Ninja and Allison were both sitting on the edge of Ninja's bed when he pushed through the door. He shot a frown in Ninja's direction then closed the door behind him.

"Tim's dead."

Allison shot from the bed, tears already filling her eyes. "What? No. He can't—what happened?"

And fuck, why had Ryder just blurted it out like that? Because he'd forgotten his sister had a 'thing'—whatever the fuck that meant—for the guy. He blew out a deep breath then gentled his voice.

"I'm sorry, Allison."

Hannah stepped in for him, going over to his sister and pulling her into a comforting hug. "Ryder found him in the water. He—he tried to help him but it was too late."

"I don't understand. Why was he in the water? What happened?"

Hannah glanced over her shoulder and met Ryder's gaze. Then she turned back to Allison, her voice even gentler as she tugged her toward the door. "Let's go back to our place. I'll tell you what I know then."

Ryder waited for both women to leave before turning back to Ninja. There was no guilt at all on the man's face—but then, Ryder didn't expect to see any. Not with Ninja. But he hadn't missed how close the two had been sitting, or the way Allison had jumped just the slightest bit when he opened the door.

"So what happened?" Ninja asked the question before Ryder could, giving him the perfect opening.

"I could ask you the same thing."

The damn man actually had the nerve to laugh. Just a small chuckle but coming from Ninja, that was about the same as a full-blown belly laugh. "I've been a perfect gentleman."

Did Ryder believe him? Yeah, for the most part. But he'd definitely keep an eye on them over the next few days, make sure the mini-vacation didn't turn into a romantic interlude.

He peeled the damp shirt over his head and tossed it to the side, then bent over to work on his boots. He'd only brought the one pair, which was going to suck later when he put them back on.

"You going to tell me what happened, or you going to keep me in suspense while you practice your striptease routine?"

Ryder got one boot off and worked on the next, loosening the Kevlar laces enough that he could get his foot out. "Just what Hannah said: I found Tim in the water."

"And?"

Ryder looked up, met Ninja's questioning gaze with his own steady one. "The back of his head was caved in."

"Accident?"

"That's what they'll probably call it but no, I don't think so."

"Any ideas who might have done it?"

"Not a fucking clue. Nobody else was missing when Hannah saw him floating—which doesn't mean anything because I have no idea how long he'd been missing." Ryder grabbed a fresh change of clothes—his last—from the pack and tossed them on the bed before moving to the small bathroom. "Do me a favor, go make sure Hannah and Allison are both packed. We're leaving in the morning."

"Didn't we try just that this morning?"

"Yeah—but we don't have to sneak away this time. The weasel's kicking us out."

Ninja pushed off the bed with another chuckle. "No shit. How'd you manage that?"

"Just one of my many hidden talents, I guess." He started to close the bathroom door then paused, all humor gone from his voice when he met Ninja's gaze. "Don't make me snap your fucking neck for messing around with my sister."

The other man actually laughed again, the sound cut short when he closed the door behind him. Ryder mentally rolled his eyes then wedged himself into the small shower. He stepped out five minutes later, clean and salt-free and with only a few bruises to show for the effort. A total win in his book.

He dried off as best he could by running the threadbare towel over his wet hair and chest and legs. Then draped the damn thing around his neck because it wasn't big enough to wrap around his waist. Not that he needed to—he was the only one in here and he wasn't exactly the modest type to begin with.

Or so he thought until he stepped out of the bathroom and saw Hannah sitting on his bed.

He blinked, wondered if maybe he was fucking hallucinating. No, it was definitely Hannah. His eyes might deceive him but his body's immediate reaction to the sight of her sitting there, staring at him, sure as hell didn't.

And she was getting one hell of an eyeful.

CHAPTER EIGHTEEN

She stared at Ryder for several long minutes, her gaze riveted on the perfection of his body. Broad shoulders. Thick arms with defined muscles, from his biceps all the way down to his wrists. The dark scrollwork of his tattoos called to her, just waiting to traced.

Sculpted chest, sprinkled with dark hair that begged to be touched and teased. Flat nipples, the points small and sharp. A drop of water trailed down the center of his chest. She watched, mesmerized, following it with hungry eyes as it cascaded down his chest to his ridged abdomen. Lower, following the thin line of dark hair that pointed the way to his erection. Long. Thick. Hard.

Growing even harder under her gaze.

His body was a study of pure masculinity, despite its imperfections. Or maybe *because* of them.

A scar ran diagonally across his side, just above his hip, the line faded with age. She remembered how he'd gotten it. He'd been fifteen at the time, had tried to jump a fence with his bike—unsuccessfully. She remembered the way he had tried to shrug it off and reassure her he was fine, even though she could see the pain in his eyes as he held his hand against his side. Even though blood dripped between his fingers while she and Allison had helped him back home.

Another scar, this one thick and jagged, marred the flesh of his right thigh. She had no idea how he'd gotten that one, wasn't sure she wanted to know. There were other scars as well, small signs that hinted at a life filled with risks taken with no hesitation.

Imperfections? No, far from it. If anything, they only added to the pure masculinity on display in front of her. They were a sign of who he was, a testament to things he had done. Things she couldn't imagine.

Things she probably didn't want to know.

Hannah dragged her gaze from the scar on his thigh, up to the thick erection jutting toward her. Need filled her, hot and heavy. She wanted to reach out and curl her hand around him, to feel the velvety softness of hot skin stretched tight. Feel him grow even harder in her gentle grasp as she stroked him.

She curled her fingers into her palms instead. Dragged her gaze up higher, away from the temptation staring her in the face. Higher still, finally meeting his own gaze.

Pure hunger, stark and powerful, stared back at her. Then he blinked and the hunger was gone, carefully hidden behind a mask of caution. He could put on any mask he wanted, it didn't matter, not when she had already seen the truth in those deep brown eyes.

He didn't move. Didn't look away. Made no effort to cover himself. If she didn't know better, she'd think he was indifferent to her presence.

His body said otherwise.

He reached for the towel draped around his neck, gripped the ends in each hand and cleared his throat. His gaze dipped to the bed then quickly met hers again. "You should be packing."

"I'm finished."

His brows shot up in surprise. "Already?"

No, not really. Maybe not even close. But she didn't have much, knew it wouldn't take long. And seeing Ryder was more important.

"I came to apologize."

His brows moved again, this time lowering in a confused frown. "Apologize? For what?"

"This morning. For overreacting."

"You did that already. Back at the building site."

Had she? Yes, she had, but she'd forgotten all about it. She shrugged, offered him a fleeting smile. "Then I'm apologizing again."

"Okay." He slowly nodded, glanced down at the bed again then back at her. "Was that it?"

"No. I—" She hesitated, not sure how to say what she'd come here to say. It shouldn't be that hard, not when she'd been rehearsing it in her mind all morning.

She took a deep breath, exhaled and let the words come out in a rush. "I didn't mean to say what I said earlier. About not being like you. I—I didn't mean it, not that way. Not the way you took it."

"I didn't take it any way."

"You thought I was talking about the day you left. I saw it in your eyes, just for a second." And she had. He'd probably deny it but it didn't matter—she'd seen the flash of surprise. Of hurt. Of regret.

"Hannah—" He stopped. Shifted. Looked down at the bed again then back at her. "If we're going to talk about this, I should probably get dressed."

Disappointment washed over her. Had she read him completely wrong? No, she didn't think so, not when his erection still stood proudly between them. But maybe that was just his *body's* reaction. Maybe it had nothing to do with *her*.

And maybe the sun would rise in the west

tomorrow.

No, she hadn't read him wrong. Hadn't misinterpreted the hunger she'd seen in his eyes only moments ago. Which meant he was trying to be noble. Or honorable. Or...or something.

Could she blame him, after the way she had acted the other night? After the way she had acted this morning? No.

She forced herself to act nonchalant and shrugged, like she didn't care what he did. "Sure. No problem. You can get dressed, I'll wait."

He watched her for a few long seconds then motioned to the bed with a quick nod. "You're sitting on my clothes."

His clothes? Was *that* why he'd been looking at the bed? She almost jumped to her feet, actually started to move—

And then she stopped.

She tilted her head to the side then leaned back, bracing her weight on her hands. Her mouth curled into a teasing smile. "Then I guess you're going to have to move me to get to them."

Ryder didn't say anything. He didn't move. And the blank expression on his face told her nothing. Embarrassment washed over her, the heat of it prickling her skin. She shifted, thought about just getting up and leaving. Coming here had been a mistake. After everything that happened the last few days—this afternoon—she had wanted nothing more than reassurance. An hour or two with Ryder. To feel his strong arms around her, to feel his warm breath against her ear as he told her everything was going to be okay. To forget, just for a little while, all the craziness that still didn't make sense.

To forget everything.

She thought that maybe he wanted the same thing. She thought...well, it didn't matter what she thought. What she wanted.

Ryder finally moved, just the slightest shifting as he slid the towel from around his neck and wrapped it around his waist. At least, he tried to. The towel wasn't big enough, not even close, so he had to hold it in front of him with both hands—

And it didn't do a damn thing to hide anything.

The insane urge to laugh swept over her and she choked it back. Stood and reached for the clothes she'd been sitting on. She'd go back to her bungalow and finish packing then get some sleep—at least, try to.

She shoved the clothes toward him, unable to meet his dark gaze. "I didn't mean to interrupt. I'll let you get back to whatever it was you were doing."

His gaze dropped to the clothes in her hand then lifted to hers. There was an intensity in his dark eyes that she didn't understand, the force of it holding her in place when all she wanted to do now was run away.

His fingers brushed against hers as he reached for the clothes. Just that little touch was enough to make her pulse quicken. She stepped back, knowing she needed to leave. Now. Yes, coming here had been a stupid idea—and for reasons that went far beyond what she had already admitted.

Ryder pulled the clothes from her hand but instead of backing into the bathroom, he carelessly tossed them back to the bed. His gaze never left hers the entire time. Holding her in place. Studying her. Watching.

Seeing too much.

"Why?"

The ragged word hung between them. Rough. Hoarse. Hannah just stood there, unable to do anything more than shake her head.

"Why apologize?"

Apologize? What was he—oh. He was talking about what she'd confessed only a few minutes earlier, when she had told him she hadn't meant what she said this morning. Hadn't meant the words the way he'd taken them.

"I—Because..." Her voice faded, swallowed by the thick tension hovering between them. Was it her imagination, or had he moved closer?

"Why apologize, after what I said to you that day?"

Yes, he *had* moved closer. She started to step back, stopped when realization washed over her with new found clarity. He was trying to intimidate her. To use the size of his body and the force of that dark stare to push her away.

Just like he'd done eleven years ago with his hurtful words. Pushing. Always pushing—because he thought he knew what was best for her.

She lifted her chin and met his stare with one of her own. "Because you didn't mean what you said. And it wasn't fair of me—"

"I meant every word."

"No, you didn't. I know you were trying to protect me—"

"Hannah—"

"—but I don't need protection. Not then. Definitely not now." She inched forward, reached up and pressed her hands in the center of his chest. She could feel the powerful beating of his heart, deep and heavy, strong and powerful—and maybe just a tad too fast.

Dark hair teased her palms. She slid her hands along his chest, entranced by the contradictory sensations of soft hair against hot, firm skin. Need filled her, making her touch bolder as she trailed her hands lower—until he reached up and captured her wrists. There was a soft whisper of material as the towel he'd been holding dropped to the floor. The tip of his erection brushed against her waist and she shifted closer, pressing against him, needing to feel more.

"Hannah, you're playing with fire."

She leaned forward, pressed a gentle kiss against the center of his chest. "Am I?"

"Yeah, you are." He maintained his gentle grip on her wrists as he stepped back, putting distance between them. "And we're not doing this. Not after the other night. Not when I know you'll regret it before we're even finished."

Surprise cooled some of the desire running through her. Surprise—and confusion. "Regret? What are you talking about? I didn't—"

"Bullshit." He released her hands and stepped away. "I saw your face, remember? My damn cock was still inside you but you couldn't get away fast enough."

She ignored the crudeness of his language, knew the words were meant to shock her. To push her away. And oh God, was that what he thought? That she *regretted* what they'd done? If she had regretted it, she wouldn't be here now.

"What you saw was embarrassment!"

"Hannah, I know the difference."

"Apparently not. I was mortified because Colter walked in on us!"

"It was more than just being mortified." He

backed up another step, stopped and folded his arms across his chest. Big. Strong.

Stubborn as hell.

Did he realize he'd just backed himself into a corner? Literally. The bathroom was tiny and there was no place for him to go, no way for him to get past her unless he forcibly moved her out of the way—something he was certainly capable of doing with very little effort. But would he?

She stepped forward, close enough that her breasts brushed against his crossed arms. Need flared in his eyes then just as quickly disappeared behind that careful mask. It didn't matter because she had seen it—and seeing it gave her the confidence to stay. To go after what she really wanted.

What she'd always wanted.

Tension gripped him, making his body even harder. The muscles of his forearms flexed under her touch and he tried to step back, to escape her trailing fingers.

There was nowhere for him to go.

And he didn't push her away. Thank God, he didn't push her way.

Hannah's hands closed over his wrists, much the way his had done to hers only moments ago. She tugged, smiled to herself when Ryder allowed her to uncross his arms and place them at his sides. She threaded her fingers through his, holding his arms in place. Then she dipped her head and pressed a kiss against his chest, right over the steady pounding of his heart. Crisp hair teased her lips as she dragged her mouth over tight skin and hard muscles. His muffled gasp of surprise ended on a small groan as she playfully nipped the sharp point of one flat nipple. His fingers tightened around hers as she slowly made her way down that hard body, kissing every inch of bare skin. His chest. His ridged stomach. Lower, until she dropped to her knees and gently pressed her mouth against his hip. His erection brushed against her cheek and she turned her head, ran her tongue over the tip. Once, twice. Tasting. Teasing.

His body stiffened and he tugged on her hands, tried to pull her up. She yanked one hand free and placed it against his hip, fingers pressing into hot flesh. Pulled her other hand free and curled it around the hard length of his thick erection.

"Hannah—" Her name was nothing more than a hoarse growl that ended in a low moan as she closed her mouth over him. He stiffened again, his hands fisting in her hair.

Not pulling her away, as she had feared, but holding her in place.

She sighed, pulled him deeper into her mouth and sucked. Slow. Teasing. Reveling in the taste of him, a combination of soap and salt and pure male musk. A thrill shot through her at the sound of his groan, low and deep. Damp heat pooled between her legs, the ache growing, need spiraling outward.

Raw. Hungry. Consuming.

One rough palm cradled the back of her head. The fingers of his other hand tangled in her hair, guiding her, holding her in place as his hips rocked. Slow at first, then a little faster.

The air around them grew more humid. Thick with desire. Heavy with need. Filled with the sounds of their harsh breathing, with Ryder's rough groans and her own smaller gasps.

Hannah reached between his legs, cupped his soft

sack in her palm. Gently squeezed, sighed when another low growl echoed around her. She lifted her gaze, feasted her eyes on the sight of Ryder's head tilted back, eyes closed, jaw clenched.

And then he looked down at her, pure hunger dancing in his fiery gaze. She didn't look away, held his gaze with her own as she swirled her tongue around his length. She curled her fingers around him. Sucked. Stroked. Harder, filling her mouth with him.

His eyes grew hotter, fanning the desire consuming her. Power filled her at the raw need in his gaze, power at the knowledge that she had put that hunger there.

She trailed her fingers along his powerful thighs, muscles clenching and jumping under her touch. More. She wanted more. Needed more.

Needed all of him.

Needed his surrender.

His hands tightened around the back of her head and he started to tug, to pull her to her feet. "Hannah—"

She wrapped one arm around his hips, sighed when he stopped tugging. His head fell back, his chest rising and falling with each ragged gasp ripped from his lungs. His hips rocked against her mouth then suddenly stilled. A low groan, harsh and desperate, echoed around them. Heat exploded in her mouth, unleashing something wild and untamed inside her as he climaxed. She drank him in, reveling in his complete surrender, sighing when he slowly eased away from her.

His hands closed over her arms, hauled her to her feet. Dark eyes held hers for several long seconds, the intensity in their depths taking her breath away. Then his mouth crashed over hers, his tongue sweeping in to dance with hers.

This was no gentle kiss. This was a claiming. A conquering. A demand that would accept nothing less than her own surrender.

She wrapped her arms around his neck and pressed herself closer, giving him the surrender he was asking for. Hands closed over her waist and lifted, carried her to the bed and gently eased her down on the mattress. Ryder broke the kiss, dragged his mouth along her jaw. Her throat. Her ear. His teeth closed over her lobe and gently bit, the sensation nearly catapulting her from the bed. Then he was gone. Rough hands tugged at her, peeling off shoes and clothes and tossing them to the side.

Then he was back, his hard body stretched along hers. The crisp hair on his chest teased her breasts and she arched her back, pressing herself closer as she spread her legs. Hands drifted along her sides. Her hips. Her outer thighs. Gentle. Teasing.

Hannah didn't want gentle. She didn't want teasing.

She wanted *him*. Ryder. All of him.

That's all she had ever wanted.

Did he know? Could he tell from the way she moved against him? From the tiny whimpers of need that fell from her mouth? He must, because he shifted his body to the side and eased one large hand between her legs, cupping her. Just that small touch was enough to make her gasp and cry out.

But not enough for him.

He slid the tip of one finger along her clit. Back and forth, back and forth. Slow. Teasing. Hannah dug her heels into the thin mattress and raised her hips, rocked against his touch. Cried out when he slid that finger inside her.

"You are so fucking wet. So fucking tight."

She cried out again, bit down on her lip when he lowered his mouth to her. When his tongue slid across her clit. Licking. Teasing. Faster and faster. Pushing her higher, so high she knew she'd never survive the fall.

But he didn't let her fall. He held her there, just on the edge. Knowing where to touch, knowing when to pull back. Her body writhed under his touch, seeking the completion that hovered just out of reach. She moaned in desperation, in pleading, unsure how much longer she could withstand the sweet torture.

Then he was gone and she moaned his loss. Reached weakly with one arm, searching for him. She heard the rustle of material, a small thud followed by the faintest sound of tearing, the noise nothing more than a soft whisper. The bed dipped under her and she finally opened her eyes, her lids heavy with need.

Ryder knelt between her legs, his dark gaze hungry as he stared down at her. He reached between them with one hand and stroked her and just like that, she was once again hovering on the edge, her body demanding the release he so carefully kept her from reaching.

His gaze lifted to hers, held it—

And then he drove into her. Hard. Deep. Filling her. Stretching her.

She cried out. Reached for something to hold onto, something to anchor her against the sudden onslaught of sensation. Ryder's hand caught hers, holding tight as he drove into her. Hard. Fast. Faster still, until she was flying.

Exploding.

Losing herself as her body shattered into a thousand little pieces that would never be found again.

CHAPTER NINETEEN

Rain pattered on the roof overhead, a gentle drumming that filled the darkness of the room. Hypnotic, teasing him with the lure of blissful sleep. The sound was so different from the heavy rain that had passed by an hour ago, pounding the roof with such force that he expected it to crash in on them.

Hannah had slept right through it, not even stirring when lightning cracked nearby, immediately followed by an angry rumble of thunder so loud, he felt the bed shake with it.

She had slept through dinner, too, barely stirring at the knock on the door. It had been Ninja, who'd taken one look at Ryder's disheveled appearance, rolled his eyes, and told him he'd save them both a plate.

Those plates were sitting on the dresser now, untouched even though Hannah had awakened an hour after they were delivered. They had both been hungry—but food had been the last thing on either one of their minds.

She needed her sleep, needed to recover from their marathon bouts of lovemaking. It was like they couldn't get enough of each other. Like they were desperate to make up for the time they'd been apart during the last eleven years. And he'd been anything but gentle, even though he had tried. He'd been seized by a desperation he didn't understand. A burning need to touch her. Brand her. Make her his. To leave his mark on her so no other man would even think of going near her.

And Hannah had acted the same way, demanding and coaxing responses from him that no other woman ever had.

That desperation—his, hers, *theirs*—scared the hell out of him, even now. It wasn't like him, not even close. And he refused to consider what it meant. Refused to entertain the idea that nothing had changed between them, that he still felt now what he'd felt all those years ago.

Bullshit. It couldn't mean anything. He wouldn't allow it. He was older now, better able to control himself. His emotions. This—whatever the hell they were doing—was nothing but temporary. They had tonight. If they were lucky, they'd have a few more days when they took the ferry to the other island in the morning. And thank God, too, because they'd gone through his small supply of condoms already.

But then he'd leave. They both would. Ryder would be going home, preparing for the next mission, whatever the hell that might be.

And Hannah would be going in a different direction, doing what she could to save the world in her own way.

After Sunday, there would be no more nights like tonight. Not even if he ran into her on his rare trips home. As tempting as it would be to hook up with her, he wasn't going to relegate her to the status of a part-time fling, available only when he was. She deserved more than that, a hell of a lot more. She deserved someone who could be there for her full-time. Someone who could take care of her and give her everything she wanted, everything she needed. Permanency. Commitment. A house filled with kids and a happily-ever-after.

All the things that Hannah had always wanted.

He curled his hand into a fist, ready to strangle the unseen man who'd even *think* of fucking touching her. And Christ, he needed his fucking head examined. He couldn't have it both ways. Couldn't wish for her to find what she wanted with someone who could give it to her in one second, then want to kill that same someone in the next.

But that's what Hannah did to him. What she'd always done to him. Make him think crazy thoughts and want crazy things. That was just one of the many reasons he'd walked away the way he had all those years ago. If he hadn't, she would have waited for him.

And yet, here they were. Eleven years later.

In his bed.

Where he swore she'd never be again.

He looked over at her now, her body nothing more than a shadow in the darkness. It didn't matter—he didn't need light to see the way her thick hair fell over her shoulder. The way she slept with one hand curled under her cheek. The way her lashes formed a dark crescent under her eyes. He'd committed all that to memory, watching her for a long time before he finally leaned over and turned out the light.

He reached for the hand splayed across his chest, smiled when her fingers automatically closed around his. He held that hand for a few minutes then eased it to the side and slid from beneath the covers. A sleepy murmur fell from her parted lips but she didn't stir, not until he reached down and pulled the thin blanket over her shoulders. She shifted, automatically finding the spot warmed by his body, then settled into stillness once more.

Ryder found his clean clothes on the floor near the bathroom and quietly dressed. He slipped his feet into his damp boots, grimacing at the chill, then quickly laced them up and tied them.

Hannah still slept, even when he eased his weight onto Ninja's bed and carefully unzipped his pack. There were a few things he wanted to take with him: the small penlight; the pathetic knife he'd taken the other day; a notepad and stainless-steel pen that doubled as a small screwdriver. He slipped the knife into his boot and placed the other things into the side pockets of his pants. He zipped the pack and sat it to the side, then stared down at Hannah's sleeping form.

His stomach knotted, the almost-painful sensation surprising him. Temptation seized him and he almost climbed back into bed with her, the need to hold her close, for as long as he could, nearly overwhelming.

Nothing was stopping him from doing just that. He didn't *need* to go out in the rain, didn't need to go poking around. Ninja had already pulled what information he could from the weasel's computer, had already moved the funds around with help from Chaos. There was absolutely nothing stopping Ryder from climbing back into the bed with Hannah. He could kiss his way down her sweet body. Watch her come alive as she slowly came awake under the touch of his hands. His mouth. Hear her soft sigh as he entered her. As he buried his cock inside her and lost himself in her tight heat.

He'd lean forward, swallow her cries with his mouth as she exploded around him. As muscles clamped down on him. Squeezing him. Drawing him in deeper. Pulling him closer, until his own cock exploded and—

Shit.

He reached down, pressed a palm against his raging hard-on, and took a deep breath. Christ. Hadn't he used her enough tonight? His damn dick should be fucking sleeping, not rearing up, ready to go again.

He took another deep breath. Forced himself to think of anything except the woman in his bed. Forced his damn dick to behave.

As tempting as it was to climb back into bed with Hannah, he couldn't. There was something he needed to check out. Something that had been niggling at the back of his mind all day.

The hell of it was, he didn't know *what* that was. All he had was the uneasy sensation that he was missing something and that whatever it was might be important. He'd been able to ignore the feeling throughout the night because he'd been distracted—fuck yeah, he'd been distracted, and damn glad of it, too—but he couldn't ignore it any longer. Not when it was pulling at him. Tugging him. Demanding he chase it down.

He finally turned away from Hannah and went outside, quietly closing the door behind him. Rain still fell, adding an eerie quality to the dark compound. Ryder stood there for several minutes, blending into the shadows as he looked around, searching for anything out of place. Anything unusual or suspicious.

Searching for anyone who shouldn't be there. But he was the only one lurking in the shadows, the only one foolish enough to venture out into the wet night.

He made his way around the perimeter, pausing at each bungalow to listen. There was nothing but silence coming from each one—including Allison's. A damn good thing, too, because he really didn't want to snap

Ninja's neck.

Then again, just because it was quiet *now* didn't mean nothing had happened earlier. Ryder narrowed his eyes and stared at the door, actually moved toward to it with the intention of slamming it open just to make sure Ninja wasn't in bed with Allison. He caught himself at the last second. What the hell would he do if he was? Drag Ninja out and beat him to a pulp?

Yeah, that's exactly what he would do.

Except he couldn't because Allison would get upset. Because if Ninja *was* in her bed, it was at her invitation.

Besides, if he dragged Ninja's sorry ass out here and started wailing on him, everyone else would wake up. That would pretty much defeat the whole purpose of sneaking around now, searching for whatever piece of the puzzle he was convinced he was missing.

If there even *was* something missing. For all he knew, that niggling sensation tugging at him was from nothing more than a lack of critical blood supply to his brain from all the time he'd spent with Hannah.

He stared at the door a few seconds longer then swallowed back a growl and moved on.

But there was nothing to see. Nothing that stood out. Even the weasel's office was locked up tight, silent as a grave. Had he figured out that the money was gone yet? Ryder doubted it. If he had, the man wouldn't be sleeping. He'd be pacing around, tearing his hair out. Throwing things.

Crying.

Yeah, Ryder could definitely see him as the crying type. The spineless piece of shit.

He moved toward the pavilion, paused just inside and leaned against one of the support posts. What the hell was he missing? What was it he wasn't seeing? It was there, just out of reach of his mind's eye. Something important. Something that didn't quite fit in.

He stared into the darkness, his gaze unseeing as he forced his mind to clear. As he focused inward.

Was it something from this morning, after Ninja had returned to the bungalow? No, that didn't feel right. Whatever it was had happened later. But when?

He closed his eyes, mentally retraced the events of the day, starting with tracking down Hannah. He'd searched the entire compound, only finding her when he ventured further away. There'd been nothing between here and there, nothing except lush vegetation and an old storage shed.

Was it something about the shed? No, it couldn't be. He'd looked inside, saw nothing but rusty tools and equipment. A stack of paint cans. A tarp, tossed haphazardly in the corner in the corner. There'd been a faint odor of marijuana, the smell fresh enough that he figured someone had been in there smoking recently, probably Tim.

What about later, after he'd chased down Hannah and gone with her to the sorry excuse for a building site? There'd been nothing out of the ordinary then, not that he'd seen. But he'd been watching the beach below as he worked on the fence, waiting on the authorities to show up and descend on that cave Hannah and Allison had found. If something unusual had happened anywhere else, would he have even noticed?

Maybe.

Maybe not.

Had he seen something without realizing it? Was

that why the niggling sensation was pulling at him now?

Dammit! He needed to *think*. To figure this out. Now. What the hell was eluding him?

He pulled in a deep breath, exhaled slowly. Cleared his mind and let the day come back to him in a series of mental snapshots.

Sunlight reflecting off the water as he watched the beach.

Sweat beading his brow as he worked. Rough wood beneath his hands as he pounded posts into the ground.

Hannah, coming up and offering him water. Asking if he thought anyone in her small group could be responsible for the guns as she looked out over the horizon.

Ryder turning, studying each member of her band of volunteers.

The weasel, standing off to the side with his hands on his hips, doing absolutely nothing.

Katie Miller, her expression distracted and fearful as she slapped paint on the concrete walls under the direction of her grandmother, Eva Miller.

Cindy and Darla, the paint brushes in their hands forgotten as they bent their heads together, quietly arguing.

George Miller, fanning himself in the shade, red-faced and sweaty from overexerting himself moving paint cans.

Moving paint cans.

Ryder opened his eyes, focused on the darkness as he mulled that last bit over in his mind. Why had he had that specific thought at that specific moment?

Because Miller had a smudge of paint on the edge of his sleeve and the hem of his shirt. Yeah, because they'd been painting, that was why. It had been nothing more than a logical conclusion. Even Tim's shirt had been stained with paint. Ryder had noticed it when he pulled the man's body from the water and quickly checked for other injuries.

Not because he was under the mistaken assumption the man could be helped, but because he wanted to see if there were any signs he might have slipped or fallen.

There hadn't been any. No scrapes, no cuts, no bruises. No rips or tears in his clothing. Just the bashed-in head and the paint stain. A pale mint green, just like the stain on Miller's shirt.

Except the school they were painting was *blue*, not green. The only thing that had been painted green anytime recently was the weasel's bungalow—which happened to be the same shade of green he'd noticed on the men's shirts.

And the same shade of green covering the sides of the old paint cans he'd seen in the shed.

Ryder swore to himself and stormed away from the pavilion, his angry strides carrying him away from the compound and toward the storage shed. Shit. Why the hell hadn't he noticed it before?

Because he hadn't been paying attention.

Because he'd been too worried about Hannah.

Because he hadn't been looking for it, hadn't even thought it was possible. He'd fucking assumed the guns had nothing to do with anyone here.

He'd been wrong. Christ, had he ever been wrong.

The creak of rusty hinges and swollen wood echoed around him, making him wince. Had anyone heard? He glanced behind him, looking for movement in the shadows, but there was nothing there. He waited, holding himself still. One minute. Two. Still nothing.

He eased the door open a little more, slowly this time, just enough so he could squeeze through. Something sharp tore his shirt and scraped his back and he swore under his breath, angry at himself for not being more careful.

Angry at himself for not seeing any of this sooner. For not putting it together before it was too late to make a difference.

He dug the small penlight from his pocket and made his way to the back of the shed, not turning it on until the absolute last second. The paint cans were to his left, tossed in a haphazard pile. He glanced at them only long enough to confirm his suspicions then moved to the tarp.

The tarp wasn't just tossed in the corner, the way he'd first thought when he saw it this morning. It was covering something, thrown over in such a way that it merely looked like it had been tossed to the side.

He grabbed a corner and pulled it back, swearing softly when he saw dark green. It was another crate, just like the ones in the cave.

Fuck.

Questions raced through his mind. Where had they come from? What were they going to do with them? How were they getting them from here to the beach?

The only question he could answer was *who*. Everything else would have to be figured out by the authorities. Not the local authorities but someone else, someone who had the manpower and the resources to handle it.

Which meant it was time for another call. Daryl would just have to get his ass out of bed and start reaching out to his contacts and get something moving. Now, before it was too late.

Ryder replaced the tarp and turned off the penlight, shoved it back in his pocket then quietly retraced his steps. Was the sat phone in Ninja's bag, or did he have it on him? Didn't matter, Ryder would find out soon enough.

He eased his body through the small opening then hesitated. Should he leave it open, or close it? Close it. He couldn't risk Miller coming out here in the morning and finding it open. Maybe he'd question it, maybe he wouldn't. But he'd already killed one person—no, *two*, if Ryder counted the one-legged man his sister and Hannah had seen. There was nothing saying he wouldn't kill again.

He placed his hand against the door and gently closed it, wincing again as the hinges creaked in protest. There was another noise, nothing more than a small splash, the sound nearly lost in the rain.

Ryder turned but he wasn't fast enough. Searing pain exploded in his skull. There was a bright flash as lights flared behind his eyes—

Then nothing but darkness.

CHAPTER TWENTY

Consciousness came slowly for Hannah. It tugged at her with gentle hands, urging her to open her eyes. To hit the ground running as she usually did. There was always so much to do and never enough time in which to do it.

Shower. Change. Get the coffee started before everyone else woke up. She might suck at cooking but her coffee more than made up for it.

Usually.

Go over reports. Review the schedule for the day and make sure any supplies they needed were loaded up. Make sure lunch was packed and loaded into the van—although Allison usually handled that chore.

She huddled deeper under the blankets, her usual enthusiasm dampened. She didn't want to wake up. Didn't want to hit the ground running. For once, she just wanted to lay here and do nothing. Wanted to forget about her responsibilities and everyone who was waiting on her.

She wanted to cuddle against Ryder and let the heat of his body lull her back to sleep. Wanted to rest her head against his shoulder as her hand drifted across his chest, as her fingers played with the hair covering that gorgeous expanse of hard flesh.

He'd roll her over, his heavy weight stretched out on top of her as his mouth claimed hers. As he kissed and licked and nibbled his way down her body, the way he'd done once before in the middle of the night.

Dampness spread between her legs, surprising

her. How could she want him again, so soon after everything they'd done the night before? She should be sore and tender from their lovemaking, not eagerly anticipating his touch.

It didn't matter. She wanted him. Couldn't get enough of him. His touch. His taste. The soft words he murmured in her ear and against her skin.

No, she could never have enough of him. Would never get tired of his touch. Of the way he made her feel. Yes, it was foolish, she knew that. She was setting herself up for heartbreak again.

She didn't care. She still wanted him.

That had never stopped, not in all these years. She'd been telling herself all this time that she'd been too young back then to be in love. That what she felt for Ryder was nothing more than an infatuation, one made even stronger because he'd been her first.

She'd been lying to herself all this time.

That didn't matter either. Maybe it would when he left. Maybe her heart would break for good this time when they parted ways. But she didn't want to think about that now. She had survived before, she'd survive again. Right now, she just wanted Ryder. Wanted to cram a lifetime of loving into the little time they had left.

She wanted...him.

She reached out with her hand, searching for Ryder. For his warm body. For what only he could give her. But the bed was empty, her hand closing on nothing more substantial than a cool sheet.

She swallowed back a sleepy sigh and lifted her head from beneath the covers. She blinked, yawned, blinked again. Was he in the bathroom? No. The door was open, showing her nothing but an empty room.

She shoved the hair out of her face and turned her head—then nearly screamed when she saw a pair of brown eyes staring back at her.

"Allison! OhmyGod." Hannah held the sheet tight against her body then pushed herself to a sitting position. A tangle of hair fell into her face and she brushed it away, her eyes scanning the room, searching for Ryder.

He was gone.

She turned back to Allison, frowned at the broad smile on her face. "What are you doing here?"

"I came to make sure you were still alive."

"Yes, I'm still alive." The memory of Tim's body floating in the water flooded back to her and she shivered. "And that's not even funny. Not after what happened yesterday."

Allison's smile faded. "I know. I'm sorry. It's just—you're usually the first one up. I wanted to check on you, make sure everything's okay."

"Yeah. Fine." Hannah adjusted her grip on the sheet and looked around the room again. "Where's Ryder?"

"No idea. He's probably out looking around, being nosy."

"You haven't seen him?"

"Nope."

"What about Colter?"

"He's been making phone calls all morning."

"Oh." Hannah glanced out the window. Watery light filtered in through the dirty glass. Now that she was awake and slightly more coherent, she could hear the rain hitting the roof overhead, a steady pounding that filled her with an uneasiness she didn't understand. She turned back to Allison. "What time is it?"

"Almost seven."

"That late?" She scrambled out of bed, searching for her clothes. "I need to get the coffee ready, get packed so we can—"

"The coffee's already made. And you don't need to worry about packing."

"But—" A crack of lightning crashed nearby, followed by a low roll of thunder.

"The ferry isn't running in this weather, you know that. We're going to be here for a while. A few hours at least. Maybe more, depending on the storm."

Hannah sank onto the bed, uneasiness filling her. Was it from the storm? Possibly. Storms always made her uneasy. The wind. The lightning. There was something wild and untamed about them that always unsettled her. Not in a bad way—they didn't frighten her or make her want to cower under the covers or anything like that. They just made her...edgy.

Or maybe that edginess came from knowing they wouldn't be leaving as soon as they had planned. They'd be stuck here, at the mercy of the weather, with yesterday's events hanging over them.

But maybe that wouldn't be as bad as she thought. There was nothing to do here when the occasional storm rolled in. They couldn't work outside. There was no community room or anywhere to congregate. Sometimes they would go to the pavilion and play cards, or maybe a board game, or just sit around and talk—but not when it rained like this. The pavilion was open on three sides and did little to provide protection from anything more than a light rain.

Which meant they'd be stuck indoors. Not a bad place to be—if Ryder was here.

And why wasn't he here? Why would he be

roaming around outside in weather like this? She asked Allison but the other woman only shrugged.

"Who knows? The weather doesn't mean anything to him, not with everything he's done. You know that."

She didn't, but she wasn't about to admit that to Allison. There was a lot she didn't know about Ryder. About the things he done in the past. About what he did now.

Maybe she could rectify that today. They could talk, *really* talk—if they weren't busy doing other things.

"Why don't you shower and get dressed, then meet me next door? I brought a change of clothes for you. And your poncho." Allison pointed to the pile at the edge of Colter's bed then stood. "We can figure out what we're going to do next."

"Next?"

"Yeah. You know—since we won't be working here anymore." Disappointment filled Allison's voice, the same disappointment that swept over Hannah when she thought about how completely they'd been conned. The disappointment was quickly replaced by anger and she ruthlessly pushed both emotions away. She didn't want to deal with it, not now. Not when she knew she'd be second-guessing herself in the months to come, wondering how she could have been so stupid and naive.

She nodded absently then called out to Allison before she closed the door behind her. "Are you sure I should come over there? Won't I be, um, in the way?"

Disappointment of another kind crossed her friend's face. "No. Colter was a perfect gentleman."

Hannah bit back a smile at the muttered *damn him* that followed Allison out the door. She shouldn't laugh, not when she knew exactly how her friend felt.

Hannah took a quick shower and quickly dressed, grateful that Allison had thought to bring a long sleeve shirt instead of a regular one. The temperature wasn't close to being cold but the rain always left her chilled and she was thankful for the thin material covering her arms.

What Allison *didn't* bring was a brush. Hannah dried her hair as best she could with the towel, finger-combed most of the tangles out, then pulled it back into its usual ponytail.

Ryder still wasn't back by the time she finished. Had he come in while she was showering then left to give her privacy? No, she couldn't see him doing that, not without at least letting her know. Besides, she would have heard him come in.

Maybe he was in the pavilion, getting coffee. Or maybe he was in her bungalow, talking to Allison and Colter. Or maybe he was—she didn't know where else he could be, couldn't even begin to imagine what he might be doing.

Thunder rolled in the distance again, sharpening that uneasiness that had been hovering over her since she first woke up and realized Ryder was gone. It didn't matter where he was, she wouldn't find him by sitting here and waiting.

She grabbed her poncho and pulled it over her head then headed outside. Coffee first, then she'd check with Allison. If she didn't run into Ryder by then, she'd start looking for him. Yes, he'd probably laugh at her for worrying. On second thought, no he wouldn't. He'd probably be upset that she wandered around by herself. Considering what had happened to Tim yesterday, that was probably a valid concern.

Okay, fine. She'd ask Colter to go with her.

The pavilion was empty when she reached it, just as she'd expected. At least there was still some coffee left. She poured herself a cup and had just taken the first sip, sighing as warmth spread throughout her, when she heard the sound of someone calling her name.

She turned, frowning when Mr. Miller hurried into the pavilion. Rain dripped from his flushed face and wet hair. He wasn't wearing a poncho or raincoat and his clothes were soaked. Not just soaked—they were streaked with mud, as if he had slipped and fell.

She placed her mug on the makeshift island countertop and hurried to meet him. "Mr. Miller! Are you okay? What happened?"

He grabbed her hand, started tugging her from the pavilion. "Oh, Hannah. Thank God. Hurry."

"What is it? What happened?" The panic lacing his breathless voice was contagious, turning the edginess into sharp anxiety. "Is it your wife? Katie? Are they okay?"

He kept pulling her, not even bothering to look at her as he dragged her away from the pavilion. "No, it's him."

"Him? Who? Kevin?"

"No, your friend. Ryder. Something's wrong. I think he's hurt."

Fear, deep and cold, froze her in place, but only for a second before it propelled her forward. She was no longer behind Mr. Miller, she was beside him, moving ahead of him in her desperation to reach Ryder.

No. Please, no, don't let anything happen to him. He's fine. He'll be fine.

He *had* to be fine. Hannah couldn't bear to think

otherwise.

Mr. Miller veered to the right, toward the van. She didn't question him, just blindly followed, thinking only of Ryder.

Until they moved past the van and Mr. Miller reached for the sliding door. Hannah slid to a stop, confusion cutting through the panic that had gripped her moments before. She backed up, frowned when the man's hand tightened around her arm.

"What's going on? Where's Ryder?"

"I'm going to take you to him."

The edginess and anxiety turned to full-blown fear. Something was wrong, very wrong. Every instinct she possessed screamed at her to run. To get away from the man watching her with cold eyes. Hannah shook her head, tried to free her arm and take a step back.

"I don't think—"

"I don't care." His grip tightened and he pushed her forward, causing her to stumble. She reached out, tried to catch herself but it was too late. He used her forward momentum to shove her into the van. She rolled to her back, tried to kick out with her feet. To scream for help. Anything—

Until she saw the gun in the man's hand, aimed directly at her.

"Sit down and shut up. If you don't, your friend is going to pay."

Ryder.

Oh God, what had he done to Ryder? Where was he? Or was this nothing more than a bluff?

That wasn't a chance she could take.

She sat back and kept her mouth shut.

And prayed that Ryder was still alive.

CHAPTER TWENTY-ONE

The first thing Ryder noticed was the splitting pain shooting through his skull. He shifted, tried to roll onto his back. Nausea rolled over him in cold waves and he immediately stilled. Waiting for it to pass. Waiting for the cold sweat coating his body to stop. He sucked in a deep breath but even that fucking hurt.

He lay there. Not moving. Not breathing. Not doing anything except waiting for the pain to disappear.

The sharp pain faded to a dull throb, one that didn't threaten to push his brains out through his ears. He moved again, tried to push himself to a sitting position—and promptly wished he was dead.

Because *fuck*. Being dead had to be better than the fucking pain bouncing around inside his skull.

Or maybe he *was* dead and this was his personal hell. Instead of eternal flames, he'd been sentenced to eternal cold and never-ending pain.

He must have *really* pissed off somebody to be sentenced to this eternal torture.

He waited again for the pain to subside then slowly opened his eyes. Or maybe he closed them because all he saw was darkness. Cold, absolute darkness. Where the fuck was he? Not Hell. At least, he didn't think so. He may have done some shit in the past that probably didn't sit well with the Man upstairs but nothing to warrant this, and nothing that hadn't been done for the greater good.

Okay, so not Hell.

But damn close to it.

Why the fuck was it so fucking *black*? Was he blind? Had that fucker hit him so hard he lost his vision?

Hit.

Snippets of memory flooded back, nothing more than flashes.

The shed.

The crate.

Fucking George-fucking-Miller coming up behind him and crushing his skull in. What the *fuck* had the man used? Whatever it was, Ryder wanted it because he was going to use it on that fucking asshole twice as hard.

As soon as he got out of here.

And to do that, he needed to fucking *move*.

Shit.

Ryder pulled in a deep breath, his mind finally registering the damp air. Okay, that was a clue. So was the rough ground under his cheek—which meant he was laying in his side. Another clue. They didn't make sense because hell, his head was still threatening to split open. Didn't matter. He'd file them away in the back of his scrambled brains and use them later. As soon as he sat up.

He closed his eyes—maybe—pulled in another deep breath, then tried to get his arms in front of him.

They wouldn't move.

What the fuck? They were there, he could feel them. He wiggled his fingers, just in case. Yeah, they were right there, behind his back.

He tried moving his legs but had the same problem—they were there but he couldn't move them, not the way he was supposed to. And whenever he tried, all he felt was pain in his arms. That didn't make sense. Why would his arms hurt when he moved his legs? They weren't attached. Unless his scrambled brain was sending mixed signals to the wrong limbs.

He frowned, focused on his fingers. Told them to move. Yup, they moved. So his poor brain was sending the right signals but something was getting lost in the transmission.

He tried again only he moved too fast. Searing pain shot through him, just as intense as the last time but not nearly as long. Was that a good sign? Christ, he hoped so. He could use a good sign right about now.

He waited another few minutes then tried moving his legs *and* his arms at the same time. It didn't work. At least, not the way it was supposed to—and it had nothing to do with scrambled brains or mixed signals.

The damn fucker had hogtied him.

He swore, long and loud, not caring that the sound bounced back at him. The pain gave him something to focus on besides the burning anger erupting inside him.

The bastard had hogtied him.

Son-of-a-*bitch*.

Something caught his attention and he immediately stilled, breath held as he strained to hear. There it was again, just a faint noise. A soft scraping sound, like something sliding across loose stone and sand.

Scrape-slide.
Pause.
Scrape-slide.
Pause.
Scrape-slide.
Pause. Longer this time, so long that Ryder started

to wonder if he had imagined the noise to begin with. Maybe he was hallucinating. Maybe he'd been walloped in the head so hard that he was lying in a coma somewhere and all of this was nothing more than his imagination.

No, he wasn't buying it. The pain he felt when he tried to move was too fucking real.

"Ryder?"

Or maybe he *was* hallucinating because that had been Hannah's voice, coming from the same direction as that odd *scrape-slide* sound he'd just heard. The voice had been weak, uncertain, pitched just above a whisper. That didn't make sense. Why would Hannah be here?

"Ryder?"

There it was again. And no, he wasn't hallucinating—that had definitely been Hannah's voice.

Son-of-a-*fucking*-bitch.

Rage tore through him, white-hot and searing, eclipsing the pain in his skull. He was going to kill the fucker for even daring to touch Hannah. And if she was hurt in any way—

Ryder pushed the fury away—for now. His first concern had to be Hannah. He'd deal with everything else later.

"Hannah? Are you okay?"

Scrape-slide.

"Yeah. Yeah, I'm okay."

"You sure? He didn't hurt you?"

Scrape-slide.

"No." Her voice was closer now, a little steadier. "Just...no, I'm fine."

Rage swept over him again when he heard the hesitation in her voice. He pulled in a deep breath, winced. Was it his imagination, or was the pain in his skull subsiding? Probably his imagination—rage had a tendency to make everything else fade a bit.

He ran his tongue across his dry lips, forced a calmness he didn't feel to his voice. "How did he hurt you, Hannah?"

"He didn't." *Scrape-slide*. "It—just my arm. When he grabbed me."

Was she telling the truth? Maybe. It didn't matter because he was still going to kill the fucker. Later. They had other things to do first.

Like get the hell out of here.

"Hannah, do you know where we are?"

Scrape-slide. Scrape-slide.

She was close now, close enough that he could feel her body heat. Close enough that he could smell the mingled scent of rain and soap on her skin. *His* soap.

Christ, now was *not* the time to be feeling all possessive and shit. Didn't mean he couldn't appreciate the image of Hannah in his shower, using his soap, that popped into his head.

Later. Much later.

He cleared his mind and focused, realized he had completely missed what Hannah had said.

"Where did you say we were?"

"The cave."

The cave. Of course. Those two little clues he'd latched onto earlier popped into place, finally making sense. What didn't make sense is why they were here. Why hadn't Miller just tossed him off the cliff or into the water? Ryder would be fish bait by now if he'd done that. And why bring Hannah here? Why grab her at all?

There could be several possibilities but Ryder had no idea what they were, not when they hovered just out of reach of his frazzled brain.

"Are you sure you're okay?" Hannah's voice, low and filled with concern.

"Yeah, fine. Just a concussion."

Her surprised gasp filled the damp air. Hands touched him, their touch awkward and fumbling as they stroked the back of his head. Ryder winced, sucked in a sharp breath and did his best to move away. Hannah gasped again, this time in horror, an apology tumbling from her mouth.

"I'm sorry. I'm sorry. I didn't mean—"

"It's good. I'm fine." At least, he would be. "Hannah, are you tied up?"

"What?"

"Are you tied up? Restrained at all?" He thought she must be but he wasn't going to assume anything, not when his brain was still trying to unscramble itself.

"Oh. Yeah. He, um, he put those plastic things around my hands and feet." She paused. When she spoke again, her voice was lower and laced by a touch of anger. "It's George Miller. He's the one—"

"I know. I'll deal with him later." And whoever the hell else was helping him. His wife? Maybe. The granddaughter? Maybe. Didn't matter because they'd all fucking pay. "Hannah, are your hands in front of you or behind your back?"

"In front. Why? Aren't yours?"

Ryder actually laughed, just a soft chuckle that caused another burst of pain in his skull. The son-of-a-bitch wasn't as smart as he thought he was; if he was, he would have tied Hannah's hands behind her back—not that Ryder wouldn't have been able to talk her through what needed to be done. "No, I'm hogtied."

"Why would he—"

"Doesn't matter." Ryder shifted his body, trying to move closer to where he thought Hannah was. "Sweetheart, can you reach my right boot?"

"I think so." There was a soft sliding sound as she moved closer, then her hands brushed the back of his head again. He swore and she immediately moved back, once again apologizing."

"Hannah, it's okay. I'm fine."

"No, you're not. You're hurt." Was that anger in her voice? Yeah, it was. And yeah, the fucker must have hit Ryder harder than he thought because the idea of Hannah being angry on his behalf actually made him smile.

"I'll survive. Just—slide a little closer."

"I'm afraid to touch you. What if I make it worse?"

The only thing that would make it worse was if Miller and whoever was helping him showed up before they could get out of here. He couldn't allow that to happen.

And he sure as hell couldn't tell Hannah that.

"You won't."

She muttered something under her breath then slid closer. Hands touched his thigh, gingerly moved down his leg, following the bend of his knee and moving along his calf to the top of his boot.

"Okay, I found your boot."

"My right boot, sweetheart. See if you can reach your fingers inside."

She shifted behind him, moving closer as her fingers played with the top edge of his boot. "Why do I need to reach inside your boot?"

"Because there's a knife in there." Maybe. If Miller hadn't taken it when he hogtied him.

Her fingers stilled. Ryder heard her unasked

question in the damp air, gave her credit for not actually voicing it. She wedged her fingers deeper into the boot then let out a small gasp of surprised triumph.

"Got it!"

"Okay, good. Now, I want you to cut the restraints holding my hands and feet."

"You want me to what?"

"Cut the restraints."

There was a long pause, one filled with hesitation and doubt. "Ryder, it's pitch black. I can't see anything. What if I cut you?"

"You won't."

"You don't know that. I can't see—"

"Hannah, I need you to do this."

Another pause, followed by muttering he couldn't quite make out. Her hands moved from his leg, fingers gingerly touching him until they stopped at his hands. She took a deep breath, shifted, then cold metal brushed across his wrist. Ryder held himself still, barely breathing as she tried to saw through the restraints. There was brittle crack then the sound of metal hitting stone, followed by a soft oath.

"The knife broke."

Yeah, of course it did. *Fuck*. He knew that knife was a piece of shit.

"Not a big deal, Hannah. We can still do this."

"But it broke. I can't—"

"I need you to untie my bootlace."

"What?"

"Untie my bootlace and pull it out. Doesn't matter which one."

"Why?"

"I'll explain later."

Hands closed over his boot again, fingers

fumbling to untie the laces. They were wet, which would make it harder for her, but Hannah didn't stop. A few minutes later, he felt a tug against his foot as she pulled the long length of lace free.

"Got it. Now what."

"Tie a loop at each end, one big enough to fit around the toe of your shoe."

"My shoe?"

"Yeah. Doesn't have to be any bigger than that. A small bowline will work."

"Um, Ryder?"

"Yeah sweetheart, what is it?"

"I, um, I don't know how to tie knots."

Shit. He could talk her through it but that would take too long. "Then just put the lace into my hands. I'll tie it for you."

"But your hands are behind your back! How are you—"

"Just a little trick I know. I'll teach you when we get out of here." He wiggled his fingers, caught the bootlace in his grasp when she gave it to him. He closed his eyes, slid the lace through his fingers until he reached the end.

Made a loop. Slid the running end up through the loop. Around the standing end. Back down through the loop. Pulled it tight. He checked the size of the loop by inserting two fingers and spreading them. Yes, that should be just the right size for Hannah.

He slid the lace through his fingers and tied another loop in the other end. Checked it again then nodded.

And *shit*. Another flash of pain exploded in his skull. Not as bad as it had been but still there. Tough shit. He'd have to deal with it. Ignore it. Push through it.

He didn't have a choice.

"Take the bootlace from my hand. I want you to put one loop around your foot, feed the lace over the restraints around your wrists, then put the second loop around your other foot."

Her fingers brushed his as she took the bootlace from him. He heard her shift, her heels kicking against the ground as she followed his directions. There was some more muttering, followed by a curse of impatience, then a feminine grunt of satisfaction.

"Okay, got it. Now what?"

"Make sure there's tension on the lace then saw through it with your feet."

"Saw? I don't understand."

"Move your feet. Pedal them back and forth."

"But won't the lace break?"

"No."

"How do you know that? It's just a shoelace. It won't—"

"It's Kevlar. Trust me, it's not going to break. Just watch your skin, you don't want to get a friction burn."

"Like I'm worried about that." He smiled at the impatience in her voice. Listened as she started pedaling her feet back and forth. There was a small snapping sound and then—

"Oh my God, it worked. It worked! How did—"

"Just another little trick I know. Now grab the loops in your hand and saw through the restraints on your feet. And when you're done that, get me the hell out of these things."

A small murmur drifted over him as Hannah quickly got to work. A few minutes later, there was another snapping sound as she cut through the restraints around her feet.

"I need to get me some of these."

Ryder chuckled, held himself still as she kneeled behind him and threaded the lace around the restraints holding him in place. One snapped, then another. One more and he was free.

Free.

Now it was time to make the fucker pay.

CHAPTER
TWENTY-TWO

"Three of a kind." Allison tossed the cards on the bed between them and looked up with a wide grin that stole his breath away. "That means you owe me another hundred bucks."

Ninja tossed his own cards down then grabbed the pad and pencil they were using to keep track of their bets. Holy shit, she was robbing him blind. He would have never suggested playing poker as a way to pass the time if he had realized she was a damn card shark.

He wanted to blame it on being distracted. He hadn't seen Boomer all morning and that worried him. He hadn't been able to reach Mac or Daryl and that fucking bothered him. He was sitting with his back to the door and that just fucking freaked him out.

But most of all, he was distracted by that kiss Allison had laid on him the night before. He hadn't seen it coming at all—although in hindsight, he probably should have. He had just ignored the subtle signs—mostly for his own sense of self-preservation. Allison was Boomer's kid sister. A woman, yes, but still his buddy's sister.

Which put her squarely in the hands-off column.

It was his own damn fault, though. He should have never caressed her back when they'd been hiding in that damn cave. Should have never leaned over and whispered in her ear.

You deserve better than him. Someone who values you for the treasure you are.

It was a damn foolish thing to say and he should have kept his fucking mouth shut. But he'd sensed her upset, had felt her entire body tense with anger and hurt at the little show going on outside the cave. Had she slept with the guy? He didn't think so. It didn't matter if she had or not. She was upset and all he'd been focused on was reassuring her—

And trying to tamp down her anger so she didn't do something foolish like storm out of the cave and go after the asshole.

Didn't matter that he'd meant the words, he still shouldn't have said them. He should have done something else, like maybe sit on her.

Yeah, sure. *That* would have gone over really well. About as well as the hug he'd given her last night. All he'd meant to do was comfort her. She was upset over Tim's death, a perfectly reasonable reaction no matter how she may have felt about the douche.

In hindsight, it had been a stupid thing to do. But in a completely uncharacteristic move on his part, he hadn't stopped to think. She was upset so he hugged her.

And then she kissed him.

For one heart-stopping second—okay, it had been more than a second, maybe a minute or five—he'd kissed her back. Cradled her face between his palms and slanted his mouth over hers. Ran his tongue over the seam of petal-soft lips and swallowed her soft sigh as he deepened the kiss.

And then he remembered where he was. More importantly, he remembered who he was with. He jumped back, the image of Boomer snapping his neck more effective than being doused with a bucket of ice-cold water. And then he just pretended it never happened.

Yeah, because he was smooth that way.

But pretending sure as hell wasn't helping him at all because he'd been distracted ever since.

"So what's the total up to?"

Ninja glanced at the two columns of numbers and quickly did the math. "Minus the one hand I won, I now owe you nine-hundred and sixty-eight dollars."

Damn good thing they were only playing for fun.

Allison scooped up the cards and shuffled them. "One more hand?"

"No, I need a break." He swung his legs over the side of the bed and stood, pausing to stretch. "Isn't Hannah supposed to be joining us?"

Allison glanced at her watch. A small frown creased her forehead then quickly disappeared. "She was supposed to but that was an hour ago. Ryder probably showed back up, which means we probably won't see either one of them for another few hours."

"Maybe." Except he wasn't buying it. Boomer would have at least stopped by to touch base and discuss alternate plans before locking himself in the other bungalow. "Let's go check."

"Check? Now? Um, ew, no. I totally don't need to see any of my brother's body parts, thank you."

"We'll knock first."

Allison looked out the window, at the rain that was still coming down. Not as heavy as earlier, and there hadn't been any lightning or thunder in the last thirty minutes, but it was still more than an inconvenient drizzle. She looked back at Ninja and shook her head.

"How about you go knock and I'll stay here?"

"I want you to go with me." He reached for her

poncho and held it out to her. "Humor me."

It looked like she wanted to say no but she must have seen something in his gaze that changed her mind. She slid off the bed and grabbed the poncho, then slipped her feet into a pair of flimsy flip-flops.

"Do me a favor: put your shoes on instead." She didn't have work boots, not like the ones he'd seen some of the others wearing, but her shoes were thick and rugged. Sturdy.

And a hundred times better than those silly flip-flops that showed off her brightly-painted toenails.

Maybe she was starting to sense something wasn't quite right. Or maybe she was picking up on his own uneasiness. It didn't really matter because she simply gave him another odd look then kicked off her flip-flops. She didn't say anything as she grabbed a pair of socks from the oversized backpack she had mostly packed last night and pulled them on. A minute later, he was leading her toward the bungalow he shared with Boomer.

His heavy knock went unanswered. He knocked again, just in case, then turned the knob. If they were in there, it would be locked, especially since he'd walked in on them the other night. No way in hell would Boomer make that mistake twice.

The door was unlocked.

He pushed it open and walked in, Allison right behind him. Boomer's bed was unmade, the covers rumpled, the sheet hanging halfway off the mattress. Boomer's pack was resting on Ninja's bed, zipped up tight. A pile of clothes that definitely didn't belong to his buddy was sitting on the faded dresser just outside the bathroom.

That uneasiness swept over him again, a little

stronger this time.

Allison moved past him, did a quick survey of the room, then turned. "The clothes I brought over for Hannah are gone so she must have taken a shower. Maybe they went to grab something to eat. Neither one of them had breakfast this morning."

"Yeah. Maybe." He didn't believe it any more than she did.

He led her from the bungalow, his gaze scanning the deserted compound as they made their way to the pavilion. It was fucking eerie, how quiet everything was. Nobody was around.

Of course they weren't. It was fucking raining. Allison had explained that everyone pretty much stayed in their own bungalows on the rare occasions it rained like this because there was nowhere else for them to go.

That knowledge did absolutely nothing to ease his edginess.

The pavilion was deserted as well, which Ninja had expected. He went over to check the coffee pot. The machine was the kind that automatically shut off after two hours. How long had it been off? There was enough coffee left in the carafe for maybe two cups. He placed the back of his hand against the carafe. Lukewarm, which meant the machine had turned off sometime in the last hour, give or take.

Allison moved toward the counter, reached for the mug sitting there. "This is Hannah's. It doesn't look like she even touched it. That's not like her. She doesn't function without her morning coffee. And she would have never left it sitting here like this."

She turned to him, the first hint of fear shadowing her eyes. "Colter, what's going on?"

"I don't know. Maybe they're in one of the other bungalows." He didn't believe it, not for a single second, but he didn't want to upset Allison more than she already was.

He grabbed her hand and led her from the pavilion. They knocked on every single door, opened each one if nobody answered.

No Boomer.

No Hannah.

In fact, the only people around besides them were Darla and Cindy, and neither woman seemed happy to see them. Ninja questioned them but it was useless—they hadn't seen anyone, hadn't heard anything, and the only thing they wanted to do was go home.

Yeah, he knew exactly how they felt.

He was leading Allison toward the project manager's bungalow when she tugged on his hand and pointed. "Colter, the van's gone. Do you think they went somewhere?"

"Maybe." *No.* "Let's check the office."

"We shouldn't go in there if Kevin's gone."

"Do I look like I care?"

She opened her mouth. Closed it. Shook her head. "Guess that was a stupid thing to say, huh?"

No. What was stupid was dragging her with him—but he'd be damned if he sent her back to the bungalow by herself. Not until he figured out what the fuck was going on.

The office was unlocked—not that it would have made any difference to Ninja. He pushed the door open then stopped so fast that Allison actually bumped into him. She peered around him then gasped in surprise.

That gasp pretty much summed it up.

The interior was in shambles. Every drawer in the filing cabinet had been opened, the contents removed. Paperwork was strewn over every surface. The floor, the desk, the small table pushed against the side wall. The few pictures that had been hanging on the walls had been thrown to the floor, frames bent and glass shattered.

What the hell?

A noise came from the back, freezing Ninja in place. He squeezed Allison's hand then released it before gently nudging her outside. She glared at him, shook her head and tried to step back in—then stopped at the steady look he leveled at her.

Had the look frightened her? Had he inadvertently given her a glimpse into who he really was? Possibly. But he'd had no choice, had no other way to communicate what a shit show this was turning out to be.

Convinced she would stay put, he moved through the destroyed office to the door of the project manager's private quarters. He paused outside the door, head tilted to the side as he listed. There it was again, the noise he'd heard earlier.

A muffled shuffling sound, followed by something that sounded like...a whimper.

What the fuck?

Ninja didn't bother with the knob. He just jammed his shoulder against the door and forced it open. Wood splintered and cracked as the door swung inward, hanging at an odd angle from the destroyed hinges.

The project manager, aka Kevin, aka Samuel Bannister, aka the sleazoid con artist from hell, was laying on the bed. Actually, he was *tied* spread-eagle to the bed, restraints securing each wrist and ankle to the frame. He stopped flopping around, stared at Ninja in wide-eyed terror, then tried talking through the strip of duct tape that had been placed over his mouth.

Thank God the fucker was dressed.

Ninja bit back a smile—a smile that only last one-point-two seconds because Allison was suddenly standing beside him. "I thought I told you to stay outside?"

She ignored him and asked a question of her own, her nose wrinkled in distaste. "What's that smell? And what happened to him?"

The smell was stale urine. As for what happened to him, there was only one way to find out.

Ninja moved closer, reached down and ripped the duct tape from the little fucker's mouth. A high-pitched wail filled the room, the sound quickly morphing to a litany of whiny words. The man was spewing them so fast that Ninja couldn't understand him.

He slapped his hand over the man's mouth, silencing him. "Shut. Up."

The man's eyes grew a little wider but he quickly nodded.

"I'm going to move my hand away. When I do, you don't say a fucking thing unless it's to answer my questions. Is that understood?"

Another nod, this one a little slower.

Ninja held the man's gaze with his own and slowly lifted his hand. A second went by, then another, each one blessedly silent.

"What happened?"

"It wasn't me. I swear it wasn't—mmph!" The words ended in a mumble as Ninja once again covered his mouth.

"Let's do this again. I ask a question. You answer it. Got it? Now, who did this to you?"

"It was Miller. He—" The man quickly shut his mouth and Ninja almost smiled. At least he was a fast learner.

"Why did he tie you up?"

"He—he thinks I stole the money, but I didn't. I swear I didn't."

"You mean the money you've collected from the con you're running? Nobody stole it—it's been donated to several charities."

"But—how did you know—"

"Uh-uh. You don't ask the questions, I do. Was Miller involved in the con?"

"No. No, he found about it though. Threatened to turn me in if I didn't—" The bastard's mouth snapped shut.

"If you didn't *what*?"

"I can't tell. He'll kill me if I tell."

Ninja leaned closer, pitched his voice so only the man could hear. "And I'll kill you if you don't."

A low whine fell from the bastard's lips. A second later, the strong smell of fresh urine filled the room. Ninja looked down, frowned in distaste at the wetness spreading across the front of the man's shorts. "Are you fucking kidding me?"

"I—don't—please—"

"Does this have anything to do with the guns?"

Bannister's eyes widened in horrified surprise. "You know? How—"

"Doesn't matter how."

"But—"

"Where's Allison's brother?"

For a second, Ninja didn't think the man would answer. One direct look from him took care of that.

"Miller found him snooping around. He—he made me help him take him away."

He ignored Allison's sharp gasp. Ignored the mingled fury and concern knotting his gut. "Take him where?"

"To—to the cave. On the beach."

"What about Hannah? Is she there, too?"

"Hannah?" The man frowned, shook his head. "No, we didn't do anything with Hannah. I wouldn't hurt her. Ever."

Was he telling the truth? Yeah, he was.

So where was she? Had Miller come back for her? But why, when she had nothing to do with any of this?

To keep Boomer in line.

Fuck.

But why would he need to keep Boomer in line? Why not just get rid of him like he had the others? Because there was no doubt in Ninja's mind that Miller had been behind the two deaths—the one last week that had prompted Allison to call her brother, and Tim's death yesterday.

So why not do the same with Boomer?

Unless he thought Boomer could be used as some kind of bargaining chip.

If that was the case, Miller had made a grave miscalculation. Hell, he'd made more than one. Dragging Hannah into it wouldn't keep Boomer in line—it would push him over the edge and unleash a side that Miller did *not* want to see.

Ninja grabbed the roll of duct tape at the edge of the bed and pulled off a long strip. Bannister started thrashing on the bed, moving his head back and forth as that inhuman whine filled the room.

"Please, no. He said he was coming back for me! Just let me up. I—mmph."

Ninja slapped the tape over the man's mouth then not-so-gently patted his cheek. "Don't whine. It's not very becoming."

He ignored the man's frantic grunts and turned, then froze at the expression on Allison's pale face.

Anger. Surprise. Denial.

Fear.

Her wide gaze met his, the muscles of her slender throat working as she swallowed. "They—they have Ryder and Hannah?"

Ninja wanted to pull her into his arms and reassure her, if only for a second. Actually moved toward her but she shook her head and backed up a step.

Great. Fucking great. Was the fear in her eyes partly because of him? Had she seen too much?

It didn't matter. He couldn't let it matter, not now. Not ever.

"Not for long."

"But you don't know that. They could already be—"

He stepped closer, refused to let her finish the sentence. "They're not. You need to trust in your brother, Al."

She was quiet for a long time, her gaze never leaving his. "Are you going to get them?"

"Yes. As soon as I get you somewhere safe."

She was already shaking her head before the words left his mouth. Dammit, he should have expected that, even after seeing that flash of fear in her eyes.

"I'm going with you."

"Al—"

"I'm going with you. What if Miller comes back? There's no place safe around here. No place for me to hide."

And dammit, she was right. If he had time, he could construct a quick structure and hide her away somewhere outside the compound—but even that wouldn't guarantee her safety. He'd need her cooperation to stay put. That wouldn't happen, not unless he tied her up, and he couldn't do that because then she'd be at the mercy of anyone who might find her.

And even if he trusted her to stay put—which he didn't—he didn't have the time to hide her away.

Fuck.

He stepped closer, let another layer of humanity drop from the carefully-constructed image he shrouded himself in. "You listen to everything I tell you. Is that clear? *Everything.*"

He expected her to stumble back. To turn and run. He sure as hell didn't expect her to meet his gaze—or to see the flash of stubbornness in her warm eyes.

"Is. That. Clear?"

"Crystal. Now let's go." She spun around and hurried outside, paused at the doorway to throw him an impatient look.

And fuck, he was in trouble.

Because that hadn't been fear in her eyes. At least, not fear of *him* as he'd thought.

He didn't know what the fuck it was.

And that worried him.

CHAPTER
TWENTY-THREE

Hannah's shoulder was wedged under his arm, supporting him. Ryder fucking hated it, wanted to nudge her away and tell her he didn't need it.

If he did that, he'd probably keel over backward and hit his fucking head again.

Each step was agonizing, detonating small explosions at the back of his head.

Step.
Boom.
Step.
Boom.
Step.
Boom.

He braced his hand against the rough wall of the cave, sweat beading his forehead and dripping into his eyes. Fuck.

He had to push through the pain. Fucking ignore it until he got them out of here. He didn't have a choice.

How far back in this damn thing were they? Not too far. At least, he didn't think so. The echo of the surf roared around them, adding to the pounding in his head. Unless that noise *was* his head.

The penlight was still in his pocket. He could always pull it out, take a quick look around to get their bearings.

No, it was too risky. There was no way of telling if anyone else was in here with them. He didn't think so—he hadn't heard anyone and with all the damn swearing he'd done, he was positive someone would have said something if they'd been in here. And just because they were alone now didn't mean they would be. For all he knew, the fucker was on his way back now.

Which meant they needed to *move*. Hannah was his first priority. He had to get her to safety. After that—

Well, after that, it was game on, fucker.

"Ryder, you need a break. You're going to hurt yourself."

Another step. Then another and another, each one as painful as the last. "No. Not until I get you out of here."

"You have a concussion. You shouldn't be—"

"I said no. It's just a concussion. I've had worse." Which was the truth. But damn if he remembered ever feeling like his head was about to roll off his shoulders. Give him a stab wound or bullet wound any day. This concussion shit was for the fucking birds.

He eased away from Hannah, ignored her exasperated sigh as he took a halting step on his own. Christ, did she think he was fucking helpless? Yeah, probably. Could he blame her?

No, not in this case.

"Ryder—"

"How far back did they bring us? Do you remember?"

She hesitated, no doubt wondering if she should keep giving him hell or just answer the question. She finally settled on the latter, although her answer wasn't as informative as he would have liked.

"A little past where we were hiding the other night. I think."

Well, at least he was leading them in the right direction. That much was helpful. His brains were still so fucking scrambled, he'd been worried they were going in the wrong direction. All he had to do was keep the wall to his right and they'd eventually work their way to the entrance.

He hoped.

"Do you remember taking any other turns? Were there any tunnels or anything?"

"No. No, I don't think so. I remember that bend where we were then it was mostly straight."

Mostly.

Well, there was nothing he could do about that now. Even the light wouldn't help, since he had no fucking clue where they were to begin with.

He reached for Hannah's hand, accidentally hit her arm instead. She made an odd noise then her fingers closed over his and squeezed.

"Ryder, please—" Her voice broke, surprising him. She sounded suspiciously close to tears, which made no sense. Was she really that afraid that he wouldn't get them out?

He braced his back against the cave wall and pulled her toward him. Wrapped his arm around her waist and held her close. He couldn't see her but he didn't need to, not for this.

He released her hand and trailed his fingers up her arm, across her shoulder. Up higher to cup her cheek. Then he dipped his head and brushed his mouth across hers—except no, that was her nose.

Close enough.

"Hey. No crying, okay? I'll get us out of here. Promise."

Her hands trailed across his chest, her fingers

trembling as they twisted in the material of his shirt. "I'm not crying. And even if I was, that's not why."

He almost laughed at the stubbornness he heard in her voice. "No? Then why?"

She was quiet for so long, he was beginning to think she wasn't going to answer him. And when she spoke, her voice was so soft, he almost didn't hear her.

"I don't want anything to happen to you, Ryder. Not after—I mean, I know we're not together anymore. I know nothing's going to happen between us when this is all over. But—" She hesitated, only long enough to release a hushed sigh. "I couldn't handle it if anything happened to you, Ryder."

And *shit*. He hadn't expected that. Maybe he should have, but he hadn't. If he were smart, he'd just utter a quick reassurance then start moving again. That was the smart thing to do. Get them out of here and worry about the rest later—especially that part about nothing happening between them when this was over.

But the truth was, he wasn't sure he *could* get them out of here. Not a hundred percent sure. Eighty percent, yeah. It was that other twenty percent that was giving him a problem. There were too many unknowns, too many things that could go wrong in the blink of an eye. He had to get them out of the cave. Then he had to get them up that fucking trail, where they'd be completely exposed.

After that—well, he wasn't sure what came after that, not yet. Go back to the compound? Maybe. Ninja would be there. They'd be able to cover each other's six until they figured out what to do.

Or maybe it would be better to take her to the small village. Call the authorities and let them handle things.

Except they'd already done that and the authorities still hadn't shown up.

And then, on top of all that, he had to pray that Miller and whoever else was working with him didn't show up while he was trying to get Hannah to safety.

That meant putting a lot of faith in too many unknowns and hoping the odds were with them. Ryder didn't like playing the odds, not when he'd rather be in control. But he wasn't, not here—and that made him twitchy.

If he were smart, he'd keep his mouth shut and keep going. But he couldn't, not now. She deserved to know. If he failed at getting them out of here, at least she'd know the truth.

He tightened his arm around her waist. Gently ran the pad of his thumb along her cheek. Took a deep breath.

Opened his mouth, then quickly shut it again.

Fuck. Was he really going to do this?

Yeah, he was.

"You remember the day I left? All those years ago?"

Hannah stiffened in his arms and he expected her to pull away. He didn't blame her—that day hadn't exactly been a shining point in his life.

"Um, yeah. Why?"

"I didn't mean to be such a dick. Well, actually, I did. But I didn't mean what I said. All that shit I was spewing? It was just that: bullshit. I didn't mean any of it."

Silence, thick and heavy, wrapped around them. He still expected her to pull away but she didn't. In fact, some of the tension actually left her.

But she didn't say anything. She just stood there,

like she *knew* he had more to say.

He almost didn't. Now wasn't the time. But he had to because if he didn't, he might never get the chance again.

"The truth is, I—" The words stuck in his throat, damn near choking him. He sucked in a deep breath and forced them out. "I love you, Hannah. I never stopped loving you. I just..."

And *shit*. She'd gone stiff against him, her fingers twisting his shirt so hard he thought she was actually going to rip it. Maybe he was wrong, maybe he should have just kept his fucking mouth shut. He didn't expect her to say them back—too much time had changed. *They* had changed. But—

"You think we're going to die, don't you?"

"What?"

"This is a dying declaration, isn't it? You don't think we're going to get out of here."

"Hannah, that's not—"

"Yes, it is. It's either that or you're hurt worse than you're letting on."

"I'm *not* hurt." He forced the words between clenched teeth, which only made his head throb again. Dammit.

He reached up and peeled her fingers from his shirt then started moving. "Come on. Let's go."

"Ryder—"

"I said *let's go*."

She threw her arms around him, the force of her body hitting his nearly pushing him back against the wall. Then she kissed him. Just a quick meeting of the lips, almost desperate.

"I love you, too."

"Hannah—"

"Just—we'll talk later, right? After we get out of here."

The unasked question in her words hung between them, demanding reassurance. Ryder reached for her hand, squeezed her chilled fingers with his own.

"Yeah. When we get out of here."

He led them forward, each step slow and uncertain. Time tended to slip away in the complete darkness and he had no idea how long they'd been walking. It felt like forever but couldn't have been more than ten minutes.

And then two things slowly dawned on him.

The first was that his head no longer felt like it was going to explode. It still hurt like hell, but not as bad. It was either getting marginally better, or he was just getting used to it. Either one worked as far as he was concerned.

The second was that he could *see*. Not much, nothing more than shadows, but it wasn't that inky darkness that swallowed everything around it. Rather, it was just a gradual lightening, so faint he almost didn't notice it. And the more they walked, the better he could see.

He stopped and looked around, recognition washing over him. They were just around the bend, in the spot where they'd hidden the other night.

Which meant the cave opening—and potential freedom—was yards away.

He motioned for Hannah to stay back then eased around the bend. The watery light pierced his eyes, caused a splintering pain to shoot against his skull. He blinked, blinked again, letting his eyes adjust.

It was still raining, sheets of it falling from the leaden sky. If it was a bright day like the last few had been, he'd be in trouble, didn't think his head would be able to handle it. Hell, just this amount of light was painful.

Too bad. He'd suck it up and deal.

He inched forward, his eyes scanning the interior of the cave, his ears attuned to any sound. It was silent, except for the roar of the surf and the falling rain.

And even better, there was nobody in sight.

He scanned the cave one more time then looked toward the right wall. There had been three chests the other night when they were here and now—

Now there was only one.

Fuck.

They were moving them. To where, he had no idea. He didn't even know how. Were they carrying them up that fucking hill? No. No fucking way. Not in this weather. That was a lot of weight, it would be too risky.

He kept saying *they* but he didn't know who *they* were. Miller, yes. But who else? He couldn't be the only one.

Miller's wife? Probably. It was doubtful that the man could be carrying something like this off right under her nose. Not impossible—but doubtful.

The girl, Katie?

No, he couldn't see it. She was barely eighteen and entirely too shy.

Which didn't mean shit. That could all be an act.

So all three of them were presumably involved. That still wouldn't make it any easier for them to move those trunks up that fucking trail. And even if they did get them up there, where would they take them? The island had no airstrip. What were they going to do, hide them again?

Yeah, maybe, if they thought their hiding place had been compromised. But they'd still have to get them off the island.

Unless they were planning to overtake it—and Ryder couldn't see that happening. There was nothing here to overtake.

So how would they get them to wherever they were going? It was an island, they didn't have that many options—

Island.

Yes, it was an island. Surrounded by water. Accessible only by boat.

Everything *clicked*—probably a lot later than it should have. Fuck. Had he missed anything else?

No, he didn't think so.

He looked back at the crate. Two of them were already gone, which meant they were being moved *now*. Was there a boat anchored offshore somewhere? Yeah, probably. That's what he would do—commandeer a fishing vessel of some kind and anchor a hundred yards or so offshore. Nobody would pay much attention to a trawler, not around here. Then he'd use a small dinghy to go back and forth.

Now he just needed to figure out where they were. Had they just taken the second crate—or were they on the way back for the third?

Only one way to find out.

He motioned for Hannah to stay put then dashed toward the entrance. Pain hit him, nearly knocking him over, but he ignored it. Ignored it, yeah—but fuck, it hurt.

He paused at the entrance, eyes open to half-slits against the gray light as he studied the horizon. There, about sixty yards out. Closer than he'd expected, especially in the storm-tossed water. He squinted, searching the waves for a smaller boat, finally found it.

Heading toward the bigger boat, not the shore.

Things were finally looking up.

He turned back, swallowed an oath when he saw Hannah making her way toward him. "I thought I told you to stay put."

"I just wanted—"

"Never mind, we don't have time." He held his hand out to her. "Come on."

Her fingers closed over his and he started to lead her from the cave. Stopped when his eyes caught sight of that last crate. Did he have time to check? Yeah, he did. Especially if it meant finding something he could use to protect them.

He pointed toward the horizon. "Do you see that boat?"

Hannah followed the direction of his finger. Squinted then slowly nodded. "Yeah."

"Keep an eye on it. If you see the dinghy heading this way, let me know."

"What are you doing?"

"I'm checking something." He didn't say anything more—there wasn't time. He hurried over to the crate, knelt in front of it, and grabbed the small set of tools from his back pocket. He wasn't as fast as Ninja when it came to picking locks but fast enough.

Less than a minute later, the lock popped open. Ryder pulled it from the clasp and opened the crate—then stared down in disbelief.

Holy fuck. If he'd been anywhere else, he would have felt like a kid in a fucking candy store. But seeing the explosives neatly stacked in the crate didn't fill him with excitement. Not this time.

What the hell were they planning on doing with this shit? Were they selling it on the black market for a quick buck, or had they stumbled into some kind of terrorist plot? And if so, who was the target?

He didn't know. All he knew was that there was no way in hell he could let this shit make it to its final destination.

He carefully studied the contents, moving things around as little as possible. Everything he needed was right here—everything except a timer.

Shit.

He peeled the watch from his wrist and grabbed the small tools, quickly removed the back and went to work. "How are things looking out there, Hannah?"

"I can't tell. It doesn't look the dinghy has moved."

Shit. Not good.

He worked a little more quickly, made some final adjustments then stared at the makeshift timer. What should he set it for? Not enough time, and he risked this whole thing going off in the cave. The fireworks show would be spectacular but what happened after that wouldn't be. If he set it for too long, he ran the risk of it being found.

Would they be able to disarm it if they found it? Maybe. Maybe not.

"Ryder?"

"Yeah?"

"They're coming back. They're already about halfway." Panic laced her voice, made the words tremble in the air between them.

Fuck.

Well, at least he knew how long to set it for now.

He made the last adjustment, closed the lid and replaced the lock, then pushed to his feet. He moved too fast and a small explosion detonated in the back of his head, this one followed by a wave of nausea.

Fuck.

He held himself still for two seconds—that was all the time he could afford and even that was pushing it—then made his way over to Hannah. Shit. He must look worse than he thought because she reached for him, her brows pulled low over concerned eyes.

"Ryder—"

"I'm fine. Let's go."

"Can't we just wait here? They might not even look for us. We could hide. Wait for them to leave."

"Bad idea, sweetheart." *Really* bad. She had no idea how bad—and he wasn't about to tell her. The last thing he wanted was for her to freak out. "When I say go, we go. Stay down low and move slow."

"Slow?"

"Yeah. If we move too fast, we might actually draw their attention to us. Remember, they won't be looking for us. They think we're still tied up."

She nodded. "Okay. That makes sense. Slow. Um, what if they see us?"

"Then we run like hell."

"Ryder, you can't—"

"I can." He leaned down, claimed her mouth in a quick kiss—and hoped like hell it wouldn't be their last. "We're due to have that talk, remember?"

"But—"

"No *buts*." He grabbed her hand. "You ready?"

She took a deep breath, nodded, then followed him out of the cave. Ryder moved slow, keeping Hannah between him and the tangle of foliage and rock that lined the cliffside. The minutes dragged out, each one tenser than the one before it. They were halfway there. If their luck held out—

A shout echoed behind them, the sound quickly followed by the sharp retort of a gun. A pistol, not a rifle. They were out of range—for now. That would change in a matter of minutes.

He grabbed Hannah and pushed her ahead of him. "Run!"

CHAPTER
TWENTY-FOUR

They had just reached the building site when Ninja heard the shot. Years of training kicked in and he dove on top of Allison, pulling her under him when they hit the ground. She screamed—not out of fear but from indignant surprise—then immediately tried to roll out from under him. He tightened his arms around her and held her still.

"Stay down."

She must have heard something in his voice because she immediately stilled. Ninja spared a brief second to give thanks for that minor miracle then lifted his head, his ears attuned for any sound, no matter how small.

Except the fucking rain made it next to impossible to hear anything.

Or did it? He closed his eyes, concentrated—

Shouts, too far away to make out. And was that the sound of someone running? No, it was more than one person.

But who?

He needed to get closer. Whatever was happening was happening down on the beach, too far away for him to figure out. Was it Boomer and Hannah?

Or Miller?

He started crawling backward, dragging Allison with him. The fact that she went along willingly—and quietly—told him that she finally realized something was going on. Something definitely *not good*.

"Get inside the building."

"But—"

"I can't help Boomer and worry about you at the same time, Al. I need to know your safe."

She twisted her head to the side, stared at him over her shoulder. And damn, what he saw in her eyes made his pulse jump. She was actually *worried*. About *him*. The novelty of it surprised the hell out of him. When the hell was the last time anyone had ever worried about him?

Never.

And as much as the novelty amused him, he didn't have the time to enjoy it. Not now. He had to make sure Allison was safe then go bail Boomer's ass out of trouble—

If it wasn't too late.

"When I tell you to, run toward the building. Stay low until you get there. Get to the back corner behind a wall and stay low. Got it?"

She nodded, her gaze still glued to his. He ignored what he saw in the depths of her eyes and eased his weight off her.

"Go."

"Colter?"

Damn the woman! Why wasn't she going already? "Yeah?"

She reached up, gently touched his cheek. "Be careful."

He couldn't help himself—he turned his head and pressed his lips against her palm then smiled. "Always, doll. Now go."

She pushed to her feet and ran toward the building, staying low as he'd instructed. Holy shit, the woman *did* know how to follow instructions. Imagine that.

Ninja belly crawled toward the cliff, his body slithering through the wet sand and mud like he'd been born to it. He peered over the edge and swore.

A dinghy was pulling up to the beach, helped ashore by the rough waves. One figure jumped out and pulled it further onto the sand then wedged an anchor into the soft ground. What kind of fucking moron would be risking his life in a fucking dinghy in this weather?

A desperate one.

No, make that two.

The person in the back raised their arm. A split second later, another shot rang out, the crack muffled by the distance and rain. Ninja looked to his left, swore again when he saw two other figures running like hell up the trail.

Hannah, with Boomer behind her.

Only *running like hell* wasn't exactly right. Boomer was moving too slow, his steps off-balance so that he was weaving like a drunk man. Fuck. He was hurt. Had he been hit? Ninja didn't think so. At least, not that he could see from here.

Which meant jack shit.

He crawled toward the trail, following the edge of the cliff. He stayed far enough back so he wouldn't tumble over if the wet ground gave way, but close enough that he could still see what was going on.

And what was going on worried the hell out of him.

The two figures from the dinghy were standing on the beach, staring after Boomer and Hannah. Another shot rang out but Ninja didn't think they'd been aiming. Who the fuck was down there? Miller—at least, he thought it was the older man judging from the gray hair but he couldn't be sure. He had no fucking clue who the other person was, if it was male or female, young or old.

Did it matter? No, not when the unknown raised their arm and fired again.

Fuck.

If the unknowns took off after Boomer and Hannah, the shit was not going to end well. With the way Boomer was stumbling and weaving, the unknowns would catch up to them in no time.

And there wasn't a damn thing Ninja could do. He was unarmed, with only a handful of rocks to use as a weapon. In close quarters, he could do a hell of a lot of damage with a rock. But from this distance?

All he could do was create a minor distraction.

He gathered a few good-sized rocks around him, ready to do just that. But the unknown pair didn't take off after Ryder—they turned toward the cave instead.

He waited for the pair to disappear then jumped to his feet and tore off toward the trail. Leaves slapped at his face and arms as he descended the slope, gravity adding some much-needed speed. Boomer must have heard him coming—yeah, because Ninja wasn't worried about staying quiet, not right now—because he grabbed Hannah and pulled her behind him.

Then sagged in relief when he realized who it was.

Yeah, there was definitely something wrong for Boomer to show anything on his face—especially relief.

He pushed Hannah toward him. "Take her. Get her out of here."

"No! Colter, help him. He has a concussion."

Ninja didn't hesitate. He grabbed Hannah and

pushed her up the trail, then reached for Ryder. He shoved his shoulder under the man's arm, grabbed him around the waist, and started hauling ass.

And damn if the ass didn't start fighting him.

"Get Hannah out of here."

"How about I get you both?"

"You don't get it." Boomer shook his head then hissed in pain. "Explosives."

Ninja stumbled to a halt, his blood turning cold. "What?"

"The last crate was filled with explosives."

"And you just had to fucking play with your toys, didn't you?"

A quick grin curled the other man's mouth, but only briefly. "You know me."

"Yeah, unfortunately. How long?"

"Fifteen minutes."

Ninja glanced toward the cave, nothing more than a dark speck further down the beach. The unknown pair were just exiting, dragging the crate between them. Neither one of them even looked back at the trail.

"Doesn't look like we need to worry about it now."

Ryder glanced at the beach then met Ninja's gaze with a slight grimace. "That fifteen minutes?"

"Yeah?"

"Could maybe be five. Hard to say."

"What the fuck?"

"It was a patch job with a makeshift timer."

"Fuck." Ninja started moving forward again, dragging Boomer with him. "How much explosive we talking about?"

"Enough."

"Damn you, Boomer. If you blow me the fuck up,

I will never forgive you."

"Don't think I'll be forgiving myself, either."

Ninja swallowed back a laugh and kept going, picking up the pace until they finally reached the top of the trail. Hannah grabbed hold of Boomer, the grip she had around his waist strong enough to cut off his breathing.

Boomer didn't seem to mind.

They watched in silence as the dinghy pushed away from the beach and headed toward the waiting boat. Waves crashed over the bow and more than once, Ninja expected it to capsize.

But it didn't. Ten minutes later, the crate was being hauled aboard, followed by the two people in the dinghy. A few minutes after that, the dinghy was hoisted on deck and the boat turned into the waves, moving further into the distance.

Ninja glanced down at his watch and frowned.

"I thought you said fifteen minutes."

"I also said it was a patch job."

"You sure you set it right?"

Boomer scowled at him, opened his mouth to say something—

And a fireball exploded on the horizon, big enough that Ninja felt the ground beneath his feet shake.

Ryder clamped him on the shoulder, a wide grin on his face.

"And that, my friend, is how I earned my name."

CHAPTER TWENTY-FIVE

Three Days Later.

Sun glinted off the clear blue water and silky white sand. There was no sign of the storm that had battered the islands a few days before.

No sign of the death and destruction he had caused.

Ryder slid the sunglasses onto his face and stepped outside onto the patio. Warm air washed over him as the sun caressed his skin. It was a welcome change from the chill that had seized him the other day, when he'd thought that neither he nor Hannah would make it up that damn trail alive. The only thing that had kept him going, that had kept him pushing through the excruciating pain exploding in his skull, was Hannah. No matter what he did, no matter what he said, she wouldn't leave him. She had stayed by his side, her hand twisted into the waistband of his pants, refusing to let go.

Everything after that was still a blur.

Yes, he remembered the explosion. As impressive as it had been, he couldn't forget it. And it wasn't as if he didn't remember everything else that had happened—he did. But some of the details were fuzzier than they should be because of the damn concussion.

The hours after the explosion had been the worst, dragging on and on as the authorities finally showed up. Question after question, explaining what they knew for fact, speculating on what they didn't. Thank God Daryl had reached out to some of his contacts when Ninja finally got hold of him. If he hadn't, there was a good chance that all four of them would still be sitting in some dingy little office somewhere, answering the same questions over and over and over.

It also helped that the weasel came clean—about everything. He'd been drawn into the weapons smuggling by pure accident, had been forced to cooperate in exchange for Miller keeping quiet about the con he was running.

That didn't make him any less guilty, not as far as Ryder was concerned. If he had come clean at the very beginning, things wouldn't have gone as far as they did.

Then again, if he'd come clean, the Millers might have gotten off instead of serving time. Stranger things had happened. Find the right lawyer, spread some money around in the right places—yeah, they could have gotten off. Or at least been released to await trial somewhere and then promptly disappear. There was no chance of that happening now, not with both of them—and whoever else had been out on that boat with them that day—dead.

Tim had been killed simply because he'd accidentally stumbled onto that fourth crate while looking for a quiet place to get high. Ryder actually felt sorry for him.

Katie was yet another casualty but in a different way. She wasn't the Millers' granddaughter, wasn't related to them at all. Apparently, she'd been kidnapped more than ten years ago and forced into slavery. The Millers had purchased her four years ago. *Purchased*. What kind of sick fuck bought and sold another human being? The girl had been abused and frightened to the point that she simply did what she was told. Ryder didn't even want to think what she might have suffered at their hands to break her to such a point.

But she'd fought back, on that last night. Had somehow found the courage to escape. That had been the catalyst that forced the Millers into acting when they did. Miller had been looking for her during those early morning hours in the storm—and found Ryder instead.

Ryder still didn't know why he wasn't fish bait at the bottom of the ocean right now. There had been nothing stopping Miller from tossing him into the water after bashing his head in—and there would have been nothing Ryder could have done to save himself.

Maybe it had been the storm. Maybe Miller was afraid his body would wash ashore too soon.

Maybe.

And maybe Ryder would never know the reason.

Could he live with that?

He turned his gaze to the woman stretched out in the lawn chair on the beach a few yards away.

Yeah, he could live with not knowing—as long as he had Hannah.

They still hadn't had that talk yet. They'd been too busy, answering questions and piecing together what had happened. They'd finally left the isolated island yesterday afternoon, taking the ferry back here and checking into the private resort. Allison and Ninja had flown home this morning but Ryder was staying here for a couple more days to fully recuperate.

Hannah insisted on staying with him.

Which was perfect, because they had what they

needed right now: privacy. Time to decompress. Time to deal with everything that had happened.

Would it be enough?

Ryder had seen the disappointment and sadness in Hannah's eyes as she watched the small island she had called home for the last six months fade into the distance. She hadn't said as much but he knew she felt like she was abandoning the people she had come to love. That she was quitting what she had gone there to do before her job was finished.

Would she be able to walk away for good? She might convince herself she could but Ryder knew better. Hannah had been born to help others. That was who she was and nothing would change that. He didn't want anything to change that.

That was why he loved her, even after all these years.

And that was why he had walked away from her eleven years ago.

He adjusted his grip around the two mugs of coffee he'd made and walked out to the beach. Sand warmed his bare feet, the grains shifting beneath him with each step he took.

She looked up at his approach, a small smile curling her mouth. He handed her one of the mugs then eased his weight onto the lounge chair beside her and stretched out.

"How's the headache?"

"Gone. Finally." This morning had been the first time he'd awakened without it. He knew better to push himself, though. A few days of doing absolutely nothing would work wonders.

Not that he was accustomed to doing nothing— he wasn't. But this, just sitting here gazing out at the water—yeah, this was nice.

He took a long gulp of coffee then placed his mug on the small table set up between the lounge chairs. The air around them was peaceful, the silence between them relaxed and companionable.

And he was about to ruin it.

He had to. It was time.

He swung his legs over the side of the chair and braced his arms on his knees. Clasped his hands together and studied Hannah for a long minute. She was looking at him, had turned toward him as soon as he moved, expectation clear on her face.

He cleared his throat, stared down at his clasped hands. "Have you given any thought to what you're going to do now?"

She was quiet for a long time. Too long. She finally looked away, lifted one shoulder in a small shrug. "Go home, I guess. That's what I was planning to do anyway, with the holidays coming up."

"And after that?"

Another long minute of silence. Another small shrug. "I don't know. I had planned on coming back here but..."

There was nothing to come back to. Not anymore.

Ryder clenched his jaw, wondered again if he'd regret saying what he was about to say. Hell yeah, he'd regret it.

But he'd regret it more if he didn't.

"There are other volunteer organizations around. Other people who need your help."

Hannah nodded, reached up and brushed a strand of hair from her face. "I know."

"You shouldn't let what happened here stop you from doing what you want."

She tilted her head to the side, a frown marring the smooth skin of her forehead. "It almost sounds like you're trying to get rid of me."

"No." Ryder shook his head, "No, not even close. I just—you have a lot to offer, Hannah. I don't want you to stop doing what you love."

She nodded, looked away for a long minute then turned back to him. "Speaking of love..." Her voice trailed off thoughtfully. Warm eyes focused on him, the intensity in their depths enough to make him squirm.

He nodded, looked away even though she couldn't see his eyes behind the dark lenses. "Yeah."

"Did you mean it? When you said you loved me? Or did you only say it because you didn't think we were getting out of there?"

He could lie. Force the words through his lips with enough false sincerity that she'd believe him. He'd done it once before, there was nothing stopping him from doing it again.

But he couldn't. Not this time.

"I meant it."

"But?"

"No *buts*."

"Then why do I get the feeling that there's something you're *not* saying?"

He took a deep breath, released it slowly as he mulled the words over in his mind. No, there weren't any *buts*—just one hell of a big obstacle standing between them that she either couldn't see...or refused to acknowledge.

"Hannah, what I do—" He hesitated, searching for the right words. "What I do isn't pretty. It's not—"

"You help people, just like I do."

Ryder laughed, the sound short and brittle. "Help. Yeah, sure." He lowered his sunglasses and captured her gaze with his own. "And sometimes I don't."

"Are you talking about the Millers?"

"Yeah." But not just the Millers. There was a long list of people just like them. People he'd helped meet their end. He wasn't about to tell her that, though.

Ryder swallowed back the sharp disappointment crashing over him when Hannah swung her legs over the side of the lounge and stood. But instead of walking away like he'd expected—like he'd been sure she would do—she sat next to him and reached for his hand. Her touch was warm. Strong. Comforting.

"You really think what happened to them upsets me?"

"When I'm the one who did it? Yeah, I do."

"You're wrong, Ryder. What they did—you didn't have a choice."

"I did. We could have just left. We *should* have just left. I put your life at risk—"

"And how many lives did you save by doing that? How many more lives would they have taken if they'd gotten away?"

Ryder didn't have an answer to that. Nobody did.

"Ryder, you did what you had to do. I can't believe you'd think that would upset me."

"Sweetheart, it's not just that. Our lives are exact opposites. What I do and what you do—it takes us in two different directions. Maryland is my home now. I can't leave Cover Six Security, not knowing what I know. Not when there are so many more people like the Millers out there."

Hannah tilted her head to the side and frowned. No, that wasn't a frown—that was a scowl. "Did I ask you to leave?"

"No."

"No, I didn't." She kept talking like he hadn't answered. "And I wouldn't think of it, either. I don't know the details about everything you do but I know enough to realize it's important. I would never ask you to stop. That would just be selfish."

"And that's the point, Hannah. I'd never ask you to give up what you wanted. I'd never ask you to put your dreams and goals to the side. I never could. That's why I walked away all those years ago."

"Why do you think I'd be putting anything on hold?"

"Because what you do takes you all over the world."

"It doesn't have to. There are plenty of people who need help at home, too. I'd already thought about staying stateside after I was finished here."

Was she telling the truth? Or was she merely telling him that to make him feel better? Ryder didn't know—and that worried him. He'd already given her plenty to resent him for, from that stunt he'd pulled eleven years ago. He sure as hell didn't need to give her more reasons to resent him.

"What about everything else you wanted?"

The confusion marring her brow was genuine. "Like what?"

"Like happily-ever-after and a house full of kids."

She blinked. Blinked again. She covered her mouth with her hand but not before he saw her smile. And then she laughed and instead of easing his mind, that clear sound twisted his guts into knots.

"Why would you think that's what I want?"

"Because that's what you told me. Eleven years

ago. When you *proposed* to me. Or don't you remember that?"

"Yes, I remember. Ryder, I was barely seventeen at the time. I had no idea what I wanted out of life—except for you."

He leaned back, unable to keep the skepticism from his eyes. "So that's not what you want anymore?"

"I don't know. Maybe. I haven't given it much thought. Having a partner to share things would be nice, but marriage? No, that's not in any plan I have right now. As far as kids..." A shadow passed in front of her eyes, quickly blinked away. "I'm not sure I want any, not with everything going on in the world today. Not when there are kids out there who have nobody."

"But you said—"

Her lips brushed against his, silencing him with the gentle kiss. "That was a long time ago, Ryder. And don't you think you're getting ahead of yourself?"

"Am I?"

"Yeah, you are." She pressed another kiss against his mouth, this one lingering. "Do you love me?"

"Yeah, I love you. I always have." The words came with no hesitation. No regret. With nothing but honesty. Hannah smiled, tightened her hand around his and stood.

"And I love you. Everything else can wait."

He pushed to his feet, let her lead him back to their suite. "Wait for what?"

"For us to get to know each other again. To figure out who we are together and what we want—together." She slid the patio door closed behind them and kept walking, a beautiful smile lighting her face as she led him into the bedroom.

"And I know the perfect place to start."

CHAPTER
TWENTY-SIX

Two Months Later.

Hannah eased her thumbs under the strap of her backpack and readjusted the weight as she stepped off the dock. It had been two months since she'd been here but nothing had changed.

Should she be surprised? No, of course not. It was, after all, only two months. Not much time at all.

Should she be disappointed?

Probably not. Life moved forward, the way it always did.

The way it was supposed to.

But she still felt as if she had missed something.

It was a silly feeling, one that made no sense. She *knew* that—but knowing didn't make it go away. Just like it didn't make the realization that this was probably nothing more than a fool's errand go away.

And yes, that's exactly what this was. Two months had gone by—not a considerable length of time, but more than enough to undo everything they'd managed to accomplish here. The compound had been empty that entire time. The building they'd worked so hard on with so little had been empty that whole time. Would anything be left? Or would the vacant structures which had been left abandoned already show signs of neglect and decay in the humid, tropical weather?

"Are we going to stand here all day or are we going to move?"

Hannah turned, offered Allison a quick smile then started moving.

She had no idea what they'd find, had no illusions about what she might accomplish now—but there was only one to find out.

They moved toward the old van waiting for them. That, at least, had survived. Ryder had made some phone calls—to who, she had no idea—and told her someone would make sure it was waiting for her. And here it was, just like he said it would be.

She opened the door, wincing against the creak of rusty hinges. The interior smelled musty, the odor heavier than she remembered from the last time she'd been inside it.

When Miller had pushed her inside at gunpoint.

A chill danced across her skin at the remembered fear from that day. Fear for herself but more than that, fear for Ryder. Not knowing what had happened to him. Thinking, for more than a few terrifying minutes as the van bounced and jostled along the road, that he was dead.

But he wasn't.

Thank God he wasn't.

And that terrifying day had been a new beginning for her. For both of them.

They'd gone home after that brief interlude at the resort. Not together. At least, not right away. Ryder had to go back to Maryland for a few days but then he'd flown back to his parents' house and they'd been able to spend the holidays together. And yes, they'd even managed some alone time, away from their families.

She'd flown back to Maryland with him, had spent two weeks there while she looked into a few different programs closer to home.

His home, in Maryland.

No, she wasn't living with him. Not officially, anyway. But it was just a matter of time. She knew what she wanted to do now, had already made arrangements with another program based out of Washington DC. The program worked with wounded veterans, helping them to transition back to civilian life. Helping them adapt their homes to their needs and providing support on their journey to recovery.

They were ready for her to start right away—a paying position this time. But she couldn't. Not yet.

Not until she came back here to finish what they'd started.

Ryder had been surprisingly supportive when she told him what she wanted to do. Yes, she knew it would be next to impossible. It was just her and Allison, after all. But she planned on enlisting help from some of the villagers, the ones who had been eager to help before but had been turned away by Kevin, aka the weasel.

It hadn't made sense to her then but it did now—perfect sense. And once again, she mentally berated herself for being so stupid. So naive and trusting. If she had followed her instincts—

No. She couldn't let herself get caught up in those regrets again. If she did, she'd never get anything done.

And they had a lot to do. She was at least honest with herself about that. Ryder was going to come with her—had offered as soon as she had told him what she wanted to do. But he'd been called away on some mission or operation or whatever it was called almost two weeks ago. She'd talked to him once, the call fading in and out because of the sketchy cell service wherever he was. She had hoped to at least see him one more time before she came back here but it hadn't worked out that way.

She missed him.

She loved him.

Hannah tossed her pack in the back with Allison's then climbed into the driver's seat. The engine started on the first try, surprising her. Even the engine's purr surprised her. It had never sounded so smooth before.

She was going to take that as a good sign instead of questioning it.

Allison climbed into the passenger seat and closed the door with a tired sigh. "I think I could sleep for the next twelve hours."

"You're not the only one." Hannah put the van in gear and pulled away from the small gravel lot. It had taken them eighteen hours to get here, thanks to a missed flight and an extended layover. The delays had caused them to miss the morning ferry, resulting in lost hours they wouldn't get back.

They didn't have the time to spare. She only had two weeks. Two weeks to accomplish the impossible.

Allison lowered her window and rested her elbow on the frame. A soft breeze blew in, filling the van with much-needed fresh air. She closed her eyes, sighed again, then turned to Hannah.

"Where to first? The camp, or the building site?"

"I was thinking of the market in the village first to pick up a few things. Unless you want to eat those MRE's Ryder made us bring."

Allison wrinkled her nose in distaste. "Eww. No."

"Didn't think so."

The van hit a rut and veered to the side. Hannah tightened her hands on the steering wheel, corrected the van's course, then followed the bend that would take them to the small village.

Allison slid another glance her way. "We should stop by the building site first."

"Why? There's nothing we can do there. Not today."

"Maybe not but we're going that way. Might as well stop by and look."

"And see how impossible this job is going to be?"

"Since when are you so pessimistic?"

"I'm not being pessimistic—I'm being realistic. There's a difference."

"If you say so. I still say we should swing by. Maybe it won't be as bad as we think."

Hannah snorted. "Yeah, okay."

"Look at it this way: if we swing by, we can at least take an inventory. Make a list of what needs to be done—"

"Which would be everything."

Allison ignored Hannah and kept talking. "Once we have a list, we can prioritize."

"*Prioritize?* Since when are you into making lists and prioritizing?"

Allison shrugged and looked out the window, but not before Hannah saw the small flush on her cheeks—and the brief shadow of disappointment in her eyes. She sighed and tightened her hands around the steering wheel again, pretending it was someone's neck.

"You still haven't talked to Colter at all?"

"Not since we left here after the explosion."

"But I thought—"

"Nope. Like I said, he was the perfect gentleman. Tough not to be when there's nothing there."

"I think you're kidding yourself." In fact, Hannah was positive of it. She'd seen the way Colter had looked at Allison in the few days they'd spent together. He wasn't overt about it, not even close, but there'd been more than one time she had seen the interest in his eyes. The yearning.

"It doesn't matter." Allison brushed off her concern with a brief wave. "Not like anything could come of it anyway, not with us living in two different states, hundreds of miles apart."

"You decided to stay home then?"

"I thought about it but...no. I've already got something lined up two months from now."

"Allison, why didn't you tell me? That's great!"

"Maybe."

Hannah frowned at her friend's lack of enthusiasm. She was ready to ask her about it, to push for more information, but Allison pointed to the road that would take them to the old building site.

"We *are* right here, you know."

Hannah hesitated. Did she really want to depress herself this soon after arriving? No, she didn't. But maybe Allison was right. Maybe they could look around and make that list while they were here. If nothing else, it would give them something to do tonight when they made it back to the compound.

"Okay, fine. But we've only got thirty minutes. If we stay any longer than that, the market will close before get there."

"Deal."

Hannah made the turn, breath held in anticipation of the huge rut they'd bounce over in a few yards. But there was no rut. In fact, the sand-and-gravel road was smoother than she'd ever seen it.

"What—" She never got the question out because the building site was now in view.

Except it wasn't the building site she'd been expecting. It wasn't a building site at all.

Her foot slammed against the brake, the sudden stop throwing her forward until the seatbelt caught. She blinked. Had she somehow taken a wrong turn? She must have—except she hadn't. She knew she hadn't—there were no other turns to take.

"What—" She choked the word out again but that was all she was able to do. In place of the half-finished, shoddy concrete building she'd seen the last time she was here, there was a brand-new school. Bigger than the original, constructed of sturdy concrete blocks painted a bright blue that matched the clear waters surrounding the island. Yellow shutters were hooked in place next to windows thrown open to catch the breeze coming in off the water. The lines of the finished roof were level, without a single dip or uneven ripple. Tropical flowers and bushes lined the walkway leading to the double doors.

And a sturdy fence ran around the entire perimeter.

Her gaze shot back to the double doors, and to the men standing in front of them. Some were strangers to her—but some she had already met.

Daryl Anderson, the head of Cover Six Security.

Mac MacGregor, a big guy with a scarred face who had frightened her the first time she met him—until she realized he was nothing more than a teddy bear.

Colter Graham, his face a mask of cool indifference—until his gaze drifted over to Allison.

Derrick "Chaos" Biggs, the man with impossibly blue eyes framed with impossibly dark lashes. The man who had made sure Kevin's ill-gotten funds had been donated to those who needed them the most.

And Ryder. Tall, broad, his inked arms folded across a wide chest. She felt his gaze through the windshield of the van, saw his mouth curl in the barest hint of a smile.

"But—" The word stuck in Hannah's throat, trapped by the tears she was trying so hard not to cry. Trying—and failing. She reached up, brushed at her wet cheek, and opened the door. The van lurched forward and she stifled a scream, slammed her foot on the brake again and placed the van in *Park*.

Allison's laughter echoed around her and she looked over, her eyes wide with surprise.

"You knew?"

"Yeah, I knew."

"But—"

Allison cut her off with a quick motion of her head. "I think someone's waiting on you."

Hannah nodded, stumbled out of the van and walked toward Ryder. He met her halfway, grunted when she launched herself at him. "I can't believe you did this. Without telling me!"

He swung her around, pressed a hard kiss against her mouth, then set her on her feet. "It was important to you."

Such simple words—but they meant so much. More than he could ever know. She threw her arms around his waist and buried her face in his chest. It didn't matter that they had an audience, didn't matter that people saw her crying. Nothing mattered except what Ryder had done.

She sniffed back the last tear and looked up at him with watery eyes. "I thought you were on a mission."

"I was."

"You've been down here all this time?"

"Mostly. It took two days to get everything in motion but after that, yeah."

She hugged him again, reveled in the feel of his arms around her. Breathed a small sigh of disappointment when he stepped back and reached for her hand.

"Are we going inside?" She wanted to see the inside, wanted to see what it looked like.

"In a minute." He led her around the building, away from the small crowd. They stood there for a long minute, not saying anything until he dropped her hand and reached into his pocket. Her heart slammed into her chest when she saw the small box and she took an involuntary step back.

"Ryder—"

He opened it up, turned it around so she could see. Inside, nestled against dark blue velvet, sat a gorgeous ring with a blue stone the color of the ocean surrounding them. A trio of small diamonds was clustered on either side of the stone.

"It's beautiful."

"It's Larimar. They call it the Atlantis Stone. It's only found in a square kilometer in the Dominican Republic." He pulled the ring from the box and reached for her left hand. Her fingers tightened around his then slowly relaxed. He must have noticed her reaction—of course he had, Ryder didn't miss anything—because he smiled and offered her a quick wink.

"It's not an engagement ring."

Her eyes shot to his. "It's not?"

"No. This is just a promise ring. A pre-engagement ring, I guess."

"Pre-engagement?"

He slid the ring on her finger with a teasing smile. "I know you're not ready."

"But—"

"I don't want to push you into anything."

"But—"

"And if you decide that marriage isn't what you want, I'm fine with that. I love you. I'm always going to love you. And I'm always going to be here. I don't need a piece of paper to make what I feel for you real."

Hannah snapped her mouth closed and stared down at the ring. It was beautiful—not just the ring, but the words he'd given her with it. The gift he'd given her with it.

Time.

Time to make sure this is what she wanted. The assurance that he wouldn't push her into anything too soon.

The assurance that he'd be there for her, no matter what she decided.

But she already knew. Had always known.

She wanted Ryder.

Always.

She threw herself into his arms, sighed when his mouth claimed hers in a long kiss that took her breath away. That stole her heart and filled her with promise.

And that was all she wanted.

For now.

EPILOGUE

Six Months Later.

"You are so easy."

"I am *not* easy."

Ryder wrapped his arms around Hannah's waist and walked her backward into the opulent bedroom of the honeymoon suite. "You're totally easy."

Her mouth pursed into a cute little pout, too irresistible not to kiss. Minutes later, he was dragging his lips from hers, his breathing harsh and ragged.

"Now who's the easy one?"

He smiled, silently conceding her point. But he still felt the need to tease her. "I figured you'd hold off for at least a year."

And that was an optimistic estimate. He'd been afraid to push her, had been willing to wait forever—because he'd meant what he said on that isolated island six months ago.

He loved her. He always would.

And he didn't need a piece of paper to prove it.

"Are you complaining?"

Ryder shook his head and caught her mouth with his as he slowly undid the zipper at the back of her simple gown. Creamy silk hugged her curves and fell in a soft drape around her shapely legs.

It was beautiful on her. *She* was beautiful—

And he couldn't wait to get her out of it.

The wedding had been a small one here at the five-star hotel in Chicago overlooking Lake Michigan. Her family and his. His teammates from CSS. A few close friends.

That was all either one of them wanted. It had been a compromise, mostly to make their families happy. Nothing fancy. Nothing over-the-top. Simple. Understated.

He didn't need fancy or extravagant, not when he had Hannah.

He peeled the dress from her, watched with glazed eyes as it slid down her body and fell in a soft pool of silk around her feet. The breath caught in his lungs as his gaze drifted over her, from her shapely calves to her shining eyes.

Eyes filled with a love so sharp and sweet it hurt.

He scooped her into his arms and carried her to the bed. Gently placed her in the middle and slowly followed her down.

Complaining? No, never.

Not when he had the only thing he'd ever wanted, right here with him.

Forever.

~ The End ~

About the Author

Lisa B. Kamps is a *USA Today* Bestselling Author who writes steamy romance with real-life characters and relatable stories that evoke deep emotion. She likes her men hard, her bed soft, her coffee strong, her whiskey neat, and her wine chilled...and when it comes to sports, hockey is the only thing that matters!

Lisa currently lives in Maryland with her husband and two sons (who are mostly sorta-kinda out of the house), one very spoiled Border Collie, two cats with major attitude, several head of cattle, and entirely too many chickens to count. When she's not busy writing or chasing animals, she's cheering loudly for her favorite hockey team, the Washington Capitals--or going through withdrawal and waiting for October to roll back around!

Interested in reaching out to Lisa? She'd love to hear from you:

Website: www.LisaBKamps.com

Newsletter: http://www.lisabkamps.com/signup/

Email: LisaBKamps@gmail.com

Facebook:
https://www.facebook.com/authorLisaBKamps

Kamps Korner Facebook Group:
https://www.facebook.com/groups/1160217000707067/

BookBub:
https://www.bookbub.com/authors/lisa-b-kamps

Goodreads: https://www.goodreads.com/LBKamps

Instagram: https://www.instagram.com/lbkamps/
Twitter: https://twitter.com/LBKamps

Amazon Author Page:
http://www.amazon.com/author/lisabkamps

THE PROTECTOR: MAC
COVER SIX SECURITY BOOK 1

These men never back away from danger—and always fall hard for love in *Cover Six Security*, an explosive new series from *USA Today* Bestselling Author Lisa B. Kamps

Gordon "Mac" MacGregor swore an oath to protect and defend—an oath he continues to uphold as a former Army Ranger specializing in dark ops private security with Cover Six Security. Danger is a constant companion—and one of the few things that make him feel alive. He doesn't expect that danger to come in the form of the Tabitha "TR" Meyers, the only woman who sees him for who he truly is—and the only woman he's ever sworn off.

TR rarely abides by the rules, not when there's something she needs—and right now, she needs Mac. She enlists his help for one night, thinking she can simply walk away when it's over. But that one night is just the beginning, thrusting both of them into a dangerous web of scandal and cover-up with roots that run deeper than either of them expects.

When TR becomes an unwitting pawn in a game of deception and revenge, Mac will do anything to protect her—even if it means risking his own heart.

Don't miss the exciting launch title of the Cover Six Security series, *The Protector: MAC*, available now.

THE GUARDIAN: DARYL
COVER SIX SECURITY BOOK 2

These men never back away from danger—and always fall hard for love in *Cover Six Security*, an explosive new series from *USA Today* Bestselling Author Lisa B. Kamps

Daryl "Zeus" Anderson walks the edge of danger. Strong. Dependable. Always in control--except for that one night in a tropical paradise that still haunts him. When an old friend calls in a favor, Daryl answers the call, never expecting to come face-to-face with the woman who damn near shattered his restraint--and his heart.

Kelsey Davis has been running for the last three years: for her safety, for her sanity, for more than just her life. The dangerous game she's been thrust into is nearing an end and she's forced to turn to the man her father swears will guard her with his life--the same man she's already run away from once.

The clock is ticking and Kelsey needs to decide if she can trust her new guardian with more than her heart. Because in this game, there's more at stake than love-- and making the wrong decision could cost them much more than just their lives.

Don't miss the sizzling second title of the Cover Six Security series, *The Guardian: DARYL*, available now.

THE WARRIOR: DERRICK
COVER SIX SECURITY BOOK 4

These men never back away from danger—and always fall hard for love in *Cover Six Security*, an explosive new series from *USA Today* Bestselling Author Lisa B. Kamps

Don't miss the next exciting title in the Cover Six Security series, *The Warrior: DERRICK*, available everywhere in August 2019.

Made in the USA
Middletown, DE
30 August 2019